THE BRIDE
MUST BE STOPPED!

A MEAN CITY MYSTERY

STEPHEN ROSS

Clan Destine
PRESS

First published by Clan Destine Press in 2025

Clan Destine Press

PO Box 121, Bittern

Victoria, 3918 Australia

National Library of Australia Cataloguing-In-Publication data:

Ross, Stephen

TITLE: THE BRIDE MUST BE STOPPED!
ISBN: 9780987553911 (paperback)
ISBN: 9780645042627 (eBook)

Cover Art by Andrea L. 'Altocello' Farley
Cover typography by Willsin Rowe
Design & Typesetting by Clan Destine Press

Clan Destine
P R E S S

THE BRIDE
MUST BE STOPPED!

STEPHEN ROSS

CHAPTER ONE

THIS TALE OF WEIRDNESS AND MYSTERY BEGAN WHEN THORNTON Thacker walked into Caroline Greer. Matheson High, between classes, busy corridor, boy slams into girl. You know the type of thing. And Thacker had never met a girl quite like Caroline Greer before. Something about her sparked inside his head and, as the poets say, it was love at first sight.

And trouble thereafter.

But before we get into that, we need to cut across town to the *Blue Bear Hotel* – a cheap, rundown pile of bricks a few blocks from the waterfront. Because this story really began with a telephone call...

'I've been watching you,' whispered a dark-haired man into a telephone receiver. He was about thirty, had an unshaved jaw, and stood at a payphone in the *Blue Bear Hotel's* empty lobby. He wore a worn-out seersucker jacket, white shirt, loose tie, navy pants, and scuffed shoes. It was summer, and a film of sweat coated his brow.

'Yeah, it's that man again.' His smile was smug.

'You're leaving too many clues.' He took a slip of notepaper from his top pocket. A series of pictographs lay scribbled across it. 'You wrote a clue on a wall, and I worked out what it said. Want me to read it back?'

The person at the other end of the line didn't like this conversation. An angry voice echoed in the empty lobby.

An old man with a lumpy face and deep-set eyes seated behind the lobby desk looked up. And then returned his attention to the sports section of his newspaper. The *Blue Bear* wasn't the kind of hotel where people liked to witness anything (alibis were available on request).

'No, I haven't told the police,' the man whispered into the telephone. He put the slip of paper back in his pocket. 'I thought I made this clear the first time I called you.'

He grinned.'Yeah, this is blackmail, baby.'

Yelling came down the line.

The man waited until the anger had eased off. He spoke quietly and firmly. 'I want a slice of the pie, the golden pie, the one you and your family have been hiding away all these years. And I'm tired of waiting.'

Silence.

He noticed a cockroach. It ambled its way across the lobby's cracked, checkerboard floor. It stopped to inspect a discarded finger of cheese that not even the mice were interested in. It passed.

'Are you still there?'

The voice at the other end started talking.

The man in the seersucker stopped grinning. 'How do you know my name?' He looked about. 'How do you know I'm a newspaper reporter?'

'I've been watching you,' said the voice.

'This isn't an idle threat,' the reporter barked into the telephone. 'I'll go to the police. I'm not the one who killed somebody.'

The other end hung up.

'Hello?'

The man tapped the payphone's hook a couple of times. 'Hello?'

The call was over.

He threw in another dime and redialed. The number picked up, but no one said anything.

'Hello?'

Silence.

'I'm not fooling around here.'

Silence.

'Do you hear me? Do you hear what I'm saying?'

The other end hung up.

The reporter had a bad feeling about this. His instincts had been screaming at him all day to drop it, to forget about it; there was easier bread in the world. But that kind of money had the strongest, sweetest smell of all.

He put the phone back in its cradle and returned to his room on the sixth floor.

A sliver of afternoon sunlight through drawn curtains lit an unmade bed, armchair with torn upholstery, chest of drawers with a washbasin on top, and books. Books lay scattered everywhere. One of them talked about Ancient Egyptian hieroglyphics.

A thin column of smoke rose from a forgotten cigarette smoldering in an ashtray. The ashtray sat on a narrow table shoved up against a wall to use as a desk. Across it lay a mess of handwritten notes, wine bottles, more books, dirty plates, and a stack of newspapers.

The reporter took the last drag from the cigarette. He picked up one of the wine bottles and drank the last mouthful. He stared at the black-and-white photograph pinned to the wall above the desk: a crime scene photo. In it, a message had been written across the wall of someone's living room in Egyptian hieroglyphs.

The reporter hadn't been allowed to visit the crime scene, but he had it on good authority from the cops guarding it that the message had been written in blood, and no one had a clue what it said. But the man in the seersucker knew. That was his job as a reporter: to find things out. He was good at that.

Thud.

He heard a shattering, crashing sound downstairs. A shimmer of vibration palpitated through the floor.

The reporter's first thought was that something terrible had happened, that an automobile or a bus had smashed into the lobby.

He opened his door and peered along the hall toward the staircase.

After a moment, he heard something coming up the stairs, something heavy and fast, and it wasn't the little old lady who lived across the hall carrying that week's groceries. Every step on the staircase creaked and groaned under the something's weight.

And then the something arrived.

It stopped at the top of the stairs and stared at him. It was black, shiny, and big. It had red eyes, each one the size of a number 3 ball on a pool table, and a large set of dirty red razor-sharp teeth. Its breath looked gaseous.

The reporter had no time to question his disbelief at what he saw. He sprinted back into his room and locked the door.

He ran to the window and ripped open the curtains. His room sat at the rear of the building, six floors up. There was no fire escape. Could he jump? A dead maple tree stood five feet from the window. Could he jump to one of the branches?

A splintering noise sounded behind him. He looked. The locked door bulged at its center, pushed from the other side. In seconds, it would fly free of its hinges.

There was no could about it.

Always trust your instincts.

He jumped.

CHAPTER TWO

THORNTON THACKER SLAMMED INTO CAROLINE GREER. BOTH HAD been wandering along a busy school corridor, with their minds on other things, when wham! They wound up sitting on the floor, their books scattered, looking at each other with surprise on their faces. Sometimes, strange things can happen when two people stare directly into each other's eyes, and for Thacker, staring into Caroline's dark eyes changed his life.

After a moment, Caroline Greer and Thornton Thacker apologized to each other for their carelessness. They climbed back onto their feet and collected their books.

She had one of his. She passed it back.

He had one of hers. Likewise.

And then she was gone. She walked away, paying attention not to walk into anyone else.

'Did you see her, Stanwick?' Thacker asked.

Stanwick, well dressed in a dark jacket and white shirt buttoned to the top, stepped up alongside Thacker. 'Yes,' he said, adjusting his glasses for a sharper look. He could see the girl. He could also see how Thacker stared at her as she studied the numbers above the classroom doors.

'I think she's new here,' Thacker said. 'Do you know her name?'

Stanwick didn't.

The new girl wore red sneakers, a red plaid dress with short sleeves and a Peter Pan collar. She had long brunette hair.

Thacker and Stanwick watched as she disappeared around a corner into an adjoining corridor.

Thacker and Stanwick sat together in class, in the back row, and listened to the elderly Mrs Driscoll explain how you could tell the Earth was round. Apparently, the higher up you went, the farther you could see around its curve. The white-haired old woman then explained how the world spun on its axis before romping off into an energetic explanation about how the seasons worked.

'Why are we still here?' Thacker whispered grumpily. 'Every other school in the city is now on summer break.'

'It's only until Friday,' Stanwick whispered back.

'I suppose you passed your finals.'

Stanwick nodded.

Blackboard full of chalk diagrams, Mrs Driscoll proceeded to forecast the week's coming weather.

Thacker's mind was back in the corridor. 'She must be new.'

'The girl?' Stanwick asked.

'I've never seen her before.'

'There are twelve hundred students in this school. You can't remember every one of them.'

'I'd have remembered her.'

A piece of chalk flew past their heads, missing by inches. It hit the rear wall of the classroom behind and exploded. Mrs Driscoll may have been elderly, but she had excellent hearing, and her eyesight and aim were deadly. She requested the pair of them shut up.

They shut up.

The lesson continued.

Philip, three rows ahead, tried to get Thacker's attention.

Thacker had no interest in geometry or Philip's eager expression. He looked at the clock on the wall above the blackboard. The second hand barely moved. Maybe it was the effect of the Earth spinning on its axis, or perhaps the summer heat had worn it out.

The girl in the corridor had looked troubled, Thacker thought. There had been something important on her mind, something with gravity. She wasn't a helium-inflated child, one who might lose her mind over a fluffy rabbit or a new set of crayons. She was a serious, grown-up girl with serious things to think about.

Philip, three rows ahead, tried again. He held up a piece of paper for Thacker's attention.

Thacker's attention lay elsewhere.

Philip wouldn't get that piece of paper into Thacker's hand until after the glockenspiel announced the end of the lesson and everyone had fled the classroom for the safety of the corridors.

'It's Dashiell,' Philip said, picking crumbs out of his zig-zag wool vest.

Philip was a rotund, ruddy-faced fellow with mustard-colored hair who appeared to be permanently on the verge of unwrapping a chocolate bar. Dashiell was his dog – an elderly gentleman among dogs who appeared to be permanently on the verge of taking a nap.

Thacker leaned back against his locker and studied the piece of paper. It was a missing dog notice. It consisted of a pencil sketch of the dog and spoke of a reward. Philip was no artist, and the reward was $2.25.

'How long has he been missing?'

'Two days.'

Philip told them his dog had gone off the morning before yesterday and hadn't yet come back. And he'd left no indication of his intended whereabouts. 'Dashiell never misses his evening meal. And now he's missed two. You haven't seen him, have you?'

Thacker didn't answer. He surveyed the steady stream of students passing by in both directions along the corridor.

'Do you have any idea where your dog might have gone?' Stanwick asked, putting his books into his locker; his locker stood next to Thacker's.

Philip didn't. 'Who is Thacker looking for?'

'A girl.'

'Why?'

'I don't know. They're not my thing.'

Philip pouted. He then asked, randomly, 'When can I join your band? I've been practicing my harmonica every day.'

11

'There isn't a vacancy,' Thacker said, looking back at the missing dog notice. 'Dashiell is a golden retriever, isn't he?'

'Yes.'

'Maybe he went to retrieve something.'

Philip rolled his eyes. It was at least the tenth time Thacker had wheeled that joke out of the retirement home. 'Do you want to take the case or not?'

Thacker handed back the missing dog notice. 'I'll find him.'

Philip cheered up.

The glockenspiel rang throughout the school, heralding the start of the next class. Philip bounded away with buoyancy in his stride.

'I'm bored,' Thacker said. 'It's been three weeks since we had an interesting case.'

'Two weeks and four days.'

'Shall we leave our schoolbags here and cut classes for the afternoon?'

'And find the dog?'

'It'll be more interesting than watching the hands of clocks. Are you with me?'

'Of course.'

CHAPTER THREE

I<small>F YOU WANT TO FIND A DOG, YOU HAVE TO THINK LIKE A DOG</small>, SO T<small>HACKER</small> thought of a cat. Aside from Dashiell's color and shape (mustard, fat), Thacker knew one other important fact about this old dog: he had a fondness for the feline and in particular a cat by the name of Sultana.

Thacker and Stanwick briskly walked out through the school gates. Matheson High lay on the 'Avenue of Despair'. A power station stood across the street from the school, its seven chimneys permanently pumping thick plumes of soot-black smoke. Each morning, as a long column of glum school students filed in through the school gates, an equally long column of gloomy power station workers in overalls filed into the power station – each side of the street looking across at the other with suspicious envy.

Thacker was shorter than Stanwick by an inch. He was a narrow boy with a clump of blond hair on his head that had yet to be formally introduced to a comb. His dress sense was post-pajama: tan trench coat, untucked shirt, black stove-pipe pants, dirty-black high-top sneakers, and unmatched socks – the socks always amused Stanwick.

'This is The Case of the Missing Dog,' Thacker announced. 'Although it's not really a case, it's simply the retrieval of a golden retriever.'

Stanwick stood taller and wider than Thacker. He had a head of short, curly black hair, wore black horn-rim glasses, and had immaculate dress sense. He never left home without polished shoes, pressed pants, a dark jacket, and a clean, buttoned-up shirt.

'Do you have an idea where Dashiell went?' Stanwick asked.

'I'll bet you the $2.25 reward he went after Sultana. And where does she spend her days?'

'Asleep in a window at your house.'

Thacker shook his head. 'Down at the waterfront.'

'Is that where we're walking? To the fish market?'

'Yup.'

Sultana was a slinky black cat of undetermined origin that belonged to Fenella, Thacker's sister. Although 'belonged' wasn't the right word: cats belonged to no one. Sultana had first appeared one sunny afternoon, a year earlier, and had planted herself contentedly at Fenella's feet – having selected her as a suitable companion and dispenser of food and comfort.

It took Thacker and Stanwick 30 minutes to walk to the waterfront and another 20 to walk about the fish market. The market was a large cold warehouse with a damp concrete floor. It was a smelly room full of dead fish, ice, wooden crates, trolleys, and an abundance of burly men in frayed pullovers and boots. The men were endlessly shouting at each other about the price of fish and debating whether swordfish really carried swords or simply had sharp noses.

Neither the cat nor the dog was to be found.

Thacker and Stanwick widened their search and investigated the docks – the dozen ramshackle piers that each jutted 40 yards into the bay where the fishing boats tied up. And Thacker found a set of paw prints.

The contents of a rusty oil barrel had leaked and made a 30-inch black puddle. A dog had hit the puddle with one of its paws, and then left a trail of black prints along the deck of one of the deserted piers.

'Looks too big to be Dashiell,' Thacker said, crouching, examining the prints. Stanwick agreed. They were at least seven inches wide, much larger than the paw of a regular dog.

'And they only go one way,' Thacker added, looking along the pier. 'This dog never came back.'

'What do you make of those?' Stanwick pointed at the other set of oily prints that ran along the pier in tandem with the dog's prints. Each of these black prints was three inches in width. One side was straight, the other curved, like an uppercase letter D.

'It's a heel,' Thacker guessed. 'The heel of a man's shoe has clipped the puddle. And he didn't come back, either.'

They followed the two sets of prints along the pier, and the further out to sea they ventured, the fuller Thacker's nostrils became of salty sea air. Thacker had no interest in the nautical. He glanced back at the city skyline: a city of concrete and steel, with the upper floors of buildings disappearing into a shroud of dark clouds. It was a city of forevers: smoke, grit, and noise. And Thacker loved every inch.

'I think he has a problem,' Stanwick said.

A set of moldy concrete steps lay at the pier's end. They led down to the waterline. A dark-haired man in a seersucker jacket sat in the water, facing away from Thacker and Stanwick and looking out to sea.

'Are you all right, mister?' Thacker called out.

The man didn't answer. He raised his arm out of the water. His jacket sleeve was ripped, his hand and forearm scratched and bleeding. He pulled a slip of notepaper from his top pocket and held it in the air.

Thacker navigated his way down the slimy steps toward the man. Globules of oil lay everywhere, along with splatters of wine-dark blood. The seawater lapping around the man's waist was the same blood color. Thacker took the slip of paper and carefully unfolded it. The paper was damp and reeked of cigarettes, like the man.

'What do you make of this?' Thacker asked. He passed the notepaper up to Stanwick.

'Egyptian hieroglyphics,' Stanwick said. 'It's a message of some kind.'

'Are you all right, mister?' Thacker asked again. He crouched alongside.

The man grabbed Thacker's arm and gripped tightly. He turned to look at him. A large chunk of the man's face was missing. He inhaled and drew enough energy to speak. It was a whisper, but insistent: 'The bride must be stopped!'

He let go.

He fell back against the steps and stared at the sky, with one of those stares that would last until the end of time.

'We need to find an adult in authority,' Thacker said.

The only adult in authority they could find was a cranky, middle-aged woman. She apparently held a position of importance at the fish market. She sat behind a counter near the entrance, drinking coffee and knitting a pullover. She didn't know what Thacker and Stanwick were talking about, but she eventually climbed off her stool and followed them to the end of the pier.

Naturally, she screamed.

CHAPTER FOUR

CAROLINE GREER DID HAVE IMPORTANT THINGS ON HER MIND. THINGS of gravity, as Thacker had suspected. And the weightiest thing of all was that day's mail. She had posted three letters to her Aunt Lillian in Scotland, and she had yet to see a reply to any of them. She thought about this on her walk home from school: how long does it take a letter to travel to Plockton in the Scottish Highlands and for a reply to come back?

Caroline hauled her schoolbag into Walnut Street; a sign said, 'Dead End'. That was completely right. She'd been living in that cul-de-sac for over three weeks, and she didn't like it. She felt trapped. And it didn't matter that it was summer – the street was cold and bleak. The houses that lined it had shuttered windows and overgrown front yards. Five homes were derelict, and in front of six others stood tilted and weathered For Sale signs.

No one was ever at home on Walnut Street. Caroline had never once seen a kid outside playing, a man working on his car, a mother carrying in groceries, or even a dog or cat. She imagined there might be people at home, behind the shutters, behind the closed doors. Unmoving people. Rotting corpses caked in cobwebs.

She shook her head. Her imagination had run wild again.

She walked to the end of the street, where the Dalrymple house stood on top of a slight rise. Two storeys, set back about 80 feet from the sidewalk, the old timber home was the darkest on the street. Thick rows of towering pine trees flanked it, casting it forever in shadow.

She looked inside the dented mailbox.

Empty.

Caroline followed the broken concrete footpath that led up the rise and across the weed-wild front yard to the house's front entrance. She climbed the five chipped concrete steps and knocked on the black wooden door.

She waited.

She'd asked for a key, but her aunt had told her no.

The door unlocked, and Uncle Alvin's cheerful face greeted her.

'How was your first day at the new school?' he asked, letting her inside. He held an oil can and wore a locomotive engineer's outfit: blue-and-white-striped overalls, red scarf, and blue cap.

'Terrific.' There was zero enthusiasm. 'Did any mail arrive today?'

'You'll have to ask your aunt. I've been in the basement since this morning. I only just came upstairs.'

Caroline nodded. 'Trains running on time?'

'Yes, ma'am.'

Alvin Dalrymple was an undistinguished man in his late forties – portly, graying hair, with a bushy mustache the size and shape of a small marsupial. He had no apparent occupation and devoted his days to his model 1880s steam train set. He had spent several years constructing yards of track and acres of elaborate scenery in the basement.

'It's only a week,' he said as Caroline wandered along the hallway toward her bedroom. 'It'll be summer break before you know it.'

'Terrific.'

Caroline's bedroom lay at the rear of the house. It was a lifeless space: a narrow bed, closet, chest of drawers, and a wooden chair. A rug on the floor held no color; all essence of life had long ago been trampled out of it. The room's 19th-century wallpaper was yellow and featured swirls that gave you a headache if you stared at them. Her aunt had forbidden her from hanging pictures of her own, and the only thing hung was a crooked painting of a man in a beige suit standing in an empty field holding the string of a red balloon. He was facing the other way.

Caroline wanted to scream. She closed her eyes and inhaled. She counted to six and exhaled.

She would have preferred a room upstairs. Up there, she imagined, she would've been able to leave her window open at night and let in some fresh air. Her aunt had forbidden that. The second floor was strictly out of bounds.

Caroline dumped her schoolbag onto her bed. She fished around inside it until she found her new letter to Aunt Lillian in Scotland, then went looking for Aunt Scarlett.

Caroline went along the hall and stopped at the foot of the staircase. She took another look. Dark wood, a set of bare steps heading up. A series of oil paintings lining the walls. Portraits: old, crooked, and layered with so much dust and filth, it was next to impossible to make out the faces.

She could see no farther than the first landing, where the staircase twisted back on itself and went off into darkness. Everything in the house was old and dark and layered with dust.

'What are you doing?' growled a cigarette-stained voice.

Caroline froze. Aunt Scarlett stood right next to her. Despite the solid wood of her aunt's heels, the woman had a habit of instantaneously appearing out of nowhere.

'I was looking,' Caroline answered.

'You're not going up there,' her aunt said. 'There's nothing up there of interest to you.'

Aunt Scarlett was a thin, pale woman with protruding teeth and a head of red hair that looked like a hornet's nest had been set on fire. She was 50, but she could have passed for 70. She had a perennially sour face and often appeared as though she was about to bite something. Anything. She wore a tidy powder-blue Grace blouse tucked neatly into a pair of navy high-waist crepe slacks. Her shoes were dirty; the heels were square and looked like the ends of table legs.

'Did any mail come today?' Caroline asked.

Her aunt shook her head and walked away.

Caroline followed.

Her aunt wore an odd perfume; she smelled like burned toast. Caroline followed her into the living room.

19

Echoes filled the large, mostly empty room. The wallpaper had been stripped, and you could have rented out the floor space as a parking lot. Alongside the fireplace stood a decrepit leather armchair with a floor lamp behind it and a small, round table next to it. The table bore a coffee cup, an ashtray, and a packet of cigarettes. The lamp lit the room in a 30-watt corn-colored glow.

It was a living room for one.

And a dog.

Aunt Scarlett went for her cigarettes. She took one, lit it with a match, and tossed the match into the fireplace – a tall, broad, black orifice with room enough inside to burn a small forest. Above the fireplace rested a high mantel of dust and a solitary candlestick. Above that hung a cloudy mirror with memories of better reflections.

Aunt Scarlett sat in her armchair and put the cigarette in her mouth. 'What?' she asked, staring at her niece.

'Is there any chance I could get a little pocket money?' Caroline asked.

'Why?'

Caroline held out the letter. 'I have no postage stamps left. I'd like to buy some more.'

Her aunt took the envelope and read the address. Her lips drew back, and her teeth protruded even farther. She took the cigarette out of her mouth. 'Why do you keep writing to this Lillian Greer woman?'

Caroline thought fast. 'She's the last living relative I have. I wanted to wish her a happy Michaelmas.'

'It's June,' her aunt grumbled. 'Michaelmas isn't until September. And what about me and your uncle? Do we not count as living relatives?'

'I meant, on my father's side of the family.'

Jasper stirred and raised his head. He looked up at Caroline, and his eyes warmed to her sight. She smiled affectionately at him.

Jasper was a fluffy little white Bolognese with the dimensions of a loaf of bread. He had been sleeping on the rug in front of the fireplace.

Aunt Scarlett bent down and stroked the little dog's head.

His marble-sized eyes looked adoringly at her.

She whispered something into his ear.

Whatever she said, it at once soothed the little thing, and he laid his head back down on the rug and went straight back to sleep.

Aunt Scarlett smiled. The woman whispered all the time to Jasper. And if she wasn't whispering to him, feeding him, or grooming him, she was taking him for a walk – one of the few times she ever left the house. At least something makes her happy, Caroline thought.

The smile fell off Aunt Scarlett's face. She straightened, sat back in her armchair, and put the cigarette back in her mouth. 'Leave it on the mantelpiece.' The upward tilt of her chin indicated the envelope. 'I'll take care of it.'

Caroline stood the envelope at the end of the mantelpiece, tucked in behind the candlestick.

'Do you have any homework?'

'Yes. An essay for science class.'

'Instead of worrying about sending letters to Scotland, go to your room and start working on it.'

'I thought I would complete it tonight after dinner.'

Her aunt stared at her. 'What do you mean, complete it?'

'I wrote most of it today during lunch break.'

'Bring it to me.'

Caroline didn't know why her aunt would want to read her essay. She returned to her bedroom and rummaged through her schoolbag. She found the handful of pages she had been working on and carried them back to the living room.

Aunt Scarlett took the sheets of paper.

She took the cigarette out of her mouth and studied her niece's handwriting. 'What is this essay about?'

'Marie Curie.'

'Why are you writing about her?'

21

'She was a famous Polish scientist.'

'I know who she is. Why are you writing about her?'

'We had to pick an element from the periodic table and then write about who discovered it.'

Her aunt looked at her.

'Marie Curie coined the term *radioactivity*,' Caroline said snippily, staring into her aunt's black eyes. She was about to add more topical information but stopped dead.

Her aunt ripped the pages of her essay in half. She ripped the halves into quarters and then tossed the lot into the fireplace, throwing her cigarette in after it. Within seconds, the torn pages of her essay were in flames.

Caroline was speechless, although a selection of unprintable words assembled inside her head.

'Homework is for doing at home,' Aunt Scarlett snarled. 'It's not work for doing during the day in school. You will now go to your room, and you will do your home work.'

'Why am I here?' Caroline asked. 'Why did you want me to come and live here, in this house, with you?'

'It is the responsibility of family to look after family, no matter the circumstances.' Aunt Scarlett smiled. 'And where else can you go?' It was not a regular smile. Her eyes hung low, unblinking, and the corners of her mouth rose slowly.

It frightened Caroline.

Her aunt's face then slid back into its regular grumpy configuration, and she flicked her wrist for her niece to leave the room. Their conversation was concluded.

CHAPTER FIVE

DOWN AT THE WATERFRONT, IT TOOK A FULL 30 MINUTES TO REVIVE THE cranky, middle-aged woman clutching a half-knitted pullover. As for the man with chunks of his anatomy missing, nothing short of science fiction was going to revive him.

The police were telephoned, and a squad car of uniformed officers dutifully arrived. They confirmed that the man in the seersucker was dead. They secured the crime scene, took Thacker and Stanwick's names and addresses, and then stood around, scratching their heads and waiting for a homicide detective to turn up.

There were no witnesses.

The man in the seersucker had been attacked at the end of the pier. That much was evident from the blood. The uniforms had also seen the trail of paw and heel prints running along the pier. They concluded that the dead man had been chased by a large dog, possibly a mastiff. There were no returning prints because the large dog had likely jumped into the water and swum away.

Thacker explained to the police officers that dogs, even mastiffs, didn't have seven-inch wide paws. Given the viciousness of the attack, the paws belonged to an altogether different kind of beast.

None of the uniforms paid any attention.

Thacker suggested there were no returning paw prints because the oil had probably washed off, as the attack had taken place on the lower steps in the seawater.

None of the uniforms paid any attention.

Thacker mentioned that the dead man's last words had been: *The bride must be stopped!*

They paid no attention to that, either.

Thacker might as well have been a seagull.

Another squad car arrived, this time with two eager young police bloodhounds. The pair of them, dripping with saliva and enthusiasm, were led down to the pier's end. They were introduced to the crime scene and asked to sniff out the offending dog's scent. After one whiff, the two bloodhounds wanted nothing further to do with the matter. One ran away as far as it could with no intention of ever returning. The other returned to the security of the squad car, where it cowered in the footwell behind the driver's seat and considered an alternative career path.

Thacker said nothing on the walk home, except for a sulky, half-muttered remark about not finding Philip's dog.

Thacker was like that.

Stanwick was used to it.

Stanwick had known Thacker since their first day in first grade. Within one week of meeting, they discovered they lived three blocks apart, that they had a shared interest in music and black coffee, and a shared hatred of school, bedtime, croquet, and banjos.

Stanwick's father was a jazz musician, a bandleader. He was often away in Hollywood, working on movie soundtracks – composing, arranging, and orchestrating. The day Stanwick had told Thacker that his father had worked with Billie Holiday and that *he* had met her almost caused heart failure in the unkempt one. Thacker had instantaneously dropped to his knees and worshiped Stanwick's feet. Stanwick had found it breathtaking that Thacker knew who Billie Holiday was. They were only six at the time.

They walked into Henderson Heights and along to Thacker's building – a tall, narrow construction of gray brick.

'Have you seen Sultana?' Fenella asked as Thacker and Stanwick walked up. She sat reclining barefoot on the front steps in the late afternoon sun. She was writing in her journal – the little grass-colored notebook that went everywhere with her.

'We haven't,' Thacker answered his sister.

Fenella had the same blonde hair as her brother, only hers was combed, and she wore it in a shoulder-length bob. She lowered her journal and peered at them through the pale-green lenses of her sunglasses.

'You need to talk to the Man Upstairs,' she said to Thacker. 'He's been calling for you.'

'Look at this.' He handed his sister the slip of notepaper.

'Why is this damp?' she asked.

'It's been in the water,' Stanwick said.

Fenella sniffed the paper and wrinkled her nose at the cigarette smell. She took off her sunglasses and studied the writing. 'Pictographs.'

'Egyptian.'

She nodded. 'Ancient Egyptian hieroglyphics. Any idea what they say?'

'Nope. I was hoping you'd know,' Thacker said.

'Why?'

'You're older than me. You're meant to know these things.'

There was an incredulous eyebrow. 'I'm only older than you by five months.'

'We had different mothers,' Thacker said, from habit.

Stanwick knew the story.

Fenella shook her head. 'Very few people would know what this message says. It's a dead language. Where did you get it?'

'From a dead man.'

'Are these bloodstains?'

'Yup.'

Fenella delicately held the slip of notepaper between two fingertips. 'You'd better talk to the Man Upstairs. He's not in a good mood.'

'Is he ever?'

Stanwick always knew an excellent time to depart, and this was one. He said goodbye and headed in the direction of Mr Warren of Lincoln Street. Some new heavy, tight silk ties were due in-store. And after that, the *Rainy Night Café* and the delights of the cabinet of cake.

The Man Upstairs was Mister Thacker – father of Thacker and Fenella. He lived on the fourth floor, the top floor of the Thacker house. He had his office up there, and he rarely ventured out and seldom during daylight hours.

Thacker hung his trench coat over the banister and climbed the stairs. He hadn't seen his father in a week, although he'd heard him: groans in the night, doors slamming, footsteps pacing, relentless typewriter hammering. Thacker tucked his shirt into his pants; remarkably, it was stain-free. He checked there weren't any buttons missing. All were present, and his laces were tied.

A row of framed mystery magazine covers lined the walls of the last flight of stairs, from the third to the fourth. Alongside them were three certificates of achievement, a couple of metal dog tags hanging on a nail, a London Underground map, and an assortment of old black-and-white photographs: Mister Thacker's memories. His favorite was the night he had dinner with Veronica Lake at the *Algonquin* in New York. His grin was in Technicolor.

The door was open.

Thacker went in.

The curtains were rarely pulled apart in Mister Thacker's office. It was a chamber of perpetual murkiness. A shell desk lamp cast a sunset glow over an Underwood typewriter and an ashtray. In the corner, a pedestal fan made a slow, fat-fat-fat sound. A street map of Dublin hung on the wall behind it. A row of tall bookcases lined one wall, each one overflowing with books, magazines, LP records, and stacks of loose typewritten paper.

Mister Thacker sat in the shadows on his old red sofa; it doubled as his bed. The desk lamp's light reflected in his tiny, round, blue wire-rim spectacles. He wore an aloha shirt and Bermuda shorts. He had a full head of black hair peppered with gray and chin stubble to match; he shaved only once a week, or if it was a full moon. He patted the empty place on the sofa next to him.

Thacker took a seat.

'I hate the summer.' Mister Thacker had an Irish accent. It

rasped as though he'd swallowed a roll of sandpaper at some point in his life. He was 39, but he'd been saying that for several summers. 'It makes fruit rot.'

Thacker wasn't aware his father ate a lot of fruit.

'And things stick. It's the dampness. This is a city of the damp in the summer.'

Dampness was one of his father's favorite things to tie to his whipping post. He could gripe about it at length, and he'd always arrive at the same conclusion: that it was the end of civilization. Today, he didn't continue. He sat in contemplation; the silence filled by the fat-fat-fat of the fan as it blew a soft breeze across the room.

'We don't talk enough,' Mister Thacker finally said.

'There's not usually too much to say,' Thacker replied.

'Some people talk a lot. Your sister, for example. You, on the other hand.' He held up a hand. 'You take after me.'

Thacker noted the Colt M1911 in the Man Upstairs' hand. He hoped it wasn't loaded. 'What did you want to see me about?'

'We need to have the talk.'

'Which one?' He hoped it wasn't the one about the birds and the bees. At least once every couple of months, his father would decide they needed to have the zoological talk.

'What is it you're looking to do with your life, son?'

They'd had that talk, too. But Thacker wasn't in an adventurous enough mood to remind the old man about it. Reminding Mister Thacker often led to strong language and the moving of furniture.

'I want to be a musician.'

Mister Thacker shook his head in his resigned, exhausted way. 'I thought you were done with that?'

'Nope.'

He studied his son. 'Your mother was crazy about music.'

Thacker knew.

'She had a voice like liquid gold. That's how I first laid eyes on her; did you know that? She was singing in a nightclub.'

His father had meant Fenella's mother. Both of their mothers had been nightclub singers, but Fenella's had been the one the

27

old man had met in a club. He'd met Thacker's mother in a train dining car, but Thacker wasn't reminding him of that, either.

'What kind of life is that for a musician?' Mister Thacker asked.

Thacker looked at the floor. It was a sea of crumpled sheets of typewritten paper. He looked across at the typewriter on the desk; it had bruises. There were bullet holes in the walls.

'Don't be judgmental,' Mister Thacker rasped. 'My fiction has always paid our bills.'

There was a squeal of tires outside. The slam of a car door followed, and an angry yell: 'Thack-er!'

Mister Thacker went to the window, pulled the curtains apart, and looked down into the street. He sighed. 'Just like your mother.'

Thacker went to look for himself.

A police squad car had parked in front of the building. A short, fat, bald man in a black raincoat strolled around from the driver's door like he owned the city. He leaned against the squad car and lit a cigarette.

It was Detective Franks – he stared at Fenella's naked ankles. She ignored him.

'Why do you always land yourself in bother with the police?' the Man Upstairs asked.

'It's what I do,' Thacker said.

His father looked at him with eyes of abandoned hope. 'In my younger days, a lad could get away with all sorts of carry-on. But this is 1958, and things change.'

CHAPTER SIX

'THORN-TON THACK-ER,' BARKED DETECTIVE FRANKS, AGGRESSIVELY spitting the syllables as Thacker walked out through the front door.

'Leave my name alone,' Thacker said. He stood at the top of the steps next to Fenella. He slipped back into his tan trench coat and untucked his shirt.

'We need to talk, kid.'

'Why?'

Detective Franks had a bald head with dents, a dirty-toothed grin, and a permanent six o'clock shadow at his jaw. He wasn't any taller than Thacker, but he weighed the equivalent of eight of him. His raincoat was grimy, its four buttons unmatched. His black tie barely hid that his shirt was about to explode open.

'Because we do.' He returned his eyes to Fenella's bare feet. He licked his lips and took a drag on his cigarette. His eyes traveled up her black pedal pushers to her black sweater and the terracotta bead necklace that hung loosely around her neck. He traveled higher up, and his eyes met hers. Sapphire blue. Angry.

'Are you one of those beatniks?' he asked.

She didn't take her anger off him. She held up her hand and snapped her fingers.

Franks wasn't sure, but he had a strong suspicion there had been something rude about the way she had done it, but he didn't understand that kind of modern lingo.

He returned his attention to Thacker. 'Let's go for a walk. And before you wiseacre me, remember that I'm the grownup and the one wearing the gun.' He pulled back his raincoat to reveal a .38 parked in his shoulder holster.

Thacker could think of better things to do than sauntering along the sidewalk with one of the city's finest, but the man had bullets.

As he walked down the steps, he whispered to Fenella, 'Memorize it.'

She said nothing.

'Don't you just love this time of year?' Franks asked cheerfully as he and Thacker walked along the street.

Thacker had no opinion.

Henderson Heights was a street of tall houses. It wasn't a premium street, although there were rumors it had been in a previous century. It was the type of road where someone could leave out an old mattress or refrigerator on the sidewalk and no one would care. And it would be gone by sundown.

'It's summer in the city, kid.'

'Don't call me kid.'

'The days are long. The sky is blue. Everything is right in the world...'

He directed Thacker into the alley that ran between buildings three along from the Thacker house.

'...except for you.'

There was no one in the alley, and that was the way Franks liked them. He flicked away his cigarette. He grabbed Thacker by his throat and shoved him against the wall. 'Listen up, you little futzer. I go down to the waterfront this afternoon to investigate a murder, and one of my uniforms tells me that two kids had been there; that they discovered the body. And the description of these two – a white kid in a trench coat and a black kid with glasses – sounds exactly like you and your buddy Stanwick.'

Thacker smiled.

'And the uniform tells me he overheard these two kids talking about the dead man; that he'd been holding a piece of paper in his hand when they found him. A piece of paper with a message written on it.'

Thacker's eyes were orbs of purity and innocence.

'And where is this piece of paper?' snarled the detective. His teeth were an inch from Thacker's face. His breath smelled of pepperoni. 'Does the uniform have it? No. Does the dead man have it? No. The white kid in the trench coat has it. He walked off with it. He walked off with evidence in a murder investigation.'

'Want to let go of my throat?'

Franks let go.

'So, you think it's murder?'

Franks screwed up his face. His whole bald head became rows of creases. 'I don't know what it is, but what I do know is I've had it with you and your school friends walking around all over my crime scenes.'

'These things happen,' Thacker said. 'I'd rather not be walking around anyone's crime scene.'

'No, these things keep happening because you keep choosing to poke your nose where it don't belong.'

Thacker shrugged. 'I was at the waterfront looking for a friend's dog.'

'Is that so?'

'Yup. Tell me the dead man's name, and I'll give you the dead man's message.'

Franks slammed Thacker back against the wall and grabbed his throat again. Franks' shoulders pinched, and his free hand clenched to go in for a solid punch. He was like a boxer itching to lay into an opponent.

Thacker held out his empty hands. 'I don't have the piece of paper; you can search me, and you won't find it. But I know where it is, and I can get it for you. Who was the dead man?'

Franks sighed. He hated his job, he hated children and, most of all, he hated Thornton Thacker. He would have gleefully murdered the boy if he thought he could get away with it.

He let go.

'His name was Albert Park. He was a newspaper reporter.'

'What newspaper?'

'The *City Star*.' Franks laughed with a hint of venom. 'Park was always hanging around crime scenes, too. Today, he got one of his very own.'

Thacker nodded: message received.

'And that's all you're getting,' the detective grunted. 'The rest of it you can read about in tomorrow's news. Where's the piece of paper with the message on it?'

'My sister has it.'

Thacker led Franks back along the sidewalk to Fenella, whereupon he conveyed the slip of notepaper from her to the detective.

Franks stared at the message, baffled. 'Is this some kind of joke?'

'Nope.'

Fenella clarified. 'It's written in Egyptian hieroglyphs.'

Franks shook his head and sighed. 'Ancient Egyptians.' He took the slip of paper, put it in his pocket, and climbed back into the squad car.

'I don't like that man,' Thacker said, watching the car take the corner at the next intersection and disappear with a huff of exhaust and a squeal of tire.

Thacker sat on the steps alongside Fenella, and she showed him a page in her journal. She had copied out the hieroglyphs in full.

'We should show this to Rosa,' Fenella said.

'Yes.' He lay back, closed his eyes, and let the fading flames of the afternoon sun warm his face. He forgot all about hieroglyphics and the dead man. 'I saw a girl today in school. I think she's new.'

He waited for a comment. None came.

He glanced at his sister. She was busy writing in her journal. She wrote poetry, not that she'd ever told anyone that. Thacker only knew because he had peeked once.

He closed his eyes again and smiled. Things change.

The smile fell off his face when Fenella asked: 'Are you sure you haven't seen Sultana?'

CHAPTER SEVEN

THE DOOR WAS SHUT.

Uncle Alvin had come upstairs from the basement to retrieve a handkerchief. He'd climbed the stairs to the second floor, gone into his bedroom and, as he'd come out again into the hall, he'd noticed the door down at the end. Shut.

That wasn't right.

The upstairs hall was a featureless, dimly lit passageway that led from the top of the staircase down to a window at the other end. No pictures were hanging, no furniture or ornaments were collecting dust. There wasn't even a rug, just bare floorboards scuffed with decades of tread.

Uncle Alvin walked along to the shut door and tried the handle. The door was locked.

He blew his nose. The door wasn't ordinarily closed, and it certainly wasn't ever locked. The room was empty.

He walked back to the top of the staircase. He was about to call out to his wife when he heard what sounded like a man's laugh.

He listened.

A conversation was taking place downstairs. He couldn't make out the words, but one voice was Scarlett's – there was an atonal sharpness to his wife's voice that was unmistakable. The other voice was quieter, and it wasn't his niece.

Caroline sat on her bedroom floor, rewriting her homework. She couldn't hear anyone talking, but she could hear creaks in the woodwork. She had lived in the Dalrymple house long enough to recognize the sound of someone on the staircase.

She put down her sheets of paper and fountain pen and let out a long, frustrated breath. Completing a 600-word essay on Marie Curie and her discovery of radium was no simple task after only one day of school. What would they expect of her on day two – a 20,000-word thesis explaining the invention of the periodic table?

Caroline went and sat on the windowsill. Through the open window, she could see a handful of stars through the pine trees that flanked the house. She could hear the soft groan of branches in the chilly night breeze. She didn't want to be in this house. And it was the beginning of summer; why was it so cold in the street?

She heard a pinecone thud on the ground. They fell out of the trees like grenades that didn't explode.

She felt a sense of danger in this place. It was an odd sensation. She wasn't afraid of the dark, never had been, but she felt unnerved. She likened it to how a mouse might feel if it was sneaking through a large, quiet, empty house in the middle of the night, knowing that an enormous cat lay waiting somewhere in the darkness.

Caroline shut the window and went back to her homework.

She thought about cheese.

And pineapple.

She was painfully hungry.

The man laughed again. This time, Uncle Alvin was standing right outside the living room and heard him clearly. The door was ajar. A man was talking to Aunt Scarlett. He had a vague accent: foreign, educated. And he had been drinking. Any word above three syllables presented a challenge to enunciate.

Uncle Alvin took off his blue engineer's cap and stroked his bushy mustache. Scarlett had said nothing about anyone coming to the house.

He peered around the door.

A tall, thin, colorless man with glassy eyes stood by the

fireplace, smoking a cigarette. He looked about 90. He had a drawn, cadaverous face and an outrageous clump of stark white hair on his head. He wore black – black shoes, black trousers, a black shirt, and a black blazer.

He and Aunt Scarlett were discussing the price of something, and he sounded vaguely threatening. He sounded like the type of man you wouldn't want to meet in an alleyway after dark. Or find smoking in your living room, negotiating prices with your wife.

'I'll do it for $1000,' the man said. He finished his cigarette and lit a new one from its dying butt.

Aunt Scarlett shook her head.

He nodded his. He threw the dead butt into the fireplace.

'Will it be quick?' she asked. 'I don't want it to go on any longer than is necessary. Sometimes, these things go on and on and on, and it's unnecessary.'

The old man cackled. 'Lady, I've been doing this type of thing for years. It'll be quick and painless. That's why you're going to pay me $1000.'

'Mr Strudel,' Aunt Scarlett growled, 'I'm paying you $400. Not a dollar more.'

They debated the price for a couple more minutes. During that time, Uncle Alvin headed back downstairs to the basement and the sanctuary of his trains. He didn't know who Mr Strudel was. When it came to his wife, it was often better not to ask and not to know.

Price settled, $401, Aunt Scarlett showed Mr. Strudel to the front door.

'When do I get my money?' he asked.

'I don't have that kind of cash in the house. Come back and collect it in a couple of days.'

They shook hands on the doorstep.

'You will be sober when the time comes,' Aunt Scarlett insisted. 'I don't want any mess made of this.'

The old man with the outrageous hair smiled confidently. 'I'm a professional, madam.' He teetered on the front steps. 'I'm always sober when I do my work.'

35

He put a fresh cigarette to his lips and lit it with the butt of the one he was about to finish.

Aunt Scarlett frowned. 'Chain smoking will kill you in the end.'

Strudel laughed. 'It probably will.'

She watched the old man stagger along the broken concrete footpath to the sidewalk. Once he had passed from sight, Aunt Scarlett came out onto the steps and looked about.

'Jasper?' she called.

There was no response, only the sound of Strudel's receding footsteps at the far end of the street.

'Jasper,' she called again. 'Come inside and get your dinner.'

After a moment, the fluffy little white dog appeared out of the shadows. Panting cheerfully, he bounded across the overgrown yard and scampered up the steps and into the house.

Aunt Scarlett smiled approvingly at him as he ran by.

She took in a lungful of night air and looked at the sky and its sea of stars.

She smiled – the same smile that had frightened Caroline: eyes hung low, unblinking, the corners of her mouth slowly rising.

CHAPTER EIGHT

CREAK.

Caroline opened her eyes. She turned her head and glanced across at the alarm clock on top of the chest of drawers. It was just before seven. Daylight slipped in through the holes in the heavy drapes, casting shafts of morning sunlight across her bed.

Her essay lay on the chair next to the chest of drawers. It had taken her until midnight to complete. Afterward, her aunt had rewarded her with an indescribable dinner of potatoes, cabbage, and an undetermined meat product. Her aunt's bill of fare comprised three meals, and cabbage and potatoes featured in each of them; she grew the vegetables in her garden behind the house.

Caroline yawned.

She raised her hand and slapped the bedspread. The shafts of sunlight became rich in dust motes, a sea of floating worlds hovering above her bed.

Creak.

It was the same sound that had woken her. It had come from above; a floorboard had been trodden on.

Caroline lay on her back and stared at the yellow ceiling 15 feet above the bed. An optimist would have described its color as off-white. Caroline saw it more as off-clean, the result of the house enduring years of tobacco smoke. Her aunt was a cigarette chimney.

Creak.

The same floorboard. Someone was walking about in the room directly above.

Caroline climbed out of bed and turned off her alarm clock with two minutes to spare before it erupted into life. She hated waking before the alarm; it was a waste of sleep.

She slipped on her bathrobe and slippers and left her room.

She walked along the hallway and glanced at the photographs that lined the wall. She realized she didn't know anyone pictured apart from Uncle Alvin. There were only photos of his side of the family, none of hers. There were none of her mother or Aunt Scarlett (they were sisters), or her grandfather.

Caroline smiled. Among the photographs hung a framed clipping from *Tappers & Shunters* magazine. It was a report about Uncle Alvin's model train set. He was pictured dressed in his engineer's outfit, with a smile as radiant as the sun.

Caroline stopped at the foot of the staircase and looked up at the first landing. She couldn't see beyond it. Whoever was wandering around up there did so out of view, in the forbidden zone.

Caroline heard cutlery being laid in the dining room. Her uncle was setting the table for breakfast, and she eagerly headed toward it.

The dining room was a narrow space papered with lilac wallpaper and black wood paneling. The paneling looked damp, as though it had been sourced from the hull of a derelict ship. The dining table was a long slab of similar wood that had probably been the ship's quarterdeck. There was no tablecloth.

Aunt Scarlett sat on the far side of the table, wearing a white polyester bathrobe. A cup of coffee sat in front of her, along with a cigarette parked in an ashtray.

'Good morning,' Caroline said.

Her aunt said nothing. She picked up her cigarette.

The woman's hair was a different color this morning. She had red hair, but it now looked orange, and the hairstyle seemed more pulpy than usual. Caroline wondered if it was hair or just one big organic thing, a wad of some kind.

Uncle Alvin stepped in from the kitchen carrying two plates loaded with pancakes. He wore civilian clothes: trousers and a brown vest over a white short-sleeved shirt. He looked like he might be planning to go somewhere.

'Good morning,' he said, with a smile as radiant as the sun. He stood the plates on the table.

'Good morning,' Caroline replied, beaming.

Uncle Alvin always made breakfast. It always involved pancakes and jam: blueberry, strawberry, raspberry. It was heaven.

Caroline took her usual seat.

Her uncle returned to the kitchen and reappeared a moment later with two chilled glasses of orange juice. He stood them next to the plates and then took his seat opposite his wife.

There is much joy to be found in the smearing of jam upon pancake, and Caroline and her uncle ate heartily.

Aunt Scarlett was a slab of concrete. She did not share in the delight of breakfast. She sat rigid, an arm across her stomach, with the other standing vertical, its elbow resting on the fist of the other. She held her cigarette between the V of two upright fingers. Her eyes settled on Caroline, and they remained there.

Caroline noticed.

The woman was unsettling. She stared like a wolf, surveying for signs of weakness, and, when found, she might leap across the table and take a bite out of Caroline's neck.

Caroline drank some juice and asked, 'Who is upstairs?'

'There's no one upstairs,' Aunt Scarlett replied.

'Yes,' said Uncle Alvin. 'There's only the three of us in the house.'

'I heard someone,' Caroline said. 'In the room directly above mine, just now.'

'There's no one upstairs,' repeated her aunt.

Uncle Alvin stroked his bushy mustache. Caroline saw his eyes drift to the ceiling.

'I heard someone,' she repeated.

'There's no one in the room above yours.' Aunt Scarlett stubbed out her cigarette in the ashtray. She did so with such force that the table vibrated.

An uneasy silence fell. Neither Caroline nor her uncle took their eyes off their plates as they ate.

Aunt Scarlett sipped her coffee. Her eyes remained fixed on Caroline.

Several minutes passed.

Uncle Alvin eventually spoke. 'Would you like to take a ride on a 19th-century locomotive on Saturday?' he asked Caroline. *The Flying Volcano*, a restored locomotive from the Wild West era, was touring the country. He was going out that morning to buy a ticket.

'It'll be a three-hour trip,' he said. 'The train will travel out of the city and into the countryside. I could get tickets for us.'

'Yes.' Caroline nodded enthusiastically. The thought of being anywhere other than inside that house appealed enormously. A day trip out of the city sounded wonderful.

Uncle Alvin grinned. He'd found a compadre.

Aunt Scarlett slammed her coffee cup down on the table and glared at her husband.

He avoided her eyes.

Caroline swallowed her last piece of pancake and gulped the last of her orange juice. She didn't feel like hanging around any longer. She excused herself and went to wash and get dressed for school.

'I'm not happy about this,' Aunt Scarlett said after Caroline had left.

Uncle Alvin didn't feel like hanging around, either. 'The train ride?'

'Yes.'

'It'll do the girl some good to get some fresh country air.'

'Trains are dangerous.'

Uncle Alvin shook his head. 'She'll be a passenger. It's not as though she'll be up front shoveling the coal. Anyway, I'll be there to take care of her.'

Aunt Scarlett's eyes tightened. She spoke softly. 'I want nothing to happen to that child. Do I make myself perfectly clear?'

Uncle Alvin understood. Whenever his wife spoke softly like that, there was no mistaking the perfect clarity of her threat.

CHAPTER NINE

THE GLOCKENSPIEL ECHOED THROUGHOUT MATHESON HIGH OVER THE school's public address system. The classrooms instantly emptied, and the corridors became a tidal surge of students desperate for a five-minute reprieve from sitting still and having to pay attention. Thacker was one of them.

Matheson High was an austere five-story building of stone, concrete, plaster, and lumber. It had originally been built in 1870 as a jail. And it had remained one until 1913, when the city fathers decided it had become entirely unsuitable for human habitation and shut it down. The building sat unoccupied and slowly rotting until the spring of 1936. At which time, it underwent a minor revamp – a lick of paint, removal of some of the barbed wire, locking the door to the execution chamber – and reopened as a high school.

Thacker made his way up the sweeping central staircase with his schoolbooks, aware that a set of eyes watched him. Mr Undergarden stood on the next landing. Dressed in a long dark coat and a white shirt with an Edwardian collar, Undergarden was a peculiar, oddly shaped man with large, heavily hung, unblinking eyes. He was like a well-dressed, upright bullfrog. His age was unfathomable. He seldom spoke, and he wore a dour expression, as though his whole life had been one long, dismal transaction and he was going through the motions until his inevitable demise – most likely by getting run down by a bus.

No one knew what Undergarden taught; no one had ever been in one of his classes to report back. Thacker suspected the man had been around since the school's prison days; that he had been the one who plugged in the electric chair or sharpened the blade of the guillotine, or whatever it was they did to dispatch people in the basement.

The only thing anyone knew with absolute certainty was that the man was a tentacle for Principal Puddle.

'What instrument do you play?' Caroline asked.

Thacker was startled. He had thought all morning about the new girl, and she now stood right in front of him on the stairs. She'd been coming down while he'd been heading up.

'How did you know I was a musician?'

'There was sheet music amongst the books you dropped yesterday.'

He admired her detective skills. 'I play upright bass.'

She held out a hand. 'I'm Caroline.'

He shook it. 'I'm Thacker.'

'Do you always wear a coat in summer?' she asked, admiring Thacker's trench coat.

'I don't feel the heat.'

'You should get a hat.'

Thacker had never thought of that before.

'It would complete the picture.'

Her eyes are the picture, Thacker thought. He could think of a dozen questions to ask her, a dozen lines of conversation to pursue, a dozen thoughts to share, but not a single word came out of his mouth.

He had opened the door to an unexplored country, and he didn't have a roadmap.

Caroline smiled. 'I'll see you the next time we walk into each other.' She continued down the stairs.

Thacker sat in the back row of science class, and, for the next hour, wholly ignored a lesson about how the moon's orbit affected the Earth's oceans and tides.

He was in orbit himself.

And now he knew the new girl's name. Caroline.

Lunchtime. The noonday glockenspiel rang, and the classrooms emptied like burst bags of rice. Thacker rode the flow all the way to his locker. He stowed his books, and then he headed for the stairs.

He went up.

He headed to room 59.

Room 59 sat on the building's top floor. Its door stood near the end of a long hallway that narrowed the farther along it you went. The other doors in the hall led to storage and supply rooms: chalk for blackboards, red ink for marking pens, riding crops for discipline, and so on. The door at the very end led up into the clock tower.

The door to room 59 was shut. The metal 5 and 9 nailed to it were askew. Thacker knocked – the special knock. A moment later, he heard the chair moving. No one had a key to the door; wedging a chair under the door handle on the inside effectively locked it.

Stanwick opened the door.

Thacker went in.

Room 59 was the size of a bedroom and had no windows. It was technically a classroom in that it had a blackboard and a desk (one only), but it had never been used as such. It had probably been a jail cell. Ancient graffiti carved into the wooden floor suggested that someone called 'Little Nell' was innocent.

'The dead man's name was Albert Park,' Thacker said, walking over to the blackboard. Fenella and Rosa stood next to it. Fenella had sketched out the Egyptian hieroglyphs across the board in chalk, copying from her journal. The message was made up of more than a dozen picture-like characters dotted with a couple of odd bird-like creatures and a snake.

Thacker shrugged. 'So, what does it say?'

Stanwick laughed. He wiped his glasses with his handkerchief. 'I think it's safe to assume that none of us are fluent in ancient Egyptian.'

'And the man handed this message to you just before he died?' Rosa inquired.

'Yes.'

Rosa Delgado wore a cream blouse, a cherry-red skirt, and sandals. She had short dark hair and was the shortest of Fenella,

43

Stanwick, and Thacker. She was also the fastest and the only one among them who had any interest in sporting activities (five tennis trophies). 'And you heard the man's dying words?'

'Yes: *The bride must be stopped!*'

'Which way do you read hieroglyphics?' Fenella asked, toying with her necklace. 'Left to right or right to left?'

'You look for a bird,' Rosa explained. 'You look to see which way its head is facing.' She tapped a finger on one of the bird-like creatures. 'In this message, the birds are looking to the left; they're looking to the start of the writing. So, we read this set of hieroglyphs from left to right, just like we read English.'

Thacker read the message from left to right. 'I still don't know what it says.'

'If we had a dictionary of hieroglyphics,' Rosa said, 'we could probably decipher its meaning.'

'Is this officially a case?' Stanwick asked.

Thacker nodded. 'The Case of the Dead Man at the Pier.'

'Do we know anything else about Albert Park?' Rosa asked.

'He was a crime reporter for the *City Star*.'

The four of them returned their attention to the hieroglyphs on the blackboard.

After a moment, Fenella asked, 'So, who is this bride? And why must she be stopped?'

Thacker shrugged. 'We need to translate this Egyptian into English. Maybe that'll tell us.'

There was no argument.

Rosa spoke with authority. 'We're going to need the public library.'

Thacker smiled the freedom smile. 'Anyone else feel like cutting classes for a couple of hours?'

CHAPTER TEN

Uncle Alvin slipped on his shoes and tied his shoelaces. He applied bicycle clips to the ends of his pants, then stood up from the edge of his bed. He straightened the creases in his brown vest as he took a last look in the mirror.

Almost.

He pushed his graying hair into order.

Dapper gent.

The hands on his wristwatch approached the hour. He had spent all morning fussing about in the basement with his trains, and he needed to get underway. He grabbed his wallet and left his bedroom.

He stopped in the hall and looked toward the empty room – its door remained shut. He walked along to it and tried the handle. The door remained locked.

'What are you doing?' Aunt Scarlett asked; her voice came out of nowhere.

Uncle Alvin felt his bones attempting to leap out of his skin.

His wife stood at the top of the staircase. Despite her hard heels, the woman had somehow climbed the stairs in utter silence.

'Why is this door locked?' he asked.

'I decided to lock it.'

'Why?'

'It's a door. It has a lock. There's a key.'

Sometimes, talking to his wife was like navigating a hedge maze. He had also been married to her long enough to know when she was up to something.

'Did you put something in there?'

She shook her head. 'It's an empty room, and I chose to lock it.'

Uncle Alvin chose to give up.

He walked back along the hallway to the stairs.

'Where are you going?' Aunt Scarlett asked, staring at his bicycle clips.

'I'm going to buy two tickets for the *Flying Volcano*.'

Uncle Alvin glimpsed an odd expression on his wife's face. Her eyes seemed to look right through him as though he were invisible. The last time she had looked at him like that had been the day he proposed marriage.

He could never make head nor tail of the woman.

He went downstairs, picked up his hat, went out through the kitchen door to the rear, and retrieved his bicycle from the shed. He walked it around to the street, mounted it, and rode off.

Aunt Scarlett watched her husband pedal away from an upstairs window.

She nodded confidently to herself.

She had decided she would kill him.

CHAPTER ELEVEN

MATHESON HIGH HAD A LIBRARY, BUT IT WASN'T HOME TO A comprehensive set of reading materials. From time to time, parents had been asked to contribute books to help pad out the stock. Subsequently, the library held an abundance of repair manuals, turgid romances, and telephone directories.

Rosa knew there was a book about Egypt, however. It was a pink picture book for infants, and about as detailed as to mention that Egypt was a country, a river called the Nile flowed through it, and some pyramids were to be found there. She knew that if they wanted to work out what the ancient Egyptian writing said, they would need to translate it. And to do that, they would need a translation dictionary: Hieroglyphics-to-English.

Rosa led Fenella, Stanwick, and Thacker across the concrete courtyard in front of the school building.

None of them knew they were being watched.

Caroline stood at a window on the school's second floor. She had caught sight of Thacker's head of uncombed blond hair. He trailed along behind three others, all heading for the school gates. None of them carried a schoolbag.

The glockenspiel sounded – lunchtime was over. Caroline sighed. She had little enthusiasm for her math lesson. Her eyes focused on Thacker as he walked out through the gates.

'He's a curious boy, isn't he?' said an English-accented voice.

Caroline turned, startled to find someone standing next to her.

The voice's owner was a tall, slim girl with a warm smile, a dark bob with bangs, and large brown eyes.

'Where is he going?' Caroline asked, wondering if there was an optionality to attending classes.

'Probably off to investigate something.'

'What do you mean?'

The girl introduced herself. She was Audrey Beech-Whale, hyphenated. Yes, she was from London, England.

'Thornton Thacker is a detective,' she said.

The public library was a 15-block walk from the school. Thacker had never been to the place and didn't know where it was. He just followed Rosa and the others, and Rosa led them through the city to a large brick building. A row of tall windows ran along each of its two floors. Its entrance featured a doorway big enough to permit a Greyhound bus, and Thacker would have willingly been on one rather than enter the building. Libraries smelled suspiciously of schoolwork, and you had to be quiet. Completely quiet. They'd shoot you if you weren't.

Inside, Rosa led everyone up a flight of stairs to the second floor. She understood the Dewey Decimal Classification system for organizing books in libraries, and she led them through acres of bookshelves to a shelf labeled 493.1.

There were three books on it: *Hieroglyphics for Academics*, an incorrectly sorted volume about animal husbandry, and a pink picture book for infants – the same pink picture book for infants that sat on the shelf in the school library. Rosa flicked through the academic book, her confidence lowering with every page turned.

The flicking went on for over a minute. During that time, Fenella excused herself to look in the library's poetry section, and Stanwick headed off to see if any new sheet music had been added in the music section.

'This is useless,' Rosa growled, slamming shut the book. 'It's only a discourse on the semantics, syntax, and grammar of hieroglyphic script.'

Thacker had no idea what language she spoke.

'There's nothing in it about how to translate the pictographs.'

'Sssshhh!' demanded a random passing librarian with a stern face and a rigid finger at her lips.

Thacker looked for the gun.

Rosa returned the book to the shelf. She growled a lively sentence in Spanish; Thacker knew enough of the language to recognize the cusswords.

Rosa straightened the ruffles in her cream blouse and cherry-red skirt. Calmed, she whispered in English, 'We need to look in Ancient History.'

Rosa led Thacker through the aisles across to the other side of the building. And then along a narrow aisle to a shelf labeled 932. A reasonable choice of books on Egypt's ancient history sat on this shelf. And amongst them, another copy of the pink picture book for infants.

Rosa grunted. She grabbed the pink thing and hurled it over the stacks. It landed in 910: Geography, Voyages, and Travel.

She scanned the ancient history titles, and, after a moment, she whispered, 'There's no translation dictionary.'

'Maybe there isn't one,' Thacker suggested.

'We'll need to ask downstairs at the desk.'

As they made their way back along the aisle, a thickset man in a dark tweed jacket and polka-dot tie squeezed by them, heading the other way.

The man had cropped gray hair and a tired face. There was a broken nose, and you could have brought home your groceries in the bags under his eyes. He took a long look at both Thacker and Rosa as he passed by.

Thacker took a long look at him, too. And just before he and Rosa left the aisle, he noted that the man had parked himself in front of the same shelf they had been exploring.

Thacker and Rosa made their way down to the lobby. Fenella and Stanwick waited at the foot of the stairs. Fenella held two books, and Stanwick clutched three sheets of music.

'We found nothing,' Rosa said. She spied Percy Shelley and Christina Rossetti in Fenella's hands.

Stanwick held up his sheets: two standards and a tune that was currently popular on the radio. Thacker smiled approvingly.

The four of them walked to the library's main desk, where an elderly man was engaging the head librarian in a heated debate.

The elderly man wore glasses with lenses the size of quarters and the thickness of doors. He insisted that Edgar Allan Poe had written a book about an old Cuban fisherman, and he couldn't find it anywhere in the library. He was hitting the counter with his walking stick.

The head librarian, a severe woman dressed in funereal black, argued that Poe had written no such book. The man was thinking of Hemingway's *The Old Man and The Sea*.

The man wasn't having a bar of it.

Rosa noticed a handbill pinned to the bulletin board alongside the desk. It said something about an Egyptian exhibition at the city museum. She had no sooner started to read it, when there was a shouty commotion. An exceptionally large security guard escorted the elderly man toward the entrance.

Thacker noted the gun.

'You're from Matheson High,' said the head librarian in an accusatory tone, as the four of them approached the desk.

'How can you tell?' Rosa asked.

The woman's eyes went to Thacker's hair. 'Lucky guess.'

'We're on a field trip,' Thacker said.

Rosa told the woman they were looking for a hieroglyphic translation dictionary.

The woman knew just the book. 'You need the *Christie Big Book of Egyptian Hieroglyphics*.'

'May we see it?'

The woman shook her head. 'It's missing.'

Four faces dropped.

The woman told them it was a reference-only book and was not supposed to leave the building; however, a man had 'borrowed' it. A formal letter informing the man of his criminality had been typed and posted. The head librarian wiped her eyes with a handkerchief. They had fogged with anger.

'The horrid man simply walked out of the library with the book,' she growled. 'He said he'd bring it back later that day, and he didn't. Despicable, nasty man. We know him well here at the library. He never returns his books on time, and he stinks of cigarettes.'

'Was he a newspaper reporter?' Thacker asked, taking a punt.

That got the head librarian's attention. 'He claimed to be.'

'Was his name Albert Park?'

The boy with uncombed hair standing in front of her was clairvoyant. 'Yes! That's his name.'

'He's dead.'

The woman's pursed lips and solemn nod of acknowledgment bore a whiff of approval.

Librarians were vicious, Thacker thought. And they could legally shoot you.

'We could get the book back for you,' Stanwick suggested. 'Where did Mr. Park live?'

'I couldn't possibly tell you that,' the head librarian said. 'That information is private and confidential.' She glanced about for any other librarians in the vicinity. There were none. She lowered her voice. 'However, as there is a reference book in question...'

She went into a nearby office, and they watched through the window as she rifled through a filing cabinet.

She came back and whispered distastefully: 'Albert Park's address is listed as Room 66, the *Blue Bear Hotel*, Rutland Street. It's not an address to inspire confidence.'

'*Blue Bear*, 66,' Thacker repeated back.

'It's a large book with an olive-green cover. Do you really think you can recover it?'

'We'll certainly try, ma'am.'

CHAPTER TWELVE

AN HOUR AND A HALF AFTER HE HAD RIDDEN OUT OF WALNUT STREET, Uncle Alvin rode his bicycle back in. He wore a satisfied smile and had two tickets for a jaunt on the *Flying Volcano* in his pocket. He looked forward to an outing with his niece. Caroline was a splendid girl, much like her mother, Rebecca. Rebecca had been Scarlett's younger sister, but the two sisters had fought like cat and dog. As a result, he had seen little of Caroline as she had grown up.

Uncle Alvin parked his bicycle back in the shed at the rear of the house.

He went inside, returned his hat to the hall stand, and laid the two train tickets on the side table in the front hallway near the staircase. Caroline would notice the tickets when she arrived home from school. It might bring some sunshine to her day; in this house, they could all do with a bit more brightness.

Uncle Alvin climbed the stairs. He decided he would spend the afternoon in the basement; there were timetables and schedules to be attended to. He headed into his bedroom and changed out of his civilian clothing back into his engineer's outfit.

Walking back into the hall dressed in his blue-and-white-striped overalls, red scarf, and blue cap, Uncle Alvin stopped and once again stared at the locked door. He remembered the funny look on his wife's face when he had asked her about it.

He walked along to the door and tried the handle.

The door was still locked.

He realized he was becoming obsessed by the damned thing.

He bent over and peered through the keyhole.

He couldn't see anything.

Uncle Alvin frowned. The room was empty. It had sat vacant for years. Why on earth had Scarlett locked it?

A visit to Colorado was needed. He went downstairs.

The house was quiet. Presumably, Scarlett sat in the living room in her armchair, with one hand holding a cigarette and the other patting that little dog of hers. The key to the door probably rested in one of her pockets.

Uncle Alvin opened the narrow brown door that stood in the hallway just before the kitchen, and he descended a narrow flight of dimly lit concrete steps. At the foot of the steps stood an old white door. Its upper half comprised three vertical opaque glass panels; light from the room behind lit all three. He opened it and went into the basement.

The basement was as long and wide as the house above it, and Uncle Alvin's train set took almost every inch. He had created thousands upon thousands of acres (to scale) of the Four Corners: Utah, Arizona, New Mexico, Colorado.

Uncle Alvin wasted no time.

He walked along the waist-height landscape until he came to the Rocky Mountains. He reached across the miniature scenery and plucked the top off a papier-mâché Pikes Peak. He reached inside the hollow mountain and pulled out a large ring of keys – there was a copy of every key in the house. A good engineer always kept a spare of everything close to hand.

He put the mountaintop back in place.

Before he left, he powered up the train set, blew his whistle, and threw the lever to get the trains rolling – no sense in being behind schedule.

Uncle Alvin shut the door to the basement and went back upstairs.

He returned to the locked door, unlocked it, opened it, and went inside.

Thick drapes were drawn, and the room sat in darkness. Uncle Alvin felt about the wall until he found the light switch. He flicked it on, and a naked bulb lit up the room.

Uncle Alvin didn't blink.

At first, he wasn't sure what he was looking at. And then he realized exactly what he was looking at, and he couldn't believe it.

He forgot how to breathe.

He stepped backwards into the hall and wobbled his way back to the top of the staircase. He had forgotten how to walk.

'Scarlett?' Uncle Alvin called out in a feeble, scratched voice, with his mouth and throat dry.

He made his way down the staircase, step by step.

'Scarlett?' Uncle Alvin called out again, his voice firming.

He had imagined all manner of things hidden away in that room, but never in 100,000 years had he expected to find that.

He was angry now. His voice became demanding. 'Scarlett!'

He was completely unaware that the woman had followed him down the stairs. And he certainly didn't know she held a meat cleaver.

Aunt Scarlett gritted her teeth.

With all the energy and strength she could muster, she swung that meat cleaver at Uncle Alvin's neck.

CHAPTER THIRTEEN

THE *BLUE BEAR HOTEL* STOOD ON THE DAMP SIDE OF RUTLAND STREET – the kind of street where the kids didn't happily play hopscotch and jump rope; they leered and loitered. Where the adults in authority were routinely rounded up and taken away by adults in higher authority. The hotel was seven floors of decrepit masonry. Its windows were an array of ragged curtains and broken panes.

'What's happened to the door?' Stanwick asked as he and Thacker approached the hotel's entrance.

'Nothing pleasant, I think,' Thacker remarked.

The hotel's doorway was one of those glass-paneled revolving types, or it once had been. It looked as though someone had fired a cannon through it, and nobody had tidied up afterward. Splinters of wood and glass lay everywhere inside the lobby.

It made sense to Thacker. The hotel stood two blocks from the waterfront. There was barely a quarter mile between the place and the end of the pier where Albert Park had lain dying. It was a logical assumption that whatever beast had chased and killed him there had probably chased him from where he had lived.

'What happened to the door?' Thacker asked the old man with a lumpy face seated behind the lobby desk. 'What came through it?'

The old man didn't want to know. He didn't take his face out of the sports section of his newspaper. He did tell them that 66 was on the sixth floor, although it was more of an allegation than a statement of fact.

There was no working elevator.

Thacker and Stanwick climbed the stairs.

In the hallway on the second floor, a plump man with wide-open eyes sat in a rotting armchair. He fidgeted nervously, staring at the wall directly ahead, mumbling to himself in a southern accent about the difference between blimps and dirigibles.

A dead animal lay in the hallway on floor three. It was only a beetle, but it was big enough to be described as an animal. Ordinarily, insects were things you caught out of the corner of your eye. This one could have shared a taxi with you.

Floor four had been burned. The walls and ceiling of the hallway were black, with large patches reduced to charcoal. A small girl, a child of only five or six, stood motionless in the semi-darkness at the other end. She wore a pinafore and clutched a headless doll; both she and the doll were covered in soot. She stared with eyes of canceled hope.

There was nothing at all on the fifth floor.

Thacker and Stanwick made it to the sixth and walked along the hall. Every step of Thacker's black hi-top sneakers and Stanwick's polished black shoes made the floorboards squeak – the wood had been walked upon so often, the nails were barely holding the floor in place.

Room 66 had no door; what remained of it lay in pieces. Destroyed, no doubt, by the same cannonball that had smashed its way through the lobby downstairs. A police-line tape hung loosely across the open doorway, and Thacker and Stanwick went under it.

Albert Park's room was a nicotine-stained mess of empty bottles, dirty dinner plates, full ashtrays, and books. A door led into a dank bedroom of soiled sheets. Another door led to a bathroom of cracked tiles. Clumps of stale leftovers lay germinating in a tiny kitchenette.

'Look at this,' Stanwick said. He stood by a narrow table shoved against the wall. He pointed to the photograph pinned to the wall above it with a thumb tack.

Thacker came over.

It was a photograph of someone's swanky living room: black and white, 8 x 10. Several uniforms stood about scratching their heads, Detective Franks among them. There was a body under a sheet lying on the floor at their feet. A woman's arm stuck out. Someone had scrawled a series of hieroglyphs in a dark color across the living room wall in the background. It was the same set of hieroglyphs as in the message.

Thacker frowned. 'Let's find the Christie book.'

Park liked books. They lay strewn everywhere. And they had odd, obscure titles, such as *Analytical Analysis for Aspiring Amateurs, The Naked and the Dead*, and *The Interpretation of the Iset Writings*.

Stanwick examined the books on the table: Egyptian history, sacred ceremonies, a biography of Howard Carter, a dictionary, and a thesaurus. There also lay a fat ledger full of business and financial records.

Thacker looked out the open window. Down below, he could see the hotel's rear yard. A pile of old mattresses lay spread across a patch of dirt and weeds. A dead, leafless maple tree rose to the height of the building. A couple of its branches hung near the window.

Thacker supposed Park had jumped.

Whatever had chased him hadn't.

That gave Park enough time to climb down the tree and run the two blocks to the waterfront and then along the pier – until he ran out of anywhere to run.

'I think I've found it,' Stanwick announced. A book lay open on top of a stack of newspapers on the floor. Its pages were divided into columns of hieroglyphs and accompanying explanations. He picked up the book and held it for Thacker to see. The cover was olive green. Embossed in gold across the front was the title: *Christie Big Book of Egyptian Hieroglyphics*.

Thacker smiled.

'I think we should leave,' Stanwick said, tucking the book under his arm. He had a feeling they shouldn't stay in that room.

Thacker didn't argue. He plucked the crime scene photograph from the wall using his pocketknife, and they left.

Half a minute after they had gone, the bedroom's closet door kicked open, and out poured a thick, dirty fog of cigarette smoke. Detective Franks stepped out. He still wore his black raincoat, but his tie was undone and his shirt unbuttoned. His eyelids were red and his eyes bloodshot. Even the dents in his bald head looked ruffled. He took the cigarette butt from his mouth and dropped it to the floor. He ground it dead with his heel.

A woman with heavy makeup and a head of peroxide-blonde hair stepped out of the closet after him. She could barely breathe from the smoke. 'Who was that?' she asked, adjusting her emerald-green dress; she had recently been undressed.

Franks stormed out of the bedroom.

The woman followed him. 'This is the last time I let you take me to one of your crime scenes.'

'Don't start, Delores,' Franks grunted. He gritted his teeth. The photograph was gone.

He suspected a tan trench coat and a pair of glasses.

He was thankful they hadn't taken Park's reporter's notebook – a beige notebook full of the juiciest dirt. It lay untouched on the room's only chair.

'This used to be fun, Frankie,' Delores griped. 'But it just ain't no more.'

CHAPTER FOURTEEN

CAROLINE KNOCKED ON THE FRONT DOOR OF THE DALRYMPLE HOUSE and waited. She knew she would have to knock again, maybe even a third time.

Aunt Scarlett eventually opened the door after the seventh knock. She greeted Caroline with her usual sour face and complete disinterest.

'Was there any mail for me today?' Caroline asked, hauling her schoolbag inside.

Her aunt said nothing. She closed the door and walked back to the living room.

A faint stain on the staircase caught Caroline's eye – a patch of dark red on the wood, seven steps up.

A second stain caught her eye, two steps down from the first.

Then a third, two steps up from the bottom.

Someone had spilled something and had made a reasonable effort to clean up. All the steps looked as though they'd been recently washed and wiped, but a few spots had been missed, and their shadows remained.

Caroline noticed two tickets for the *Flying Volcano* on the side table. Steam locomotives weren't her thing, but anything that would get her away from that house for an afternoon had to be good. Her uncle was a kind man. His cheerfulness was the only pleasant thing in all of Walnut Street.

Caroline looked back at the staircase.

She spied a fourth stain, smaller, higher up.

Someone had dropped something on the stairs It had bounced. She went to her room.

AUNT SCARLETT CALLED CAROLINE TO THE DINNER TABLE AN HOUR later. A plate waited for her, loaded with barely cooked cabbage, potatoes, and carrots. It was indescribably tasteless, and its color was inexplicably beige. Caroline was too hungry to complain. She reminded herself that it was food; her only alternative was to eat the tabletop.

She ate in silence.

Aunt Scarlett sat opposite. She smoked and ate – a mouthful of food, a drag on her cigarette, occasionally a mouthful of a dark green liquid from a tall glass. She wore the same powder-blue Grace blouse tucked neatly into high-waist crepe slacks that she always wore.

Caroline asked. 'Where is Uncle Alvin?'

'Argentina.'

There was no expression readable on the woman's face, and she wasn't known for her sense of humor.

'I'm sorry,' Caroline said. 'Did you say Argentina?'

'Yes.'

'Argentina, the country?'

Aunt Scarlett grumbled, 'He's gone to Buenos Aires.' She was bored with the conversation.

'Why has he done that?'

'To learn how to dance the tango.'

Caroline waited for the punchline or for her uncle to bounce into the room with a hearty laugh.

She waited for five minutes. Neither happened. She finished her dinner, and Aunt Scarlett finished her cigarette.

'I didn't always used to be a bitch,' Aunt Scarlett said.

Caroline looked across the table at her. Her aunt had an odd face. She looked almost remorseful.

'I used to be young once, like you. I was full of enthusiasm and hope.'

Caroline had never noticed before how tired her aunt looked.

Her black eyes were flanked with a clutch of creases. It was as though the woman never slept.

'That's the difference between you and me,' Aunt Scarlett said.

'What is?'

'Your mother and father loved you.' She swallowed the last mouthful of her dark green liquid.

'What is that you're drinking?' Caroline asked. 'You have it every dinnertime.'

'It's cabbage juice. And a spoonful of dirt.'

Before Caroline could inquire more about the concoction, her aunt continued with what was becoming a monologue.

'I had a sister who didn't love me,' she said, 'and a father who only loved my sister.'

Her eyes focused tightly on Caroline.

'Rebecca always got the best. She got anything she wanted. She even got to pick her husband. Did you know she met your father on an ocean liner?'

Caroline nodded.

Aunt Scarlett stared at the knife lying on her dinner plate. She stared at its sharp edge and a stain of carrot on its blade. Without taking her eyes from the knife, she asked, 'Do you believe in true love, a love that lasts forever?'

Caroline did, but she didn't know if she should answer her aunt's question or if the woman was thinking out loud.

Her aunt raised her head. 'I was made to marry Alvin. Did you know that?'

Caroline didn't.

'Your grandfather arranged it. He selected Alvin as my husband.' She said 'selected' as though the word had been coated in battery acid. 'The Dalrymple family had distribution contracts and connections throughout the Orient, and your grandfather wanted to expand our family's business.'

She returned her eyes to the knife. After a moment, she shook her head slowly. 'Alvin could never satisfy me.'

'May I be excused?' Caroline didn't want to be having this conversation.

Aunt Scarlett sniffed. 'It'll be the summer solstice in a few days.' There was a faint smile.

Caroline didn't know what to do with that random piece of information.

Her aunt flicked her hand, dismissing her from the table.

Caroline took her plate to the kitchen and then headed back to her bedroom.

Aunt Scarlett lit another cigarette and took a deep drag. She pouted and then exhaled. Her smoke hovered above the dining table like a rain cloud. It slowly rose, dissipating as it went, its molecules joining the billions of others lodged in the ceiling's stained paintwork.

Aunt Scarlett picked up the knife she had been staring at. She put the cigarette in her mouth and stood up.

In a brutal downward thrust, she stabbed the tabletop.

She carved a triangle into the bare wood, with each of its three sides two feet long.

She dropped the knife onto the table and sat down again.

She smoked and stared at the triangle.

She smiled.

It wasn't a regular smile. It was that smile of hers, with her eyes hung low, unblinking, with the corners of her mouth slowly rising, drawing her lips back over her teeth.

CHAPTER FIFTEEN

CREAK.

Caroline's eyes opened.

It was the floorboard in the room above, again. A footstep.

Caroline rolled onto her side and half-buried her head in the pillow. Her eye that wasn't buried looked across at the alarm clock on the top of the chest of drawers – less than one minute of sleep remained on the little round dial. Another day of school ahead. Thrills.

Caroline pondered the concept of her uncle traveling to Argentina to learn how to dance.

How did he travel there? Locomotive?

The alarm clock rang. Caroline hated the sound, but that was the point of alarm clocks. Torture. She climbed out of bed and turned the thing off.

She heard sniffing; it came from under her bedroom door.

She opened it, and Jasper bounded into the room. He ran circles around her feet – it was his way of telling her breakfast was ready.

'Hello, little thing,' Caroline said.

Jasper stopped. He looked up at her with bright eyes and his tongue hanging out. He appeared to smile and then ran from the room.

Caroline put on her dressing gown and slippers.

On her way to the dining room, she looked again at the framed magazine clipping hanging on the wall and her uncle's smiling face. She looked again at the two train tickets that lay on the side table.

Argentina?

The tango?

It was frankly ridiculous. The man was obsessed with trains, not South American dance steps.

She went to the dining room.

A place had not been set at the table for Uncle Alvin.

Aunt Scarlett sat in her usual seat with her cigarette and cup of coffee. It was odd to see her in daylight – the drapes had been drawn back, and she sat caught in the morning sun. She wore a red polyester bathrobe and had washed her hair that morning. It lay slumped on her scalp like a dead beige animal.

Caroline took her seat at the table. A glass of milk and a plate with two pieces of toast waited for her. She noticed someone had carved a triangle into the tabletop.

She didn't ask.

The toast was hard and cold. The two pieces of bread had popped out of the toaster at least an hour earlier. Caroline smeared a layer of raspberry jam across one slice and ate it for the best.

Aunt Scarlett was looking upwards, her eyes veering to the right. She wasn't looking, she was thinking.

Caroline studied her.

The woman's face appeared gray and cold in the daylight – crinkled and prehistoric, as though her head had been carved from rock. She was only 50, Caroline reminded herself.

'How long is Uncle Alvin going to be in Argentina?' Caroline asked.

Aunt Scarlett stopped thinking. 'Six months.' There wasn't a trace of emotion. 'The tango is a complicated dance,' she said. 'You can't master it in one day. You have to commit time and effort.'

'This is a joke, isn't it?'

The rock face remained unchanged.

'He's upstairs, isn't he?'

Aunt Scarlett shook her head. She stubbed out her cigarette, rose from the table, and left the room.

Half a minute later, the loud, angry music of a string quartet erupted from the gramophone in the living room. The noise of it flooded the house.

Aunt Scarlett returned. She sat back in her seat and gazed across the table at Caroline, her head hanging forward like that of a vulture, her teeth protruding.

Caroline tried not to look at the woman. She finished her second piece of toast and washed the crumbs down with the last mouthful of milk.

There was a lull in the music.

'*Der Tod und das Mädchen*,' Aunt Scarlett bellowed loudly in a heavy Germanic accent.

It was so startling a broadcast that Jasper woke in astonishment and Caroline almost stood to attention.

'Schubert,' Aunt Scarlett said. 'Now there was a composer who knew how to get inside the listener's head.'

Caroline couldn't take her aunt's intense staring any longer. She excused herself and left the table. She knew enough German from school to know that the music's title translated into English as 'Death and the Maiden.'

She knew which of the two she was supposed to be.

Her aunt was the other.

CHAPTER SIXTEEN

'I MET A TRAVELER FROM AN ANTIQUE LAND,' FENELLA SAID.

Thacker glanced at her. She was reading the Shelley book she had gotten from the library.

'It's the first line of a poem.'

Thacker figured that. He drank some more coffee. There was nothing better than the aroma and taste of black coffee in the morning; the fuel of the gods. He looked out the café window. The morning sun lit up the storefronts across the street. Life crowded the sidewalk: people moving, places to go, things to get done. Automobiles shuffled by – taxis, cars, buses, trucks – with impatient drivers and car horns. On mornings like these, the city bustled. It had rhythm and kick like a drum kit.

Thacker glanced at Rosa's slender fingers; she sat across the table from him. It always amazed him how tightly she could grip a drumstick, how hard she could strike a snare.

'They're identical,' Rosa pronounced, comparing the hieroglyphs in the crime scene photograph to the copy in Fenella's journal.

The three of them sat in the *Rainy Night Café* at the old wooden table by the window. The café was open every day of the week, rain or shine, and every hour of the day. It was the best place in the city, and only two blocks from the school gates.

Fenella finished reading the Shelley poem. She had read it before; all the talk about Ancient Egypt had reminded her of it. She closed the book. 'Do words die?'

'How do you mean?' Rosa asked.

'Those hieroglyphs are words, a message, from an ancient

time,' Fenella said. 'A long time ago, most people probably knew what they said. Now, we need a dictionary to understand them.' She pointed to the *Christie Big Book of Egyptian Hieroglyphics* under Rosa's elbow.

'They're dead words,' Thacker said. He took another mouthful of coffee. 'And does the message simply say: *The bride must be stopped*?'

'I haven't looked through the Christie book to confirm,' Rosa said. 'But I think this is someone's name.' She pointed to the three hieroglyphs at the message's end.

'How do you know?'

'They're inside a cartouche.' Her finger traced the line encircling them, enclosing them in an oblong. There was a vertical line drawn at one end. 'Hieroglyphic characters enclosed inside a cartouche almost always represent someone's name – usually someone important.'

Thacker pulled his I hate puzzles face.

Fenella finished her coffee.

She glanced at the clock on the wall behind the café counter. The start of the school day was nearing. There was no one else in the café besides Mimi, the owner – she stood behind the counter adding more beans to the coffee machine. Fenella went over and asked if she'd seen Sultana. Mimi hadn't.

Thacker threw back his last mouthful of his coffee.

'Shall we go?' Rosa asked.

'Yup.'

They grabbed their schoolbags.

Stanwick stood at the top of the steps, his schoolbag at his feet. A slow-moving morning tide of students flowed in through the gates, across the concrete courtyard, and up into the school building – swallowed for another day by education.

Stanwick wiped the lenses of his glasses with a clean white handkerchief. He had once seen Louis Armstrong perform. The man had held his trumpet in one hand and a large white handkerchief in the other. A week later, Stanwick had acquired a set of similar handkerchiefs. Not that he played the trumpet; his

STEPHEN ROSS

instrument was the piano. His days began and ended at the piano keyboard in his parents' basement. Finger exercises. Practice pieces. Scales: major and minor, and the pentatonics and their blue notes – the bittersweet notes of the keys.

Stanwick put his glasses back on and set his chestnut eyes to the sky. The sunny morning had ended, and a battlement of dark clouds was assembling. The day had begun in G major 7th, but it was quickly becoming D minor.

Thacker's socks didn't match. Stanwick observed this as Thacker, Rosa, and Fenella crossed the courtyard toward him. He smiled.

'Do you know what a cartouche is?' Thacker asked him as they climbed the steps.

'It's French. It means cartridge.'

'That's right,' Rosa said.

The four of them went into the building's entrance hall. Students crowded the wide concrete concourse, their voices echoing in the cavernous space. Corridors led off to the teachers' lunchroom and the school administration office. Several sets of stairs led up to the floors of classrooms. You had to be careful on the concourse not to trip on the rusty bolts that jutted out of the floor. The space had originally housed rows of metal prison cages bolted to the floor.

Fenella spotted someone on the stairs she needed to talk to and headed in his direction. The other three huddled.

'The cartouche got its name from French soldiers during the Napoleonic era,' Rosa explained. 'Its appearance reminded them of their bullet cartridges.'

They watched Fenella. She stood on the stairs, a step below a guy wearing a bored look and sunglasses. He stood slumped against the railing with his hands in his pockets. He wore a white T-shirt, and his jeans had rips. Fenella was talking to him; he was barely replying. He barely looked at her.

'Who is that?' Thacker asked.

'Kevin,' Rosa said. 'He's a poet. He's her new boyfriend.'

'What happened to the old one?'

'She returned him to the store,' Stanwick said. 'He was defective.'

Thacker didn't like the look of Kevin. 'Her last boyfriend was nice,' he said. 'He owned a set of bongo drums.'

'You, boy!' barked an angry man's voice. It was, unmistakably, Mr Undergarden. He stood on the other side of the concourse, his drooping eyes unblinking.

The students on the concourse and stairs promptly shut up.

A bony finger extended from the frayed sleeve of Undergarden's long black coat. 'Thacker!' he barked, clarifying the finger's target.

No additional instructions were required.

Thacker handed his schoolbag to Stanwick and headed in the man's direction. And then, together, he and Undergarden proceeded to The Staircase of Doom. It only went down, and it led to three locations: the boiler room, the execution chamber, and Principal Puddle's office.

No words were spoken.

Thacker followed Undergarden into the school's bowels. It was a descent into the lowest depths of the school. A place where the sun didn't shine, the wind had no measure, and all life ended. And Undergarden never once looked back to see if Thacker trailed behind. It was understood that when a boy was summoned, he would follow.

They passed the red door to the execution chamber. It stood ten feet high and four feet wide. Thacker noted the rusty padlock was still in place.

The corridor leading to Principal Puddle's office was 30 yards long, narrow, and brightly lit. There were no other doors, just Puddle's rusty metal one at the end. Splashes of dirty brown liquid lay on the floor, and scratch marks on the walls became more apparent the closer you drew to it.

Undergarden knocked.

There was a muffled 'Enter.'

Undergarden opened the door, and Thacker entered. Undergarden didn't follow. His work was done.

Principal Puddle sat at the center of his office behind his desk – a vast plane of cedar dotted with papers and books lit by a bank of fluorescent tubes high above. His office was 80 feet wide and circular. The floor was white rubber, despoiled from decades of foot traffic. The walls were padded with cushioning – row upon row of two-foot square panels of dirty beige felt, with four inches of rubber behind each. The rows went from the floor to the ceiling, 20 feet above.

Puddle's stubby fingers beckoned Thacker to approach.

Thacker approached.

The nameplate on the desk read: P.P. Puddle.

Puddle was an obese man with a nose like a lumpy potato and a face with an abundance of loose, sagging flesh. Like Undergarden, his age was unfathomable. A bulky academic black robe flowed about Puddle's shoulders, and on his head sat a black skull cap with a square board on top; a long gold tassel hung loosely over an edge.

The Puddle, as he was known (in whispers) by the student body, was a reclusive man. He seldom ventured from his office. The most anyone saw of him was on the first day of each new school year, when the students would assemble in the courtyard at the school building's rear. He would stand on a raised wooden platform, peer down at everyone with two sloping, bushy gray eyebrows, and deliver a forty-minute speech, in Latin, about the need for civility, comportment, and cleanliness. After this, he would shrink back to the school's underbelly.

Thacker stood in front of the desk. There was no chair; the condemned were not afforded the luxury of seating.

'You are on a road, Thacker,' Puddle said. With the fingernail of his left index finger, he attempted to dislodge a piece of carcass from a cleft in his lower jaw. There was a voluminous dinner plate on his desk. A meal had been consumed. There were bones.

'What road am I on?' Thacker asked.

'Life is a long, winding road,' Puddle said. 'Along its way, there are many side streets and alleyways, thoroughfares and lanes.'

'Sir?'

70

The man cast his eyes upon Thacker's tan trench coat and untucked shirt. There was a look of disdain. 'Somewhere, Thacker, many miles back, you have taken a wrong turn.'

'Have I?'

'Yes, and you have found yourself on the highway to damnation.'

'Have I?'

The Puddle snorted with infuriation. 'It is bad enough that you are proceeding down that highway, but now you seem insistent upon taking passengers with you.'

Thacker stared at the man. He knew the man was talking in metaphors, but he had no idea what he was metaphoring about.

Meat removed from his jaw, Puddle launched into a lengthy tirade, enhancing and expanding upon his road, highway, traveling, and damnation metaphor. It took five minutes for Thacker to realize he was being told off, and, after another 500 miles of metaphor, Puddle finally arrived at his point.

'It is bad enough that you seem to suit yourself about attending classes, but it is thoroughly reprehensible when you walk away from school, before the time of leaving, and take three other pupils along with you.'

The man was talking about the previous day's visit to the public library during school hours.

'Do you want to be expelled, boy?'

'No.' However, Thacker could see the benefits.

'You can wipe that expectant smirk off your face,' Puddle roared, his jowls shuddering. 'Don't think I can't see it.'

Thacker wiped.

The big man calmed. 'You must find an alternative route and rejoin the correct road.'

Thacker thought of asking for a roadmap but thought better of it. When Principal Puddle was in a metaphor, it was best not to climb in along with him.

Puddle sat back and inhaled. He inhaled so much air his cheeks puffed up, and he looked like he might explode. He then exhaled, and a great gust crossed his desk, lifting the papers on it. 'As punishment, I'm tempted to delay summer break another week.'

Thacker's face dropped. 'You've already delayed it until Friday. You can't punish me like that.'

Puddle's eyes sparkled. 'It wouldn't just be for you. It would be a delay for everyone in the school.'

Thacker's dropped face went pale. This was migraine territory. 'You can't do that. Punish me if you want, but leave everyone else out.'

Puddle shook his head. He slid open his top desk drawer. He held up a small, rusty key. 'Do you know what this unlocks?'

Thacker had a good idea: a rusty padlock.

'I am the principal. I can do whatever I choose to whomever I please. Rejoin the correct road, boy, or I will add another week.'

Thacker was excused.

He fled for his life.

Rosa sat at the top of the stairs reading the Christie book of hieroglyphics. She watched Thacker climb the stairs from the concourse. The mess of blond hair on his head looked even more disheveled. She had known Thacker for two years, and she had never seen his hair combed or cut.

Thacker smiled at her – she had skipped class, a fellow traveler on the highway to damnation.

'I've translated one of the words,' Rosa said.

'You know the name inside the cartouche?'

'No, it's one of the other words, and I'm fairly certain I have the translation right.'

'You two should be in class,' said the elderly Mrs Driscoll, passing. She took the next staircase and headed up. She was probably on her way to the top floor to retrieve a fresh box of chalk for education and crowd control.

Thacker and Rosa shuffled along the corridor.

'What's the word?'

'Bride.'

CHAPTER SEVENTEEN

MR GREEN WAS A TALL MAN WITH A GARIBALDI BEARD AND A preoccupation with dates. He walked about the classroom, reeling off a bunch of them related to Napoleon Bonaparte and his war with Britain. Claudius, in the second row, questioned the sleeping arrangements between Mr Bonaparte and Ms Josephine. He'd heard rumors of ropes and feathers. Mr Green became red. He hurriedly began listing the days of each of the Napoleonic War's battles.

Caroline wasn't paying attention. She sat in the back row and worked on refining a letter to the Scottish Highlands. She had her own battles to worry about.

Dear Aunt Lillian,

I am writing to you with hope.

I hope you have received my other letters. As I wrote earlier, I haven't seen you since I was a child and I hope you remember me. I remember you well. I fondly remember our visits to your farm and our many picnics by Loch Carron. I still remember that afternoon when I fell into the lake, and my father (your brother) had to jump in and rescue me. I have many happy memories of our visits to Scotland.

I will be honest.

I write to you because I find myself in a mess. I am in a place of no happy memories. As I wrote earlier, I now live with my mother's sister, Scarlett. She is the only living relative I have left in this country, and I was given no choice but to stay with her.

I will be direct.

Do you still have that spare room, the one that looked out to the oak tree and the hills? I am very tidy. I am good at housework. I promise I would be of no trouble to you.

Please, please reply,

Even if your answer is to be no.

Your loving niece,

Caroline Greer

xxx

P.S. I would be more than happy to sleep in the barn. And I know how to milk a cow.

Caroline sighed. It was her fifth letter to her aunt. She folded the letter and tucked it into an envelope. With a lick of her tongue and the pressing of her fingers, she sealed it. She then thought again about her uncle.

Thacker felt folded up, himself. He sat in the back row of English class and had better things to do than listen to a lot of talk about Shakespeare. Apparently, William Shakespeare was significant, despite the fact the man had been dead for 500 years and had worn funny clothes. And there was something about a balcony. Apparently, balconies were very important in England 500 years ago. Thacker was glad he didn't live in England 500 years ago; everyone spoke in poetry.

The Stick of Severity struck Thacker about the back of his head, and he snapped back into reality.

Mrs Denton loomed over him.

Mrs Denton was a thin, middle-aged woman with bifocals and a fondness for looming. She once claimed to have read everything written by Charles Dickens, the Brontë sisters, Mark Twain, and Henry James. A claim Thacker had found deeply suspicious. And she carried a weapon: a 23-inch length of bamboo. She used it to point at things, slam down on hands, and strike backs of heads.

She asked Thacker, again, if *Romeo and Juliet* was a history, comedy, or tragedy.

Thacker didn't know. He didn't even understand the question. 'It's a play,' he guessed.

'Try again.'

Thacker put on a thoughtful expression and slowly inhaled, as though he was mulling an answer. It was a tactic that had served him well. He might not have been paying attention to the lesson, but he knew the exact time, and he could breathe in an awful lot of breath.

After a long moment of mulling and inhaling, the glockenspiel sounded. The class woke up, and, like a roomful of tightly wound clockwork devices, everyone sprang to their feet and headed for the door, taking Thacker along with them.

His next class was math. Things could only get worse.

Thacker trudged along the corridor to his locker.

A hand grabbed his shoulder from behind.

He turned about.

He was startled. The hand belonged to Caroline. 'I've been told you're a detective.'

'It's one of my hobbies,' he answered.

'I'd like to hire you.'

'Why?'

'I think something may have happened to my uncle.'

'What kind of something?'

'I don't know. Would you be interested in investigating?'

'Sure.'

'I can't pay you.'

Thacker shook his head. 'I don't do detecting for the money.'

'Could you start today?'

'How about after school?'

'Yes. Will you walk home with me?'

'Of course. We can meet at the gate after school.'

'Okay. Thank you.' She headed off to her next class.

Thacker went to his.

He spent the next hour sitting in the back row, staring out the window at cloud formations. He was oblivious to them being burnt yellow and full of rain. His conversation with Caroline had lasted 15 seconds, and in that tiny moment of time, things changed. Everything had become sunshine.

He would see Caroline after school.

He would walk her home.

Caroline.

The girl.

What was that about an uncle?

CHAPTER EIGHTEEN

THERE WAS A QUALITY OF NO-NONSENSE TO CAROLINE THAT THACKER found irresistible.

'To cut a long story short,' she said, 'I live with my uncle and aunt, and my uncle has gone missing. I'm not sure if he's still in the house, and I don't believe the story my aunt is telling me about where he's gone.'

'Where did she say he went?'

'South America.'

The two of them were walking, hauling their schoolbags. They had met at the school gates, as planned, and headed off together toward Caroline's house. It was a journey that led them into a suburban part of the city – a place where people owned tidy homes on tidy parcels of land on tidy streets. Where there lay the possibility of a picket fence, a porch, and a rocking chair. Where people smiled and waved at you, baked apple pie, and hung Home-Sweet-Home samplers on their living room walls. And where the leading cause of death was from sheer, utter, complete boredom.

Caroline opened her bag and took out the framed magazine clipping of her uncle; she had plucked it off the wall when leaving the house that morning.

'Is your uncle a locomotive engineer?' Thacker asked, looking at the man's clothes.

'Kind of,' Caroline said. 'He lives for trains and his train set.'

'He has a train set?'

'Yes. He told me that when he was a child, he wanted to grow up to be a train engineer.'

'What did he grow up to be?'

'I'm not entirely sure.'

Caroline told Thacker how her uncle, according to her aunt, went to Argentina to learn how to dance the tango. 'He doesn't have the physique,' she said. 'I'm sure he could manage a sedate waltz, but I don't picture him gliding about the dance floor in any sprightly manner.'

A blinding flash of white lit up the sky, and seconds later, a thunderous crack echoed throughout the city. It had been a week of sizzling summer days, but the arsenal of gunmetal clouds assembled in the sky was soon to say goodbye to that.

'Tell me about your aunt,' Thacker asked.

'She is an angry woman.'

'Does she like trains?'

'I don't think she likes anything.'

'Does she have any hobbies?'

'Smoking. And growing vegetables. She has a garden in back of the house.'

They turned the corner and walked onto Walnut Street. Walnut wasn't one of those tidy suburban streets.

'Which one is your house?'

'It's at the end. And there's something I want you to look at when we go inside.'

'Sure. What?'

'There are stains on the staircase. I think they might be blood.'

Thacker nodded. 'I've seen a few stains and splatter patterns before. I'll pay attention.'

They approached the house.

'Do your aunt and uncle have any children?'

'None.'

Caroline checked the mailbox. There was no mail.

'It looks crooked,' Thacker remarked.

'What does?'

'Your house.'

The large, old house seemed to lean to the left, although it may have been an illusion caused by the tilt of the dark trees that lined both sides and the overcast afternoon light.

There was a second flash and an accompanying crack of thunder.

Caroline led Thacker to the front door, and she knocked.

The front door looked crooked, too.

Caroline glanced at Thacker and said, 'My aunt will wonder why you're here.'

'Tell her I've come along to help with your homework.'

'Do you know anything about math?'

'I know a lot about music.'

Caroline knocked again. 'I should warn you: my aunt can be a little abrasive.'

The door unlocked and opened. Aunt Scarlett's eyes registered Caroline and then darted to Thacker.

'This is my friend, Thornton,' Caroline said. 'He's come to help me with my music homework.'

Aunt Scarlett reached out and grabbed Caroline by her arm. Her grip was vise-like. She yanked Caroline into the house. 'Go away,' she hissed at Thacker. 'There will be no boys coming in here.'

She shut the door and locked it.

'That was rude,' Caroline snapped at her aunt. She dropped her bag to the floor and reached to unlock the door.

Aunt Scarlett grabbed her wrist. 'I will not have boys coming into this house.'

The thin woman possessed a startling amount of strength. She marched Caroline along the hallway to her bedroom. She announced Caroline wouldn't be eating dinner that night until she completed her homework.

She left and slammed the door.

She came back a moment later, threw Caroline's schoolbag into the room, and slammed the door again.

Caroline sat on the edge of her bed. She cradled her wrist. It throbbed. There would be bruises.

There was a tapping – knuckle on glass. Thacker's face was at the window, his honey-colored eyes looking in.

Caroline went to the window and unlatched it. She slid it up.

'Abrasive as a broken bottle,' Thacker whispered.

'I'm so sorry,' Caroline whispered back. 'She was very rude to you.'

Thacker dropped his schoolbag onto the ground and perched at one end of the windowsill. 'I want the long story now.'

'What do you mean?'

'You cut the long story short. Why do you live with your aunt and uncle?'

Caroline perched at the other end of the windowsill. She took a glance across at the door. 'My mother and father are both dead,' she said.

'I'm very sorry.' Thacker sensed the need to comfort her. He wanted to reach across and hold her hand, but he wasn't sure how to do that. That kind of thing was an undiscovered country, and he didn't have a map.

'I grew up on the other side of the city,' Caroline said. 'I used to attend Hallas High. The decision for me to come and live here was made by lawyers and Aunt Scarlett. And Aunt Scarlett is the reason I started at Matheson with only one week left until summer break!' Her brow knitted. 'And why is the school still open?'

Thacker frowned. 'Almost everyone flunked their finals, so The Puddle delayed summer a week.'

'Did you pass?'

'I got an A in music. Do you have no other family?'

'Only my father's sister, my Aunt Lillian. She lives in Scotland.'

'Scotland?'

'My father was Scottish.'

'Where were you born?'

'Here, in this city.'

'But you'd rather be in Scotland.'

'How did you guess?'

'It's in your eyes.'

She smiled enthusiastically. 'Scotland is a wonderful place. There's so much to do and to explore there.'

'Countryside?'

'Yes.'

Thacker wasn't a fan of fields and streams.

'I got my love of exploring from my father,' Caroline said. 'He was an archaeologist. He was always away somewhere digging something up.'

'An archaeologist?'

'Yes.'

'Did he ever dig up anything in Egypt?'

'Yes. The year before I was born, he dug up the tomb of Sennefer the Unbelievably Magnificent, if you've ever heard of him and his ridiculous name?'

Thacker hadn't. 'Could your father read hieroglyphics?'

'Yes.'

'Can you?'

'No. Why?'

'We're having a problem with another case.'

There were creaks in the floorboards in the hall; someone was heading toward Caroline's room.

'Hide.'

Thacker jumped off the sill and dropped below the window.

Caroline sprang across the room and perched on the edge of her bed.

The door opened, and Aunt Scarlett stepped in with a sullen face and suspicious eyes. 'I heard talking.'

'I was thinking out loud,' Caroline answered.

Her aunt walked across to the bed and bent over, bringing her head two inches from Caroline's face.

She studied her niece.

After a moment, Aunt Scarlett's glum face attempted to evolve into a friendly smile. It didn't succeed. 'We have to take good care of you,' she whispered, as though it was a secret of some kind.

Caroline didn't know what to say.

Aunt Scarlett sniffed the air, and her eyes narrowed. She looked across the room. 'Why is the window open?'

'Fresh air.'

Aunt Scarlett went over and looked outside.

She inhaled a lungful of the late-afternoon air, and her nose twitched.

She could sense something, but was unsure of exactly what. Had she peered over the windowsill, she would have seen Thacker.

'I have another letter,' Caroline announced, drawing her aunt's attention away from the window. She retrieved the envelope from her schoolbag. She held it out for her aunt to see. 'Could you please post this for me?'

Aunt Scarlett came over. She took the envelope, read the address, and said nothing. She returned to the window and slammed it shut. She took the letter and left, slamming the door behind her.

Caroline breathed.

Thacker rose at the window and stared inside. He put his hand to the glass.

Caroline went to the window and raised her hand to touch his from the other side.

A flash of light lit the sky, and thunder followed. Rain was coming. Thacker shrugged. With a sad smile, he gave Caroline a small wave.

She waved back.

Thacker grabbed his schoolbag and left.

Caroline went to her bed, fell backward onto it, and blew out an exhale of frustrated air.

Aunt Scarlett sat in her armchair in the living room. She scratched a match and lit a cigarette. She then set fire to Caroline's envelope and watched it burn.

She studied the deep glow and texture of the flames.

It mesmerized her.

After a moment, she tossed the burning envelope into the fireplace.

Jasper raised his head, yawned, and went straight back to sleep.

Aunt Scarlett reached down to the floor alongside her chair and picked up a large black notebook with a red metal spiral spine. She took the fountain pen that lay on the small table next to her chair. She opened the notebook to a blank page and wrote the word 'SOON' in red ink.

She wrote the word again.

And again.

She spent the next hour smoking and writing the word over and over until she had filled several pages and the ink in her fountain pen had run dry.

SOON
SOON
SOON
SOON
SOON
SOON
SOON
SOON
SOON
SOON
SOON
SOON
SOON
SOON
SOON
SOON
SOON
SOON
SOON
SOON
SOON

CHAPTER NINETEEN

IT RAINED HARD THAT AFTERNOON AND INTO THE EVENING.

Sultana returned to Henderson Heights. Fenella found her waiting on the doorstep, soaked. The cat had been absent for three days, and she looked miffed, as though she had recently been made to suffer some great indignity. Fenella led her to the kitchen and provided her with a bowl of milk and a plateful of cheese, salmon, and blueberries – the cat's standard recovery pack.

Dashiell also returned home that evening. Philip found his dog lying on the doorstep of his building, looking rattled, wet, and somewhat the worse for wear. If the old dog could have talked, he would have requested strong liquor, a blanket, and the booking of a six-month ocean cruise.

Whatever had taken place in the preceding 72 hours, one thing was certain: the dog would no longer entertain any idea about pursuing that specific cat.

Thacker took off his wet trench coat and hung it on a hook by the kitchen door. He then took a seat at the table. 'You have a new boyfriend.'

'Yeah.' Fenella stood a plate in front of him: mashed potatoes, two sausages, a tomato, and a small acreage of green peas.

The kitchen at the Thacker house was a small room with vivid pink walls and blue-colored cupboards. The Man Upstairs had painted the room. There had been no explanation.

'Any ketchup?' Thacker asked.

'There's none left.'

Fenella took the seat opposite her brother.

'There's a new case,' Thacker said. 'The Case of the Missing Uncle.'

'Whose uncle?'

'A girl I know. Her uncle has a train set.'

Thacker noticed the Shelley book on his sister's side of the table. There was a bookmark. 'Dead words, huh?'

A door slammed higher in the house. The two of them looked at the ceiling. More noises from above reverberated down the staircase. Something had been thrown against a wall. The sound of something hitting the floor and shattering followed. They looked at the head of the table. Fenella hadn't even bothered laying out a knife and fork.

'He has a deadline,' she remarked.

Thacker nodded. 'If that typewriter were a person, we'd have to call the cops.'

They ate without talking. There was further turbulence from above – random thuds and bumps, and furniture movements.

'We have no control, do we?' Thacker said.

'What do you mean?'

He pointed upwards. 'If anything happened to him, what would happen to us? Where would we go? Where would we live?'

Fenella chewed on a piece of sausage and thought about that.

She eventually shrugged. 'I don't know. Your mother is in jail, and who knows where mine is?'

'And who else is there?' Thacker asked.

She sighed. 'The odd random uncle and aunt.'

'We don't know, do we?'

She came to the same conclusion.

The sound of a gunshot echoed through the house from the top floor.

Thacker and Fenella froze – their eyes wide and their ears listening. The silence seemed to last forever.

And then they heard it: footsteps pacing. The Man Upstairs was walking in a circle again – no doubt with angry eyes, a sheet of paper and pencil in his hands, and another bullet hole in his typewriter.

'I'd look after you if anything happened to him,' Thacker said.

Fenella looked at her brother, a skeptical eyebrow raised. 'How?'

'I'd get a job or something.'

For a moment, she considered the possibility she was hallucinating, but there was a seriousness in her brother's honey-colored eyes.

The pacing stopped, and the sound of typewriting returned. All was at peace. The Man Upstairs was back inside his latest book.

They finished eating. Fenella took their plates to the sink.

Thacker drank a mouthful of water. 'When did you know you were in love?'

'In love with whom?' That wasn't a typical question from her brother.

'Your boyfriend.'

'I don't know that I am.'

'Really?'

'I dig him, but I don't know that I'm ready to leap off the top of a building. We've only known each other for a month.'

'How long does it usually take?'

'To fall in love?'

'To leap off the top of a building.'

'You just know, I guess.'

Sultana jumped onto the table. She sauntered along it, looking for crumbs, found none, and then looked to Fenella. Fenella fed her some more fish.

After that, Fenella took a glass of water and her Shelley book and went upstairs.

Thacker gave the cat some more milk and then washed the dishes.

After that, he went up to the top of the building.

There were puddles on the roof. Thacker stepped around them. The roof was flat, higher than its neighbors, and on the street's higher side. The sky was a mess of exhausted clouds, with scatterings of stars breaking through. The rain was over, and the city lights shimmered in the damp air. It was a sultry night.

Thacker took a seat on the park bench. It was wet, but he

didn't care. His father had dragged the bench up to the roof a long time ago, along with an assortment of potted palms and a pink flamingo. There had been no explanation. Thacker sat back and looked at the view.

The city was a dense sprawl of buildings from the near to the far, umpteen columns of vertical lights with a soundtrack of traffic at their feet. He loved it. It was jazz made physical. Bebop. After the *Rainy Night Café*, the Thacker roof in the middle of the night was Thacker's favorite place in the world. And above him, glowing large in cool blue, hung the words:

LIVING ROOM

His father had hauled that up to the roof, too: a neon sign. He had duct-taped the big thing halfway up the roof's lightning rod and had run a power cable down the staircase to the first available power socket. Where he'd gotten the sign from and why he'd hung it on the roof were yet untold tales.

Thacker could hear Francine Timmins practicing her scales. Francine lived across the street, played the cello, and was into Bach. Thacker had never spoken to her. Every night in Henderson Heights, there was a soundtrack of babies crying, dogs barking, angry people griping, and Francine continuing her lessons.

The Thacker house was one of the narrower buildings in the street, and Thacker's father had never sublet. With only the three of them, it meant they had a floor each to themselves: Fenella had the second, Thacker the third, with their father on the top floor in his office. The roof was anyone's for the taking.

A streak of lightning flashed above the city. A few seconds later came a deep roll of thunder in the distance.

Thacker sighed.

'So, it's a woman, is it now?' asked a voice.

Thacker turned about.

Mister Thacker stood in the stairwell doorway, leaning against the frame. Aloha shirt, Bermuda shorts, loafers. He looked beaten up, as though he had gone 12 rounds for a heavyweight title.

He came over and took a seat on the park bench next to Thacker. He sat back, adjusted his spectacles, and looked at the city.

A car horn honked below.

'How will I know when I'm in love?' Thacker asked.

'You won't,' Mister Thacker said. 'And if you're asking, you probably already are.'

Thacker shrugged. 'How do I drive this thing?'

'You don't. It drives you.'

Thacker felt it was driving right over him.

Mister Thacker lit a cigarette.

'Back when I was a lad in Dublin,' he said, 'there was this girl. Her name was Aisling. She was the prettiest girl you'd ever seen, the cutest curls, the cutest smile. We were in school together, and I sat in the row behind her. I used to spend most of the lessons staring at the back of her head, my mind wandering in the flow and swirls of her hair. One day, she turned around and asked me if I had a spare pencil she could borrow. Her eyes looked directly into mine. Such beautiful eyes. And her breath smelled of peppermint. Aisling was the first girl I fell in love with.'

He basked in the memory.

After a moment, he stroked his chin. There was a faint rustle of his fingers across his stubble. 'I started timing my arrival at the school gate in the mornings to match Aisling. I'd stroll in from the other way and greet her with a smile. If the teacher asked me to hand out books in class, I'd always hand one to her first. If my mother put a fine apple in my lunch, I'd pop it on her desk without saying a word.'

'Did Aisling like you?' Thacker asked his father.

Mister Thacker looked at his son. There were tears in his eyes. 'She always had a grand smile for me, and I never saw her give it to anyone else.'

He looked back at the city. 'But I don't think she really knew me, not as I knew her. But I wanted her to know me, as I thought I knew her.'

He smoked his cigarette for a moment.

'I knew where she lived. I knew her bedroom was upstairs in the front, that she was mad for the reading, and that her favorite author was Sir Walter Scott. I knew her favorite color was blue.'

He flicked his half-smoked cigarette over the side of the building and into the street.

'I figured I couldn't just be sitting there. I had to do something, you know, like The Bard said: *To be, or not to be.* So, I hatched a plan to earn myself a place in Aisling's affections. And I didn't sleep a wink drawing it up.'

'What was the plan?'

'I mapped out each day, across many months, extending over several years into the future, with a task for myself each day. On day one, get her to know my name. On day two, greet her by her name at the school gate and see if she remembered mine. On day three, ask her if she had ever read Sir Walter Scott's *The Lady of the Lake.* And so on.'

He sighed.

'I put near on two months into that plan: a task for every day, day after day. And the more I planned, the more I fell in love with her.'

He sighed deeper.

'On day 18, I was to find an excuse to walk home with her after school. On day 66, a Friday, I was to ask her if she fancied spending Sunday afternoon with me on St. Stephens Green. On day 288, I was to hold her hand on a bridge in the moonlight and kiss her. It was like I was plotting a book, and, like a good book, it had a perfect ending. On day 827, I would go down on one knee and ask her to marry me.'

'What happened?'

Mister Thacker pouted. 'On day 22, she and her family moved to Galway, and I never saw her again.'

A dog barked in the distance.

'Love is all about wanting what you don't get. And it doesn't matter if you fall in love with a woman, a bottle, a system of beliefs, or a cherry tree. In the end, it'll drive you out of your mind.'

CHAPTER TWENTY

DETECTIVE FRANKS GAZED AT A RUBBER DUCK — A BIG ONE, SUSPENDED above a windowless, nondescript building's entrance. The duck had once been yellow, but after many years of sun and rain, hail, and snow, it was now vanilla. The orange of its beak was a muddy brown, and the paint of its black orb eyes had dulled.

Snore.

Franks sighed. Delores was asleep. She had her head leaning against the glass of the passenger seat window. With each exhale, she clouded a large part of it.

Franks had parked his squad car in the city's back end, where the streets were lined with uninspiring buildings, factories, and offices, and the air smelled of chemicals and smoke. It was midnight and there was no one around. Shadows danced in the faltering light of a row of flickering streetlamps. Worn-out bulbs, every one of them. Ready to give up, ready to die.

Franks flicked his cigarette butt through the window; its ash and embers sizzled in the rainwater on the street. He returned his attention to the dead reporter's notebook. He had been reading it under a flashlight.

Albert Park's notebook was a fat little volume. Its cover was food-stained and circled where Parks had parked more than one cup of coffee. The handwriting inside was tiny, but comprehensive and intriguing. Parks had written some of it in shorthand, but Delores could speak that language and could translate. Franks wasn't a book kind of guy, but the dead reporter's notebook was quickly becoming his favorite reading.

Albert Park had done a lot of snooping. Reporters like him

were almost as good as detectives. They knew how to dig up the dirt. And in the soil Park had dug lay money. Park had known it, and so now did Franks. He could smell it as though it was a plate of hot pizza sitting right in front of him.

Franks took another glance at the street ahead. No one. He glanced in the rearview mirror. No one. He had been getting the feeling someone was watching him, and he didn't like that – he was the one who was supposed to do the watching.

He took another glance at the duck. Its dull eyes stared at him.

Delores rustled back to life. She opened her eyes and sat up straight. Looking out, she realized she was still in the same boring place they had been when she'd dozed off.

'Gee,' she grunted. 'You're quite the guy. You take a girl to some really high-class joints.'

Franks started the ignition.

He slowly drove out of the street.

He didn't notice the polka-dot tie hiding in those dancing shadows.

Fenella finished reading the book of Shelley's poems. She laid it on the bed alongside her. Her bedroom had originally been two rooms, but the Man Upstairs had torn down a wall and turned it into one. Her bed was king-size – half of it she used for sleeping, the other half as a dumping ground for anything current: books, dinner plates, clothes, jewelry, LP records. Her room was lit by the soft light of five candles on the bedside table. Pinned to the wall above the bedhead was an autographed photograph of Chet Baker leaning against a wall, looking subdued and holding a trumpet.

Percy Shelley had been dead since 1822. That was a long time ago; however, his poems didn't need a dictionary to work out their meaning.

Fenella thought about that.

Maybe in a couple of thousand years, they might.

Possibly, far in the future, all the words we wrote today would be meaningless to people without some kind of dictionary to help them understand.

Fenella rolled onto her stomach, reached across the bed, and grabbed her journal.

She wrote in it:

All words die.

All words are dead the moment they are written

And they remain dead until someone picks them up.

Today, tomorrow, or in ten thousand years

It is the reader who brings life to words.

The reader breathes life into the dead and makes them new.

CHAPTER TWENTY-ONE

CREAK.

Caroline woke up.

Someone was walking above her.

Creak.

Slow, deliberate steps.

Caroline climbed out of bed. She put on her dressing gown and slippers and turned off the alarm clock – five minutes of sleep had remained. She left her room and went along the hallway to the staircase. The clank of a plate hitting another plate sounded in the kitchen at the other end of the house.

Caroline wondered how far up the stairs she could make it before her aunt grabbed her and finally bit her protruding teeth into her flesh. She noticed someone had wiped away the patches of dark red – the old wooden steps had been comprehensively cleaned: there wasn't a trace of dirt, dust, or anything else on them. She also noticed a black, five-gallon gasoline can standing in the hall by the wall. It had a built-in handle and a screw top. That hadn't been there before.

Cutlery jangled in the kitchen.

Caroline tiptoed. She peered around the kitchen doorway. Her aunt was preparing breakfast.

Caroline decided. She swiftly returned to the staircase.

She found Jasper waiting for her. The little dog sat on the second step, his little eyes studying her.

Caroline kneeled in front of him. She put a gentle hand on the back of his neck and softly stroked him. 'Don't make a sound, my little friend.'

Jasper appeared to nod. He climbed off the stairs and trotted off in the direction of the living room.

There was another clank in the kitchen.

Caroline made her way up the stairs.

She stopped at the first landing. From there, the staircase changed direction and went to a second landing – she couldn't see beyond it.

Caroline called out in a whisper, 'Uncle Alvin?'

There was no response.

She whispered louder. 'Uncle Alvin?'

'What are you doing?'

Caroline froze.

Aunt Scarlett stood at the foot of the stairs. She held a meat cleaver.

'There's someone upstairs,' Caroline said. 'There's someone in the room above mine. I've heard footsteps.'

Her aunt's stare was angry, burning.

'Is it Uncle Alvin?'

'I've told you the upstairs is out of bounds. Come down here – now!'

Caroline didn't argue with the angry woman holding the meat cleaver. She made her way down, but when she arrived at the third-to-last step, she stopped. She towered over her aunt and summoned a degree of defiance. 'Who is upstairs?'

'Get off the stairs!'

'I know someone is up there.'

'It's not your uncle.'

'Who is it, then?'

Aunt Scarlett snorted. She looked as though she might explode. She finally spat out some words. 'It's the boarder.'

Caroline was bewildered. 'A boarder?'

'Yes.'

'How long has a boarder been living in the room above mine?'

Aunt Scarlett reached up and grabbed her niece by the wrist.

She dragged Caroline from the stairs and back to her bedroom. She instructed her to wash and get ready for school. Two minutes later, she delivered breakfast: two pieces of burned toast and a glass of water. She went to the living room and turned on the gramophone. She played Schubert at a deafening volume.

Caroline skipped breakfast, got ready, grabbed her schoolbag, and left the house as fast as she could. She could still hear the music at the end of the street.

CHAPTER TWENTY-TWO

AT ONE MINUTE TO MIDDAY, MISS XAVIER FLICKED THE SWITCH THAT powered the school's public address system. She waited for the amplifier valves to warm up and for the pilot light to come to life, informing her she was on the air. Light lit, she picked up her wooden mallet and started playing the *Funeral March of a Marionette* on the glockenspiel – a dusty clump of wood and metal plates nailed to her desk in the school's administration office. A microphone hung directly above it. The sound of her playing fed out into the school through a plethora of loudspeakers. Even from her location in the school's administration office, The Bun of Doom, as she was known (in whispers) by the student body, could feel the great upheaval in the school population as everyone abandoned their classes for the sanctuary of the lunch break. The tune was the noonday gun, the restorer of life to the certifiably dead.

Miss Xavier had another task to perform: hunt for Thornton Thacker. She ventured into the stormy sea of students and looked for him. She could have broadcast a spoken request for the boy to report to the office, and, for some minor matter, she might have done so. But this was no minor matter, and she reveled in the chase. She had probably been a bird in an earlier life, something like a hunting falcon.

Within minutes, Miss Xavier spied Thacker amongst the students; his unkempt blond hair was unmistakable. He was heading up the stairs carrying his schoolbooks.

Thacker, in return, spied her.

Whenever a teacher or adult in authority was around, it affected everyone present. Conversations became hushed and guarded, nobody ran, everyone became orderly. However, what had caught Thacker's attention was the unmistakable tight bun of hair on top of the woman's head.

Thacker had been heading up to room 59.

He never got there.

The Bun of Doom swooped in for the kill, her bony hand grabbing Thacker's shoulder, forbidding any further upward movement. 'A police officer wants to talk to you,' she squawked. 'He's waiting outside.'

Miss Xavier marched Thacker down the stairs, her hand tightly gripping his collar. The sea of students parted. A student in an adult's custody brought silence, pity, horror, and often tears.

'I hear the weather at Alcatraz is nice this time of year,' Miss Xavier cackled.

Thacker glanced. Until that moment, he had never seen the woman smile.

She led Thacker to the front entrance, where she remained, observing that he proceeded down the front steps and toward the police officer waiting at the school gates.

Detective Franks pulled a cigarette butt from his lips and flicked it away. 'What do we have in common, kid?'

'We have nothing in common,' Thacker answered as he walked up. He noticed little clumps of cheese and anchovies stuck to the detective's raincoat. 'And don't call me kid.'

'What we have in common, you little futzer, is that every couple of weeks, you and I do this. We talk. We talk so much, we have history. And I don't like the fact that we have history. I'm a cop, and you're a schoolkid. We should have nothing to do with each other. And yet, here we are. For the second time in a week, I've had to come and look for you.'

Thacker was bored with the preamble. 'What do you want to talk about?'

Franks glanced at the two schoolbooks Thacker held loosely at his side.

'What were you and your buddy Stanwick doing in Albert Park's room at the *Blue Bear* yesterday afternoon?'

'Who says I was in his room?'

'I do. This is my city, Thacker. I know what goes on in it.'

'I was working for the library.'

Franks grinned with doubt. 'The public library?'

'Yup.'

'Do you even know where the public library is?'

'I do.'

'Okay, what was this so-called work you were doing for the public library?'

'Retrieving a book.'

'What book?'

'Book 493.1.'

'What kind of book is that?'

'I hunt by the Dewey number.'

Franks sighed. For a moment, he considered a quiet career working at a munitions factory. 'What was the book about?'

'Egypt.'

'Be more specific. I polished my bullets this morning.'

'*The Christie Big Book of Egyptian Hieroglyphics.*'

'Did you find it?'

'Yup.'

'Did you take it?'

'Yup.'

Franks looked again at the two schoolbooks.

Thacker held them up: a math book and a copy of *Romeo and Juliet.*

'So, where is the hieroglyphics book now?'

'It's going back to the library.'

'Going back? Where is it right now, at this particular moment?'

'In transit.'

'In transit with who?'

'The transit people. And it's with whom.'

Franks wanted to pound the boy's head into the school gates. 'Did you take anything else from the room?'

'No.'

Franks grabbed Thacker by the neck. 'You took a photo,' he roared. 'I don't care about the photo. It's a police photo. I have five copies. What I care about is you walking into a crime scene and taking things. Because this isn't the first time you've done that. You think nothing of walking away with evidence – a book, a photo, a piece of paper, a sundial, a chipped cup with lipstick on it, a red kimono. And every time I tell you not to do it, you keep on doing it.'

'What road are you on?' Thacker asked, prying the detective's fingers from his neck.

The detective stared at him. 'What?'

'Life is a long, winding road,' Thacker intoned. 'Along its way, there are many side streets and alleyways, thoroughfares and lanes. Which road are you on?'

Franks' eyes widened with incomprehension. He hadn't expected profundity. 'I'm on the road to a whole lot of money,' he answered honestly.

He snapped back to reality. He grabbed Thacker's neck again, and his face took on the demeanor of a crocodile. 'From now on,' he growled, 'keep your nose out of police business. I'm a very large grownup, and you're just a small boy.'

He let go.

'Go back to school, kid. Learn about Shakespeare, long division, and algebra. Stay away from me and police business. And don't think I can't arrest you. Don't think I can't come after you. I know where you live.'

He walked through the gates and headed toward his squad car.

Thacker frowned. Threats from grownups with polished bullets were always annoying.

He went back inside.

He had almost gotten to the top floor when a hand from behind grabbed the sleeve of his trench coat.

It was Caroline. She was troubled. 'There's someone upstairs.'

'What do you mean?'

'There's someone else in my house, upstairs, in the room above mine.'

'Is it your uncle?'

Caroline shrugged. 'My aunt says it's a boarder.'

'Come with me,' Thacker said.

'Where are you going?'

'I think it's time you met my friends.'

Thacker knocked the special knock.

Shortly after, Stanwick dragged the chair away and opened the door to room 59.

Rosa and Fenella stood at the blackboard. Rosa, holding the Christie book, had been explaining her idea of what the first hieroglyphs in the message said.

'Everyone, this is Caroline,' Thacker said.

He introduced everyone to her.

'The missing uncle case?' Fenella asked.

Caroline nodded. 'I guess you could call it a case.' Her attention was taken by the hieroglyphs on the blackboard.

'We've been attempting to work out what this message says,' Fenella reported. 'One of the words is *bride*.'

Rosa patted the board under the first couple of hieroglyphs. 'And I'm certain this says *I am*.'

'And the cartouche at the end is someone's name,' Stanwick added. 'So, the message says, *I am the bride of someone*.'

'Sennefer,' Caroline said.

Everyone looked at her.

'The name in the cartouche is Sennefer.'

Thacker was as wide-eyed as the others. 'Sennefer the Unbelievably Magnificent?'

'My father discovered his tomb. I've seen the hieroglyphs of his name many times.' Caroline's attention turned to the crime scene photograph duct-taped to the board alongside the hieroglyphs and to the woman's hand extending out from under the sheet at the policemen's feet. She became pale.

'Are you okay?' Fenella asked.

Caroline wasn't. 'That's my mother under that sheet.'

CHAPTER TWENTY-THREE

'MY MOTHER WAS MURDERED.' CAROLINE SAID IT MATTER-OF-FACTLY but was deeply upset. 'It happened a month ago. It was the afternoon, and she was alone in the house. Someone broke in and attacked and killed her. And then wrote that message in hieroglyphics on our living room wall using her blood.'

'*I am the bride of Sennefer*,' Thacker said.

Pigeons cooed above in the rafters.

Thacker, Fenella, and Caroline had relocated to the clock tower – the three of them sat on old classroom chairs, 10 feet below the great bell.

The glockenspiel had rung shortly after Caroline's shock at seeing the photograph, and she had been in no mood to go to her next class. Fenella had known exactly where to hide her, and Thacker had gone with them.

The clock tower was the highest part of the school building. Its great clock face was a large circle of dirty white, with rusted Roman numerals and hands permanently frozen at five minutes to six. Directly below, and open to the weather and the birds, hung the great bell. Once upon a time, long before Miss Xavier and her glockenspiel, the bell had rung, signaling the start or end of the jail's exercise time. Access to the tower was via a dark, narrow staircase hidden behind the door at the end of the hall near room 59. Naturally, the tower was utterly out of bounds to the students.

'Why did the killer write that message?' Thacker asked.

Caroline shrugged. 'I suppose to make people think my mother had died because of the curse.'

'What curse?' Fenella asked.

Caroline announced it theatrically, as though it was the title of some cheap B-movie: '*The Curse of Sennefer's Tomb.*'

Thacker and Fenella stared at her.

'The year before I was born, my father led the expedition in Egypt that discovered Sennefer's tomb. A curse had been placed on the tomb, so that anyone who unsealed it and opened it would die.'

'And your mother was there when it was opened?' Thacker asked.

'Both my mother and my father were present. There were four people there that day and, with my mother's recent death, they are now all dead.'

'What happened to your father?' Fenella asked.

'He died in a car accident three years ago.' She didn't hide her disgust. 'He was drunk.'

Caroline inhaled deeply.

Fenella took her hand.

Thacker noted his sister did that so naturally. He asked, 'Who put the curse on the tomb?'

'Iset,' Caroline answered.

'I've heard that name someplace before.'

'Three thousand years ago, when Sennefer was sealed in his tomb, Iset had a curse engraved onto the burial chamber's doors. It warned that only she could unseal the tomb and open it. If anyone else did, they would die.'

A crow squawked in the rafters. The pigeons shut up.

'Who was Iset?' Fenella asked.

'Sennefer's bride.'

Thacker and Fenella looked at each other.

'Why were you trying to translate the hieroglyphs?' Caroline asked.

'A dead man had them written on a piece of paper,' Thacker said.

'And why do you have that crime scene photo?'

'It was in the dead man's hotel room.'

'What man?'

'Albert Park. He was a newspaper reporter.'

'Has your mother's killer been caught?' Fenella asked.

Caroline shook her head. After a moment, there were tears. 'I don't believe in curses. That's just hooey. My mother was murdered. She didn't die because of some words written on a door in Egypt thirty centuries ago.'

Fenella hugged her.

A fluttering of wings came from above, and the crow flew past the bell and out of the tower. The chorus of pigeons resumed.

'Was your Uncle Alvin part of the expedition in Egypt?' Thacker asked.

Caroline shook her head. 'The discovery of the tomb was before he married my aunt. He didn't know our family back then, and Aunt Scarlett wasn't part of the dig, either. I don't believe she's ever been to Egypt.'

Thacker sat back. He pouted. It was complicated when there was more than one case on the go. 'Before we try to work out anything about the bride,' he said, 'we need to first concentrate on your missing uncle.'

Caroline and Fenella both agreed.

'We need to find out exactly who is upstairs in the room above yours. Is it your uncle? Is it a boarder? Does the boarder know where your uncle has gone?'

'I'm not allowed upstairs,' Caroline said to Fenella.

'And I'm not allowed inside the house,' Thacker added. 'Boys aren't permitted.'

Fenella smiled. 'What about girls?'

Caroline noted a sparkle in her eyes.

'I might be able to think of a plan.'

CHAPTER TWENTY-FOUR

AUDREY BEECH-WHALE, HYPHENATED, FROM LONDON, WAS PROBABLY the most sociable person anyone knew. If requested, she could have drawn up a list of the entire school population, including their pets, entirely from memory. Whenever her birthday came around, there would only be a single invitation: a handwritten card pinned to the school noticeboard inviting everyone. And everyone went. It was an unmissable event and talked about for weeks afterward.

Audrey was often described as the definition of gregarious.

Thacker once had to look up that word in a dictionary. It meant outgoing, friendly, and pleasant to be around. Audrey once described Thacker as sometimes being not very.

And Audrey liked to talk, which made her perfect for Fenella's plan. Fenella's plan was straightforward: if you want to find out who is on the second floor of a house, go and see. And they would do it that day after school. The only trick required was a diversion, and that was Audrey.

Audrey B-W was always keen on a lark, and at the end of the school day, she accompanied Fenella, Rosa, and Caroline to the Dalrymple house. The four of them had no sooner hauled their schoolbags into Walnut Street when Caroline spied Aunt Scarlett. Her aunt and Jasper were walking back toward the house. Jasper had legs no longer than half-chewed pencils, and the four girls quickly caught up.

Caroline introduced her three friends. She told her highly suspicious aunt they were an after-school study group, that the other three girls were going to help Caroline prepare for an upcoming math test. Aunt Scarlett was unhappy about this invasion, but not so much that she forbade them from entering the house.

Once inside the house, as per Fenella's plan, Caroline casually mentioned to Audrey that Aunt Scarlett grew all her own vegetables. This launched Audrey into an enraptured sermon on the benefits of homegrown food, which led to a vigorous discussion between Audrey and Aunt Scarlett about cabbage varieties.

A discussion that naturally saw Aunt Scarlett lead Audrey, Fenella, and Caroline out into the rear yard for a firsthand inspection of the crops.

Rosa did not join them.

As per Fenella's plan, Rosa progressed no farther into the house than the front entrance. And when she was sure they had all gone out through the kitchen door, she left her schoolbag at the foot of the staircase with the other girls' bags and ran up the steps with swift strides.

At the top of the staircase, Rosa found a dark, empty hallway. No furniture or ornaments, no pictures on the walls, not even a rug on the floor. There were five doorways. The two at the end were closed.

The first doorway Rosa passed opened into a large bedroom: a four-poster bed with the sheets torn back, a chaise longue, a dresser, a chair, and a mess of strewn women's clothes. The bedroom across the hall was smaller: a single bed, tightly tucked, with a painting of a steam locomotive on the wall directly above the head. It appeared Caroline's aunt and uncle slept in separate rooms.

The third doorway led into a bathroom.

Rosa approached the closed door at the end of the hall on the right – the room she knew to be above Caroline's room.

The door was locked.

She peered through the keyhole.

Darkness.

Rosa hated closed doors. You never knew what was lurking behind them.

She went to the closed door on the other side of the hall. It wasn't locked and opening it swirled up a room full of dust.

The room hadn't been in any use for some considerable time. A large desk and chair stood at the center. On the desk lay a dusty typewriter, three full ashtrays, a litter of books, pencils, and sheets of notepaper. Many of the books were about Egypt. Many of the sheets of paper had sets of hieroglyphs drawn across them. Books and papers littered the floor as well, and the room's bookcases overflowed.

And then Rosa saw something that made her eyes widen. It was such a surprise she had to grip her mouth to prevent a shout from erupting.

The desk faced a wall, and across the wall, covering every inch, were hieroglyphs. Hundreds of them had been drawn onto sheets of paper in black and nailed to the wall.

And they looked odd.

Rosa had seen countless hieroglyphs in the past couple of days. These were different. There was something strange about their appearance. It came to her mind they had been written in another language. Was that possible?

She recognized one set of hieroglyphs. The cartouche for Sennefer hung at the wall's center.

'Why is your vegetable garden laid out in the shape of a triangle?' Audrey asked, shading her eyes from the late-afternoon sun.

Aunt Scarlett wasn't pleased with the question. She eventually answered, 'I like triangles.'

They stood at one of the triangle's points, staring across a large thatch of produce. The garden was an equilateral triangle, with each of its three sides at least 60 feet long. It dominated the rear yard. A garden shed stood near the house, and a rusting, yellow 1940 panel truck stood next to that.

'Why not a square?' Audrey asked. 'You'd have a larger area to grow things.'

Aunt Scarlett lit a cigarette. 'The triangle is the strongest of all the shapes. If you want something to grow properly, plant it properly.'

She said nothing further about the shape of her garden.

Rosa closed the door to the room of hieroglyphics and went back to the locked door.

She knocked on it.

No one answered.

She put her ear to the door. She pressed up hard and listened.

After a moment, Rosa became aware of breathing – a slow and steady breath with a slight rasp. There was a soft afternoon breeze outside. She might have been hearing the wind through a window or a slit in the building's elderly woodwork. It was also likely someone was standing on the other side of the door, merely inches away from her.

Rosa decided she really didn't want to be inside that house.

'Why are you preparing for an upcoming math test? Aunt Scarlett grunted, staring at the girls. 'Your school is on a remedial week. Your finals were two weeks ago.'

Audrey launched into a speech on the benefits of fresh air and how being outside was exceptionally good for one's health and immune system.

Aunt Scarlett paid no attention. 'One of you is missing. Where's the fourth girl – the Mexican girl with the short hair?'

Three smiling, innocent faces.

Aunt Scarlett stormed into the house. Her destination was the staircase, but when she arrived at the foot of the stairs, she heard humming in Caroline's bedroom.

She went to it.

Rosa sat on Caroline's bed reading a mathematics exercise book. She was humming the tune *Midnight, the Stars and You*.

She looked up.

Aunt Scarlett had entered the room. Her face was incandescent, a turbulent palette of rage and suspicion.

Caroline peered around the doorway, along with Audrey and Fenella.

'Can you play a musical instrument?' Rosa asked Caroline.

'I can strum a few chords on a guitar.'

'Perfect.'

'Why?'

'We're getting together tonight to rehearse for the school's end-of-year dance on Friday night. What do you think, Fen?'

'That's crazy cool. You should join us, Caroline.'

Before Aunt Scarlett could get a word in, Rosa added, 'There will be a female parent supervising, and no boys will be present at the venue.'

CHAPTER TWENTY-FIVE

BUT AUNT SCARLETT DID GET A WORD IN. THE WORD WAS NO. UNDER no circumstances would she allow Caroline out of the house after dark to attend a 'rehearsal of music,' even if no boys were to be present, which she sincerely doubted.

She canceled the after-school study group and sent Audrey, Rosa, and Fenella home.

After dinner, she sent Caroline to her room to do her homework.

But Rosa had written the rehearsal's location on a piece of paper, complete with a quickly sketched map of how to get there. She'd left it folded in two on Caroline's bed – unnoticed by Aunt Scarlett but found by Caroline. And Caroline had thought about it throughout dinner.

Stanwick's house is at 21 Goodman Street

After 8 p.m.

(go down the stairs)

Just before nine o'clock, back in her room, Caroline decided. She put on her shoes and slipped on her coat. She remembered the envelope in her schoolbag and placed it in her pocket.

She climbed out the window.

She had no money for a bus, so she had to walk across town. But she didn't care – defiance of her aunt was the closest she could get to any kind of freedom.

Goodman Street was a tree-lined street of smart houses and expensive cars. Stanwick's house was a three-floor building of red brick with two staircases in front – a grand one led up to the front entrance, and a narrower one led below the sidewalk down to the padded, raspberry-colored door to the basement.

Caroline made her way down the stairs and could hear music: a piano and a bass; a slow, bluesy tune. She pressed the buzzer next to the door, and, after a moment, Fenella opened it. She wore a black-and-white striped T-shirt and greeted Caroline with a warm smile.

Caroline stepped inside.

The basement was lit by a couple of lamp stands with swirling paisley-patterned shades. Deep burgundy-colored rugs covered the floor. A coffee table littered with sheet music and coffee cups stood to one side of the room, flanked by a couple of old armchairs and an inviting sofa. The room's dark walls were adorned with a row of large, framed photographs of musicians, each lit with its own light. Caroline didn't recognize any of the people in them. The room was pleasingly air-conditioned, and there was a rich smell of incense in the air. The basement was immediately both a cozy and alien world to her.

And then there was the music.

There was no female parent supervising, and there were definitely boys present at the venue. Stanwick sat at a shiny black Bösendorfer grand piano in the center of the room. He had taken his jacket off. His shirt remained buttoned to the top. Thacker stood next to him; his trench coat lay in a clump on the floor. He played an Epiphone B4 – an upright bass that was as tall as he was, with four fat strings on a dark wood neck and a honey-blonde body. He provided a steady, harmonic counterpoint to Stanwick's melody.

Caroline was impressed. They weren't amateurs.

Behind them stood a set of drums – red shells with dirty white batter heads. No one sat at them. The large bass drum had a circle of pale blue for a front, and across it was printed:

The Rainy Nights

'Do you play an instrument?' Caroline asked Fenella.

'I can make a few notes on a trumpet.'

Thacker realized they had company. He stopped playing and leaned his bass against the piano. Stanwick gave his left hand a break, while his right hand lightly continued the melody.

'You came,' Thacker said, walking over to greet Caroline.

'Of course.'

She turned to Fenella and asked the question that had been on her lips since that afternoon. 'What did Rosa discover upstairs? Is there anyone in the room above mine?'

'The door was locked,' Fenella said. 'But Rosa is certain there was someone inside.'

The buzzer rang.

Fenella opened the door.

Rosa entered, carrying a wicker picnic hamper. She wore a blue checkered blouse, jeans, and kitten heels.

'Tell Caroline about the room,' Fenella said. 'The other room.'

'What other room?' Caroline asked.

'There's another room upstairs you should know about,' Rosa said.

'Why? What's it in?'

'Hieroglyphics,' Thacker said. He fell back into one of the old armchairs. It caught him like a catcher's mitt.

'It's like an office,' Rosa said. 'There is a desk and a chair, and one wall is covered in hieroglyphs.'

Caroline took a seat on the sofa. She was baffled. 'I didn't think that my aunt or uncle had anything to do with Egypt. Neither of them has ever mentioned it.'

Rosa placed her hamper on the coffee table and opened it. The aroma of freshly-baked cupcakes and lemon icing filled the room. She took a cupcake and perched on the arm of Thacker's chair.

'And the hieroglyphs look far out,' Fenella said.

'Far out in what way?' Caroline asked.

'It's hard to describe,' Rosa said. 'They didn't look like regular hieroglyphs.'

Stanwick peered into the hamper and selected a cupcake. He took a seat in the other armchair.

'My uncle has his trains,' Caroline said. 'My aunt has her garden. I can't think whose room it would be.'

'Does your uncle smoke?' Fenella asked, taking a seat on the sofa next to her.

'No. He told me once that he never has.'

'There were ashtrays in that room,' Rosa said. 'They were all full.'

'Then it's my aunt's room.' Caroline sat back, still baffled.

'I saw the cartouche for Sennefer, too,' Rosa added.

'Everything keeps leading us back to Sennefer, the Unbelievably Magnificent,' Thacker said.

'Who was Sennefer?' Fenella asked.

'He was unbelievably magnificent,' Stanwick remarked.

'I mean, what do we know about him?'

'He lived in Thebes three thousand years ago,' Caroline said.

'Was he a pharaoh?'

She shook her head. 'He was a type of magician, you know, someone who would put on a show and pull rabbits out of hats. To be honest, I don't really remember much more. I stopped listening to my parents talk about him a long time ago.'

'And his bride's name was Iset?' Rosa asked.

'Yes.'

'She placed a curse on his tomb,' Thacker added.

'Yes.'

'*The bride must be stopped!*' Stanwick said. He selected another cupcake. 'It's been three thousand years. The bride would be dead. What's to stop?'

There were footsteps above.

'It's my mother,' he remarked.

'Oh,' Rosa exclaimed. 'I nearly forgot!'

Thacker noticed her smiling in that way of hers whenever she had a wonderful surprise to reveal. And she did. She reached into the picnic hamper, and, instead of pulling out a cupcake, she produced a folded-up handbill.

'I went back to the library this afternoon,' she said. 'To get a better look at this. It was pinned to the library's bulletin board.'

She unfolded the handbill and put it on the coffee table for everyone to see. It was a printed advertisement for an exhibition at the city museum. There was an illustration of an Egyptian mummy, and below it:

The Exhibition
of the Tomb of
Sennefer the Unbelievably Magnificent

A special exhibition
to commemorate
L.L. Carnaby

'Who was L.L. Carnaby?' Thacker asked.

'He financed the dig in Egypt that found Sennefer's tomb,' Caroline said. After a reluctant pause, she added, 'He was my grandfather.'

'The museum doesn't shut until late,' Rosa said. 'Anyone feel like cutting band rehearsal?'

Stanwick put on his jacket.

Thacker headed for his trench coat.

CHAPTER TWENTY-SIX

THERE WAS A MAN ON THE NIGHT BUS. HE WAS DRUNK. HE SAT AT THE rear, dressed in a tired suit and loose tie. He insisted upon shouting ahead and asking if anyone had anything to eat. He was looking for something like Key lime pie, but he'd settle for anything – ice cream, cheesecake, lasagna.

Fenella shouted back at the man that it was late, and since he had missed the dinner gong and hadn't come to the table, he would now have to go to bed and wait until breakfast.

This confused the man. He shut up.

The bus driver was the only other adult aboard. He wasn't drunk, but he looked forward to it.

'We should have asked your uncle to take us in his taxi,' Fenella said to Rosa. 'I hate night buses.'

Rosa shook her head. 'It's Uncle Diego's evening off. He'll be in a movie theater with his girlfriend, a carton of popcorn, and soda pop.'

Rosa and Fenella sat together. Thacker and Caroline sat in the two seats directly ahead. And Stanwick sat ahead of them – across the seats with the back of his head to the window, his black pork pie hat tilted low on his head.

Caroline hadn't known there was an exhibition of Sennefer's tomb at the museum, and she wasn't keen on visiting it, but there was no question about going in Thacker's mind. Sennefer was, somehow, at the center of the mystery – of all the mysteries. He needed to be investigated.

The bus drove through the city, spewing a cloud of diesel fumes behind it, its headlamps lighting up the empty streets

114

ahead. No one was out. The city had moved indoors for the night.

'This whole thing started a long time ago,' Caroline said, 'when my mother met my father.'

'How did they meet?' Fenella asked.

'They met on a ship bound for England.'

'How old were they?'

'My mother was 20. She was sailing to London to join up with my grandfather for a holiday. He had been there on business. My father was 38. He was returning home.'

'Her father was Scottish,' Thacker said.

'He had been visiting New York to raise money for a dig in Egypt.'

Rosa asked, 'How much does a dig cost?'

Thacker pictured a shovel.

'A lot of money. It's not like someone goes into the desert and digs a single hole. A team of men dig many holes across a wide area of the desert. And when they find what they're looking for, which can take months, more people are hired to help excavate and dig everything up. There are people to document and photograph the findings, people to guard the site, people to cook for everyone, a doctor, and many others.'

'What were your parents' names?' Fenella asked.

'John and Rebecca. My mother had always been fascinated by Egypt, and my father was an archaeologist. Their meeting was fate, I guess.'

'That's sweet,' Rosa said.

'My father had spent several years in Egypt searching for Sennefer's tomb,' Caroline said. 'He believed it lay in an unexplored valley 30 miles from the Valley of the Kings – the valley where they found Tutankhamen's tomb. But he didn't have the money to fund a full expedition.'

'How did he know where to look?' Thacker asked.

'Years of research. There had been many stories about Sennefer handed down from generation to generation. Folktales, myths, and legends. The rest was, as my father described it, guesswork and luck.'

'And your grandfather paid for the dig?' Rosa asked.

'Yes. My mother introduced my father to my grandfather in London. When my grandfather learned about Sennefer and a proposed expedition to find his tomb, he offered to pay for it.'

'Was your grandfather fascinated by Egypt, too?' Stanwick asked.

'No, my grandfather was fascinated by money. One of the most famous legends about Sennefer was that he had been buried with three large chests: one filled with gold, one with silver, and one with jewels.'

'So, they found a vast fortune when they discovered his tomb?'

Caroline shook her head. 'Tomb raiders had beaten them to it. All they found were Sennefer's sealed burial chamber and three empty chests.'

Jasper poked his tiny nose into Aunt Scarlett's ankle.

Aunt Scarlett wasn't paying attention. She was seated in her armchair, staring at the clock on the mantelpiece. She hadn't heard a sound in the house since after dinner, when Caroline had gone to her room.

She looked down at her dog. 'Walk?'

Jasper nodded.

'Up to the end of the street and back. Would you like that?'

Jasper nodded.

They went out.

They walked to the end of the street in the moonlight and back again.

Coming back along the sidewalk toward the house, Aunt Scarlett sensed something wasn't right. 'You know it, too, don't you, Jasper?'

The little dog nodded, although he didn't know what the woman was talking about. He didn't speak English. He was a dog.

They went back into the house, and Aunt Scarlett went straight to Caroline's bedroom.

Caroline was not there.

CHAPTER TWENTY-SEVEN

THE CITY MUSEUM SAT MINDING ITS OWN BUSINESS ON WALLER STREET near the river. It was an imposing building of several floors, with a wide set of steps leading up to a large doorway flanked by tall, weathered marble columns. It was one of the oldest buildings in the city and, to Thacker's mind, it looked so old the whole thing itself belonged in a museum.

Thacker had been to the building before. There were a couple of displays that had caught his eye on a school trip several years earlier: knights and castles of the Middle Ages, and musical instruments from the Baroque to the 20th Century.

'Do you believe in curses?' Caroline asked him as the five of them climbed the steps to the museum's door.

'I always allow for the possibility of the extraordinary.'

'Why is that?'

'I've seen a lot of weird things in my life.'

As they approached the museum's entrance, a thickset man in a dark tweed jacket came out. Thacker recognized the polka-dot tie and the pugnacious face. It was the man he'd seen at the public library. The man held a small booklet, no doubt for some museum exhibit. At the library, Thacker had pegged the man for a cop. Now, he was sure.

The cop, for his part, was now sure the boy was Thornton Thacker.

Thacker and his friends entered the museum.

It was late in the evening and there was no one there: no visitors, no attendants. The lobby was a cavernous hall of echoes – a vast space of statues, two grand granite staircases, 20-foot-

117

high windows, and a ceiling higher than the school clock tower. It was the largest indoor space Thacker had ever set foot in. And it smelled like the Man Upstairs' sofa – decaying. That and floor polish.

A sign standing at the lobby's center reported that the Sennefer exhibition was on the third floor. A stack of booklets lay on a small table in front of the sign, and Rosa took one. She held it up for the others to see:

> *Tomb of Sennefer the Unbelievably Magnificent*
> *Exhibition Guide*

It was the same booklet the cop with the polka-dot tie had been holding.

Rosa led them to a staircase, and they went up.

'The exhibition is on loan from the Cairo Museum,' Rosa reported, reading from the guide. 'The Egyptian Department of Antiquities awarded L.L. Carnaby a special medal for his services to their country's archaeological history.'

'There's a statue of my grandfather downtown,' Caroline remarked. 'The pigeons love him.'

They arrived on the third floor.

A series of signs led them along a maze of corridors.

'Sennefer's tomb was located thirty feet underground,' Rosa reported. 'It had been carved out of the bedrock beneath the desert, and access to its antechamber was down a narrow set of steps.'

'What's an antechamber?' Thacker asked.

'A room before a room,' Stanwick said.

'A lobby,' Fenella said.

A last sign pointed them into a shadowy room. The four of them entered, and found themselves inside Sennefer's tomb.

'This is a reconstruction of the tomb's antechamber,' Rosa said.

In the dim light, they could make out gray walls simulating bedrock. The floor was gray as well, with a sprinkling of sand to give it an air of authenticity. Four large wooden chests stood in a row along one wall. They were constructed of dark wood, had no lids, and were empty. Decorating the front of each was the engraved image of an animal's head – two elongated pointed ears, two ovals for eyes, with the face descending to a sharp point.

'Is that meant to be a coyote's head?' Thacker asked.

'It's a jackal.' Rosa read directly from the guide. 'L.L. Carnaby was heartbroken to discover the door to the antechamber had been broken open many years earlier by tomb raiders. The raiders left nothing of Sennefer's treasure except for a row of four empty chests, each bearing the image of a jackal.'

'Are these the actual chests they found in the tomb?' Fenella asked.

Rosa confirmed it. 'The exhibits on display were brought across from Egypt – their first time out of the country.'

'I thought there were only three chests,' Thacker said.

'Yes,' Stanwick said. 'One filled with gold, one filled with silver, and one filled with jewels.'

Caroline didn't know. 'I was always told three.'

'What was in the fourth?'

Rosa looked in the guide. 'Flowers.' After a moment of further reading, she added, 'Poppies.'

Caroline shrugged. 'I guess poppies aren't valuable enough to talk about.'

Everyone's attention turned to the two large limestone doors that led into the tomb's burial chamber; they stood open, both engraved in hieroglyphic script.

Thacker put his hand to one of the doors. It was smooth to his touch and cold.

'These are the actual doors to the burial chamber,' Rosa reported. 'They were closed when L.L. Carnaby's expedition discovered the tomb. The doors' copper handles were bound with rope, with the knot sealed in clay and imprinted with the image of a jackal.'

'Why a jackal?' Thacker asked.

'A theme is emerging,' Stanwick remarked.

Rosa found a footnote in the guide. 'The jackal is a symbol of the Egyptian goddess Anput.'

'And the burial chamber was still sealed when they discovered it?' Fenella asked.

'Yes.'

'Why didn't the tomb raiders break it open?' Thacker asked. 'Anyone can untie a rope.'

Caroline pointed to the hieroglyphs engraved on the doors. 'Because of the curse.'

Rosa read from the guide, 'The hieroglyphic script on the burial chamber's doors announces a curse for anyone who dares to open them. They say only Iset may unseal the burial chamber and enter. Anyone else who passes through these doors will die.'

'Fantastic,' Fenella grumbled as she followed the others through the doors into the burial chamber.

The burial chamber was the size of a bedroom. The air was icy, and it was easy to imagine you were underground.

'Is that Sennefer's coffin?' Thacker asked.

'Yes,' Rosa said.

Sennefer's coffin lay raised two feet from the floor on a stone pedestal at the room's center. The casket was made of wood. It was eight feet long and three feet wide and had a shape that suggested a body's outline. It was open and empty. Its exterior was painted a luminous golden color and inlaid with rows of red jewels. Its interior was lavishly decorated and carved. Remnants of ancient linen and padding lay at the casket's bottom.

'Is this the real thing?' Fenella asked.

Rosa confirmed it.

The coffin lid stood upright, raised on a small display stand, and lit by a small spotlight from above. The lid's surface featured a protruding, life-size illustration of a man dressed in a flowing white robe. He had long, dark hair, and an intense face.

'Sennefer,' Caroline said.

Even in the illustration's faded pigments, the man's vividly rendered eyes stared at everyone.

'He looks young and handsome,' Stanwick remarked.

'He was twenty years old when he died,' Rosa reported.

Fenella cocked her head. 'I can't decide if he's handsome or creepy.'

'Me neither,' Rosa said. 'And I wish he'd stop staring.'

Caroline felt cold, as though ice cubes had been inserted into her bloodstream. She had only ever seen photographs of Sennefer's coffin and its lid. She wasn't pleased about being in the same room with the actual thing.

'It's amazing to think,' Thacker said, 'this tomb was hidden away for thousands and thousands of years, and then your father found it.'

Caroline thought of another hidden place from the past – a room she hadn't thought about since she had been a small child: a secret room and a crooked cat.

'These hieroglyphs are the same as those at Caroline's house,' Rosa said, walking over to one of the burial chamber's walls. It was covered in hieroglyphic script.

'They do look strange,' Caroline said, looking at them.

'Yeah, weird,' Fenella said.

Rosa looked in the guide. 'These walls are exact replicas of what's in the burial chamber in Egypt.'

'They're a different type of hieroglyphs to those on the chamber's doors,' Stanwick remarked.

'And the ones we've been looking at in the Christie book,' Fenella said.

'I have a question,' Thacker said. 'It may be a stupid question, but it's a question, anyway.'

Everyone looked at him.

'Isn't there meant to be a mummy inside this thing?'

Everyone gazed into the empty coffin.

'Yes, there is,' said an elderly man entering the burial chamber. 'The mummy of Sennefer the Unbelievably Magnificent.'

The elderly man wore a dark sack coat and pants, and a tangerine-colored ascot tie tucked into a check shirt. He wore well-worn hiking boots.

He joined them at the coffin.

'I'm Professor Bacon,' the man said. 'I'm the senior curator here at the museum.'

Bacon had a two-week white beard and a swept-back hairline of gray and black that looked like the shoreline of a rugged coast on a windy day. His eyes were keenly alert, and the grin at the edge of his mouth suggested he was the joker in the pack. 'Sennefer's mummy was to have been the central piece of this exhibition.'

'What happened to it?' Rosa asked.

'It was stolen.'

'Someone stole a mummy?'

'Yes. There are thousands of dollars' worth of treasures and artifacts in this museum, and all the thieves took was a dusty, three-thousand-year-old mummy.'

Thacker chortled. 'A corpse wrapped in bandages.'

'Indeed.' Bacon glanced at Caroline. Something about her face had caught his attention. 'The police think the thieves used a wheelchair,' he said. 'And that they simply wheeled the mummy out of the building.'

'Those aren't normal hieroglyphs, are they?' Fenella asked, pointing at the wall.

'No, they're not.' Bacon went over and inspected them to refresh his memory. 'They're a stylized form of hieroglyphics. They were written that way on purpose.'

Thacker got it. 'They're written in code.'

The professor's eyes beamed with delight. 'They're written that way to keep their meaning a secret.'

'Who wrote them?' Rosa asked.

'Iset. She was Sennefer's bride and a fascinating woman. She believed in reincarnation, you know.'

'She did?'

'Oh, yes. She claimed to have dreamed of many previous lives.'

'I don't believe in reincarnation,' Caroline said.

'And she was called Sennefer's bride, but they were never actually married.'

'Why not?' Fenella asked.

'Because on the morning of their wedding, Sennefer was murdered.'

That got everyone's attention.

'Who killed him?' Thacker asked.

'His sister.'

Thacker nodded appreciatively. Sisters could be like that.

Fenella nodded appreciatively. Brothers could be like that.

Professor Bacon went to the coffin lid. 'The lid's outer surface displays an illustration of Sennefer. It's quite a famous image.'

Caroline knew what the man would say next. She had been dreading it.

'But there's also an illustration on the inside of the lid.'

He took hold of the coffin lid and turned it around on its stand for everyone to see. On the inside was a life-size illustration of a woman. She wore a flowing white robe like Sennefer on the front. Her mouth was open, as though she had just said something, and her hands were outstretched to embrace. She wore a string of red poppies in her long black hair, and her dark eyes were just as intense as those of Sennefer.

The woman's face was familiar to everyone.

Bacon smiled. 'With the lid in place, she would have stared forever at Sennefer.'

Everyone stared at Caroline. There was an unmistakable similarity.

'Who is the woman on the inside of the lid?' Rosa asked.

Caroline felt numb. 'It's Iset.'

CHAPTER TWENTY-EIGHT

CAROLINE EXCUSED HERSELF BEFORE ANYONE COULD ASK QUESTIONS. She had seen enough of the exhibition. She walked briskly through the museum to get away from Sennefer's tomb, his coffin, and its lid.

Thacker hurried after her. 'What's reincarnation?'

'After you die,' she said, grumpily, 'your soul gets reborn in a new body, and you live a new life. And I don't believe in it.'

The museum was empty, its corridors dim and endless. With every step, Caroline felt as though she was being watched by history – by the faces on old statues and Grecian urns, by the eyes in old oil paintings, and even by little prehistory figurines with abstract bodies.

'My father used to joke about it,' she said. 'My mother, too. About the similarity between my face and Iset's.'

'You have the same eyes,' Thacker said.

'Yes, and that's about all. It's a coincidence. I'm not Iset's reincarnation. I didn't have a previous life in Ancient Egypt and lay my dead lover to rest in a tomb and then seal him in with a curse.'

She stopped and sat on one of the hard wooden benches that lined the corridors.

Thacker sat next to her.

'Sorry to be so grumpy,' Caroline said.

'I understand.'

She smiled at him.

They looked across at a cabinet on the opposite wall. Inside it stood an array of old marble chess pieces.

Thacker stared at their reflections in the cabinet's glass front. Caroline was deep in her thoughts – about her parents, he assumed. Important things. Things with gravity. He thought of his father, the ancient man living at the top of their building. The Man Upstairs may have been many things, but he had never made jokes about Thacker or Fenella, and he'd probably shoot anyone who did.

Caroline wasn't thinking of her mother or father. She was thinking of her grandfather and a cat. 'I found a hidden room once,' she said.

Thacker was all ears.

'When I was very young, I wandered into my grandfather's office; he owned a manufacturing business. I was in his office all by myself, and I saw a crooked cat on the wall.'

Thacker tried to picture a cat clinging to a wall.

'It wasn't an actual cat. It was a sconce – a lampshade – in the shape of a black cat's head. It was tilted slightly to one side. I dragged a chair to the wall and climbed onto it. I straightened the cat. And when I did, somehow, a bookcase in my grandfather's office near to the cat slid open and revealed a hidden room.'

'What was inside the room?'

'I couldn't see. The room was dark, and before I could climb off the chair and look, my grandfather came in. He was furious. He tilted the cat back to its crooked angle, and the bookcase slid back into place. He then carried me out of the room.'

She frowned. 'My grandfather was never a happy man.'

'Did you like him?'

She shook her head.

'Did you like your mother and father?'

'Yes. But they had some really, really, really annoying habits.'

Thacker sat back and looked at her reflection again. She was looking at his.

'Parents,' Thacker sighed. 'They name you, select your first clothes, choose your first haircut, and tell you when to go to bed. And what can you do?'

Caroline laughed. 'And life goes on.'

They turned and looked into each other's eyes.

Hers were deep brown.

His were honey.

There were no words. She smiled. He smiled.

It was a moment.

'And one day,' Thacker said, 'we'll all be old and gathering dust in a museum.'

Caroline hugged him.

He hadn't expected that.

The man in the black-and-white photograph looked to be in his late 30s and had a matinee idol smile. He wore an intrepid explorer type of hat and had skin that looked like it had long baked in the desert sun.

'That's John Greer,' Professor Bacon said.

'He was the expedition leader,' Rosa said.

'Yes, he was,' Bacon said, stroking his tidy white beard. He was delighted to have found a captive audience. He had led Rosa, Fenella, and Stanwick out of the tomb into an adjacent room, where the rest of the Sennefer exhibition was displayed. Along one wall hung a row of photographs taken in Egypt at the time of the expedition.

'And if the tomb hadn't been robbed,' Stanwick asked, 'he would have become a wealthy man?'

Bacon shook his head. 'No. Anything found in a dig goes to the Department of Antiquities. To dig in Egypt, you need an excavation license – you need the permission of the Egyptian government. The license is a contract. Anything found in a dig straightaway becomes the property of Egypt and is eventually displayed in the museum in Cairo.'

'So why do people dig?' Fenella asked. 'If they have to give up what they find, what's in it for them?'

'They dig for the glory,' Bacon said. 'Certainly, the Egyptian government compensates expeditions for their work if they find something, but the real prize in archaeology is prestige and fame. Finding Sennefer's tomb made John Greer's name as an archaeologist. He spent several years on the lecture circuit, for which he would have been well paid.'

Bacon frowned. He spoke in a whisper. 'Sadly, Greer was a heavy drinker. He died in a car accident three years ago.'

'Who is she?' Fenella asked. Next to John Greer's photograph hung one of a woman standing beside a camel. The woman looked to be in her early 20s and wore sunglasses and an enormous hat. She could have been the matinee idol's co-star.

'That's Rebecca Carnaby,' the professor reported. 'She was extraordinarily beautiful.'

After a moment's gazing at her photo with adoration, he added, 'She and John Greer were married that same year, a month after the tomb's discovery.'

'Caroline's parents,' Fenella remarked, frowning.

'So sad,' said Rosa and Stanwick.

The professor's eyes widened. He pointed in the direction Caroline and Thacker had taken.

'Caroline Greer,' Fenella said, nodding. 'Their daughter.'

'Goodness me,' Bacon exclaimed. He frowned. 'Her mother's murder was a tragedy.'

No one disagreed.

'Do you believe in Iset's curse?' Rosa asked him.

He shook his head. 'I can't say that I do.'

Some of the room's lights faded and went out.

Professor Bacon glanced at his wristwatch. 'It's just before the hour. The museum is closing.'

'Is that L.L. Carnaby?' Fenella asked. The next photograph in the row was of an elderly man. He had a fat face, a head of wispy gray hair, and a wispy gray mustache buried under a bulbous nose. He stared into the camera with an angry squint. He held a walking stick and looked like he would strike you with it if you had gotten close enough.

'Yes,' Bacon said. 'That's L.L. Carnaby. Rebecca's father and your friend Caroline's grandfather.'

'He doesn't look friendly,' Rosa remarked.

'He wasn't. I met him once. He was quite surly.'

'What did L.L. stand for?'

Bacon grinned. 'Laid Low. Did you know he financed the expedition to Egypt from the money he made selling rubber ducks?'

The three of them stared at him.

'He really did. The Carnaby Rubber Duck Company.'

'Who is that?' Rosa asked. A fourth photograph presented a bald, middle-aged man who looked thoroughly surprised he was having his picture taken.

'That's Bernard Harwood,' Bacon said. 'The expedition photographer.'

'And all four of these people were present when the burial chamber was opened, weren't they?' Rosa asked. 'The photographer, the grandfather, the mother, and the father.'

'Yes.'

'And they're now all dead,' Fenella said.

'Yes.'

'Iset's curse.'

Bacon shook his head. 'Harwood died of a blood infection a week after the tomb was opened. The newspapers put his death together with the story of the tomb's curse and sold a lot of copies. And after that, whenever one of the four has died, the newspapers have again run with the "curse" story. Rebecca's murder notwithstanding, the others died by accident.'

'How did L.L. Carnaby die?' Stanwick asked.

'He fell down a staircase.'

Fenella nodded with confidence. 'Sounds like a curse to me.'

'I think we'll leave that debate to the philosophers.'

Suddenly there was a loud noise from below, and a strong vibration rippled through the building's floors and walls. The four photographs slipped from their hooks and fell to the floor, their frames and glass smashing when they hit.

'Goodness me,' Bacon yelled. 'What in the blue blazes was that?'

'What was that?' Caroline shouted as she and Thacker sprang

to their feet. The marble chess pieces rattled in the display case. The king and queen toppled. 'Is it an earthquake?'

Thacker's instincts said no.

They stood in the corridor, ready to fight or flee, their eyes darting, ears listening for any sound.

Their eyes eventually met.

They stared at each other.

After a moment, they relaxed and smiled, amused at their hugely dramatic response to what was probably a door slamming.

Caroline shrugged.

'There's a dance at school on Friday night,' Thacker said.

'I know.'

'Would you like to be my date?'

There was no hesitation. 'Yes.'

They stared at each other...

Not knowing what to say...

Awkwardness.

Thacker operated on instinct. He moved his head in her direction.

Caroline moved hers in his direction and closed her eyes.

Their lips had barely touched when a great animal growl echoed through the hall. They jumped back, truly startled.

Caroline's eyes were wide open. 'Okay, what was that?'

They felt vibrations through the floor and heard distant thuds of heavy footfalls. There was no mistaking it. Something big was moving through the building.

Thacker's instincts now said *run!*

He grabbed Caroline's hand.

CHAPTER TWENTY-NINE

THACKER AND CAROLINE RAN THROUGH THE MUSEUM, THEIR SNEAKERS pounding on the floor like a volley of bongo drums. Thacker's trench coat fluttered behind him like a cape.

Another deep animal growl reverberated through the building. It sounded like a combination of a bear, a wolf, an alligator, and construction equipment.

'What is that?' Caroline shouted, keeping pace with Thacker.

'I don't want to know. And whatever it is, I want to keep it behind me and far, far away.'

Thacker and Caroline found their way back to the staircase and passed a glass cabinet full of Devonshire dinner plates. The lights went out, plunging the building into near darkness. The museum had closed for the night. They headed down the stairs, lit by moonlight through the windows. When they arrived on the second floor, they heard the glass cabinet smashing.

'We'll never make it to the ground floor,' Thacker shouted.

He led Caroline away from the stairs, and they ran along a long, dark corridor. They then passed a sign:

Knights and Castles

'Where are we going?' Caroline shouted.

'Shopping.'

'Huh?'

Thacker and Caroline ran into a moonlit room filled with suits of medieval armor, mock castle walls, a drawbridge, and a handful of full-sized model horses decked out in tournament livery. They could hear thunderous footfalls behind them and more display cases smashing. Whatever it was, it was big, it was galloping, and it had no regard for the preservation of history. And there was no mistaking its intended destination: the two of them.

Thacker considered the available weapons: a lance, a mace, a battle-ax, a shield, and a sword. And then he saw something even better: an exit. He led Caroline to a door at the end of the room with a sign on it: STAFF ONLY. They exited, and Thacker shut the door.

Behind the door, they found a narrow wooden staircase lit by a couple of 20-watt bulbs. They ran down the stairs to the ground floor and found a fire exit, and then they heard the STAFF ONLY door above shatter and rip from its hinges. Whatever was chasing them, it had no interest in door handles, either.

The fire exit led into an alley that ran alongside the building. Thacker slammed the door shut, and then he and Caroline ran toward the main street, about 200 yards away. They saw Rosa, Fenella, and Stanwick run past the mouth of the alley – they had fled the building from the front entrance.

Stanwick saw them, too. He stopped.

'Run,' Thacker shouted.

Stanwick disappeared after Fenella and Rosa.

Smashing noises erupted behind. The whatever-it-was was shoving its way down the narrow staircase. It was bigger and broader than the stairs, and the side of the building rattled. Clumps of masonry fell.

Thacker and Caroline arrived at the main street.

The others had gone.

'Where do we go?' Caroline asked, breathing fast.

A taxi cruised by looking for fares; its top light was on.

Thacker hailed it.

It stopped.

'Drive,' Thacker said, as he and Caroline clambered onto the back seat.

The driver did.

'Fast.'

'Sure, buddy. Where to?'

'Walnut Street. And don't take your foot off the accelerator.'

The taxi sped across town.

'What was that?' Caroline asked.

Thacker didn't know. He kneeled on the seat and looked through the rear window. There was no sign of anything hurtling after them.

He sat down again.

He looked at Caroline. She at him.

Relief.

Thacker leaned across and kissed her.

She grabbed him.

He her.

They kept on kissing.

The taxi driver snorted. He swung his rearview mirror in another direction.

Mr Strudel stepped out of the Dalrymple house wearing a long, dark coat and smoking a cigarette. The front door shut behind him. Thacker noted the man's outrageous clump of white hair. In the moonlight, it was as though a ghostly tumbleweed had latched onto his head.

'Who is he?' Thacker asked. 'Is he the boarder?'

Caroline shrugged.

They sat in the taxi parked at the curb.

Mr Strudel walked out to the sidewalk, counting a crumpled fist of twenties. He found a dollar bill among them and smirked with satisfaction. He glanced into the taxi at Caroline and Thacker as he walked by and smiled at them. They noticed the man's glassy eyes and his wizened face. He walked away into the night, humming a tune about someone possessing the whole world in his hands.

Caroline remembered the envelope in her coat pocket. 'I need a favor,' she said, handing it to him.

Thacker read the address: Lillian Greer, in the village of Plockton, in Scotland.

'I need a postage stamp,' she said.

'No problem. Want me to drop it in a mailbox?'

'Please. And can you write on the back of the envelope that the reply is to be sent to your house?'

Thacker looked at her.

'I don't trust my aunt.'

'Leave it in my hands.'

Caroline climbed out of the taxi and looked at the house.

Thacker slid across the seat to the open door. 'Should you be going in there?'

'I don't really have a choice. Will I see you at school tomorrow?'

'Yes.'

She smiled at him, he at her, and then she walked to the front door.

As the taxi pulled away, Thacker noticed a light in one of windows on the second floor. He was reasonably certain it was the room above Caroline's.

Caroline fortified herself and knocked. They tell you when to go to bed.

After a moment, the door opened. Aunt Scarlett looked as if she had eaten a case of lemons. 'You're supposed to be in your room.'

'I went to the music rehearsal,' Caroline said defiantly.

Her aunt lunged and grabbed her by her coat sleeve. She dragged her into the house and slammed the door.

'You can't imprison me,' Caroline shouted, standing her ground in the front hallway. 'You have no right to do that. I'm not a child. I'm allowed to have friends.'

Aunt Scarlett pulled her up close and sniffed her. 'You've been among boys.'

'So? What if I have?'

Aunt Scarlett screamed. 'From now on, you're grounded. You're not leaving this house unless I say so!'

'You can't be serious,' Caroline protested. 'I have rights.'

Her aunt slapped her across the face. 'You have no right to anything.'

She dragged Caroline along the hall to her bedroom and threw her into it. Caroline tumbled over her schoolbag and fell onto the floor.

Her aunt slammed the door.

Caroline got to her feet. She was speechless, breathing fast. Her mind flipping through a range of options: she wanted to cry, she wanted to scream, but, most of all, she wanted to take a heavy piece of furniture and throw it at her aunt.

There was a tap on the window.

Thacker, outside in the dark.

Caroline opened the window.

'I'm grounded,' she whispered, hyperventilating with fury.

Thacker noticed her left cheek was red. He reached out and put the palm of his hand to it. 'Your aunt?'

'Yes.' She held his hand against her face.

'There's a light on in the room above yours,' Thacker said. 'Once and for all, I'm going to find out who's up there.'

'How?'

'The drainpipe.'

'Seriously?'

'Yup.' He stood back and looked up. The window above Caroline's room was open and light lit its frame. He took off his trench coat and dropped it on the ground.

'Are you sure it's safe?'

'Yup.'

The drainpipe ran up the side of the house three feet from the windows. Getting a good grip and using the thick metal clamps that held the pipe in place, Thacker climbed it like it was a ladder.

There is something of a circus acrobat about the boy, Caroline thought.

Thacker climbed up alongside the second-floor window. He leaned across the three-foot gap to get a look inside.

His foot slipped.

He grabbed the windowsill with one hand.

His other foot slipped, and he thrust out his free hand.

Clutching the windowsill in both hands, Thatcher dangled, 20 feet above the ground.

Caroline covered her mouth. She wanted to scream.

Thacker had a good grip.

He pulled himself up.

He looked into the room and, all at once, Aunt Scarlett's angry face obscured his view.

Her left hand came at him with the speed of a rattlesnake and gripped him by his throat.

'Keep away from Caroline,' the woman barked. 'Her purity must remain!' With her right hand, she smacked Thacker hard across his face with her black notebook. Its red metal spiral spine ripped his cheek.

Thacker lost his grip.

For a heartbeat, looking past Aunt Scarlett, he caught a glimpse into the room. And he saw an Egyptian mummy sitting on a chair.

He fell.

He landed on his feet in front of Caroline's window and bounced like a spring, falling firmly on his backside.

Caroline was horrified.

Thacker was dazed. Blood flowed from the cut to his cheek. He gasped for breath.

And then he heard a deep, rasping sound.

He looked about, but whatever it was, it was shaded from the moonlight by the tall column of pine trees that flanked the side of the house.

Thacker clambered to his feet.

Two large, dark red eyes appeared in the darkness. The rasping sound was the thing's breathing, and it was getting closer.

'Shut the window,' Thacker called to Caroline. He blew her a kiss, grabbed his trench coat, and ran.

Caroline had no chance. Aunt Scarlett stormed into the room, shoved her out of the way, and slammed the window down herself.

Thacker ran across the front yard and tripped and rolled onto the sidewalk.

He sat up.

The dark red eyes had followed him.

Thacker stopped breathing.

It was an animal, jet black and barely visible in the night. It was as broad and tall as a horse. It had four long legs with paws seven inches wide. Its large, round eyes glowed like the embers of a fading fire. Its ears were tall and pointed, and its snout was elongated. Dirty, red teeth glowed in its salivating jaws.

It was too impossibly big to be a dog. It was an enormous, oddly elongated wolf, or coyote, or jackal.

The creature walked up to Thacker and stopped a few feet away. It lowered its enormous head and stared. It could have been pondering what the weather would be like in the morning or deciding which of Thacker's limbs to eat first. Who could tell? It stood close enough that Thacker could smell smoked meat on its rasping breath.

Thacker's instincts took over. He sprang to his feet, grabbed his coat, and ran as fast as he could. He was an Olympian. He ran to the end of the street in seconds.

Running around the corner, he ran straight into Mr Strudel, nearly knocking the old man to the ground and knocking the cigarette from his mouth.

'Watch who you're running into, boy,' Strudel barked, retrieving his cigarette from the sidewalk.

Thacker was pale. He looked back down Walnut Street. The creature hadn't followed.

Strudel lit a new cigarette from the old one. He inhaled, and his face lit up in a red glow. 'Seen the devil tonight, have you?'

CHAPTER THIRTY

PROFESSOR BACON HATED KERFUFFLES. AND THE NOISES HE HAD HEARD that night in the museum, and the damage to the exhibits he had surveyed afterward, were the highest caliber of kerfuffle. No reasonable explanation had come forward. There had been talk of subterranean tremors, stray ducks, and ley lines. None of it reliable. And one museum guard swore on his mother's grave he had seen a large black dog with red eyes. A hideous beast.

Kerfuffle.

Bacon opened his office window to let in the night's cool air and sneezed.

He looked for his handkerchief. It was hidden under the ocean of paperwork and books that covered the desk he had dutifully sat at for 45 years. He had the most ordered mind in the building, but finding a handkerchief on his desk was like mounting an expedition into the Amazon to find an apricot-flavored accordion.

He journeyed.

A minute later, he found it.

He wiped his nose.

Talk of a beast reminded Bacon of a story handed down from Egyptian antiquity; a servant girl's tale of three poppies. It was a story of Sennefer and Iset's wedding day.

The Servant Girl and the Three Poppies

The youngest of Iset's servants was a girl of 12. Her name was Panya, and Iset tasked her with delivering a gift of three poppies. The poppies were for Sennefer, and the young girl had to deliver them at daybreak on the morning of the summer solstice – the day Sennefer and Iset were to marry.

In the night, lit by a crescent moon, Panya made her way on bare feet across the city to the villa of Sennefer's family. The villa stood on a large tract of land surrounded by a high stone wall. The wall encompassed not only the house but an orchard behind. Panya followed the wall around to where a fig tree overhung it, with its branches reaching the ground. Iset knew of the tree, and she had instructed the young girl to climb it – to get over the wall and into the villa's rear grounds.

Panya had been hesitant to undertake such a task. The gates to the villa were locked at night. If caught, trespass meant whipping. Iset told her it was merely a game, a delight, a surprise for her lover, and she gave the young girl a small papyrus bearing her name and seal to present to anyone if found.

Panya did as she was instructed. Once inside the grounds of Sennefer's villa, she waited in the orchard for daybreak. And when the sun's first light came, she unwrapped the three poppies from the satchel she had carefully carried them in. She made her way through the orchard and across to the villa. She followed its left wall until she came to the window of Sennefer's room.

Her instructions were to place the poppies on Sennefer's windowsill, where they would be caressed by the morning sun, and he would see them.

And she did.

And looking into the room, she saw Sennefer, asleep in his bed.

And at that moment, Panya saw Sennefer's youngest sister, Beketamun, enter the room. She saw her climb onto the bed and straddle Sennefer's chest. She saw Beketamun gently place her hand on Sennefer's forehead, and, with her other hand, strike at his neck with a knife.

A hard, decisive strike.

Sennefer's eyes opened immediately.

His blood sprayed onto Beketamun.

Panya ran.

She climbed back over the wall and ran across the city.

She found Iset in the temple of Anput, where she was offering her goddess a gift of blood and tears.

Panya told Iset of the murder of Sennefer by the hand and blade of his sister, Beketamun.

Iset screamed.

It was the loudest of screams. A firestorm of sound.

And before Panya's eyes, a great beast appeared. A beast of the underworld from forgotten times – from before there was a world in which men and women breathed.

A lusus naturae.

The beast of Anput.

This creature thundered from the temple and ran to Sennefer's villa, where it unleashed utter chaos and destruction in its hunt for the sister Beketamun.

But it did not find her.

Beketamun had vanished.

She was never heard from or seen again.

Professor Bacon sneezed. He had always wondered: Why three poppies?

His mind returned to the present kerfuffle. He would have to organize a cleanup in the morning. Doors would have to be repaired. Cabinets replaced. All the broken objects would have to be carefully collected and itemized. Glue would have to be procured.

Why three? What did each represent?

Not all the details had been neatly handed down through history.

The Cinnamon River flowed through the city's neighborhoods with little logic or geographical sense. And on that night, its black currents had caught a shoe, and it gently sailed along.

Dashiell pursued it.

A human foot left an odor in a shoe, an odor as unique as a fingerprint, and Dashiell could not resist the smell of a foot.

'Wait up,' shouted Philip, following in his dressing gown and sneakers.

Dashiell was not a dog who had formally entered any owner-master arrangement. He was his own dog, and he enjoyed sneaking out for an evening ramble. So, on that night, well after midnight, with the moon high above the city, Philip trailed his dog along the tree-lined bank of the city river as Dashiell followed a shoe.

Philip didn't like the Cinnamon River; it smelled foul and there were stories of the old days. The river carved its way into the city through the foothills of the Silverdales – a ragged range at the edge of town where men had once mined for gold. There was no gold in the Silverdales (or silver), but many men had quarreled over its dirt. In the old days, the Cinnamon River had flowed crimson.

It was a man's brown leather shoe, left foot, scuffed. After traveling some distance, it eventually floated to the shore. At which point, Dashiell made his move. He clambered into the water and bit it.

He attempted to take the shoe out of the river, but there was a problem in performing that task.

As Philip strode closer, he could see what the problem was. The shoe had a foot in it, and the foot was attached to a leg.

Philip helped Dashiell drag the shoe, foot, and leg out of the river.

As Philip had feared, a body was attached to the leg; he and Dashiell hauled it onto the riverbank and into the moonlight. It was a man dressed in the blue-and-white-striped overalls of a train engineer. Dashiell took a sniff and decided it wasn't something he wished to pursue any longer. Philip didn't want to pursue the matter, either. The body had no head.

A police car arrived 10 minutes later, its headlamps lighting up the river's edge and the body on the shore. Two fat, uniformed flatfoots climbed out and took a look. The kid's telephone call hadn't been a prank – there really was a dead man, and he really didn't have a head. The cops put in a call on their radio. Ten minutes later, three more squad cars arrived, bringing the uniform count on the riverbank to 12.

Philip was told to stand by a tree. He was told he shouldn't be looking at such things as headless bodies. Philip took Dashiell and stood by the designated tree. He watched as the 12 policemen stared at the dead man, each one of them wondering why they were looking at such things.

A black car pulled up, and its sole occupant climbed out: a thickset man in a dark tweed jacket and polka-dot tie. He put on a hat. He walked over and kneeled beside the body. After a rudimentary inspection, he looked inside the dead man's pockets. All of them were empty.

The man with the polka-dot tie stood up.

He spoke to the two uniforms who were first to arrive. Glances were made in Philip's direction. The uniforms had a lot to say. Eventually, the man came over and flashed his badge. 'Lieutenant Bendix. You found the body?'

'Yes,' Philip said. 'It was floating in the river. My dog followed it until it floated to the riverbank. And then we dragged the body out of the river.'

'I've been told this isn't the first body this dog has found.'

Philip shrugged. 'This is his third. There was one two years ago, The Case of the Lopsided Tennis Court, and one last Christmas, The Case of the Too Many Christmas Trees.'

The lieutenant chuckled. 'You're a friend of Thornton Thacker, aren't you?'

Philip stared at the man, in awe of his extra sensory perception.

CHAPTER THIRTY-ONE

BANG. BANG. BANG.

Caroline opened her eyes. She had been dreaming she was on a train thundering through the Scottish Highlands, and she had been eating haggis.

Bang. Bang. Bang.

The train vanished into the distant hills of her mind.

She sat up in bed, wide awake, and daylight flooded her face.

Bang. Bang. Bang.

The drapes were fully drawn back. Aunt Scarlett had a hammer and was driving a nail through the wooden window frame.

'What are you doing?' Caroline shouted above the hammering.

'Closing the window.'

'How am I supposed to get any air if it's nailed shut?'

'There's plenty of air in the room.'

Aunt Scarlett slammed in another eight nails, and, once satisfied that no one was ever going to open the window again, she took her hammer and bag of nails and left the room, slamming the door behind her as she went.

Slamming doors had become the woman's hobby.

Caroline climbed out of bed. She tried to open the window but couldn't. She resigned herself to the fact it was shut. She knew full well that if she somehow pulled out the nails, her aunt would scream at her and drive a new set back in. And who knew with that woman, maybe she'd start driving nails into her.

Caroline pulled the drapes back into place, leaving only a tiny gap for the morning sun to sneak in. There were still 15 minutes before her alarm clock was due to erupt. She fell back onto the bed and gazed at the ceiling. She had stared at it so often, she was familiar with every line, crack, and bump in its tobacco-stained paint.

She closed her eyes and tried to remember the train in her dream and the Scottish Highlands, even the haggis. She failed. She stared at the ceiling again.

The ceiling was a map of a vast, sprawling continent. Each bump and crack where the paint was coming loose represented a hill or a mountain range. Each damp spot was a lake. Each crack or line dark with mold was a river. There were cobwebs, and she imagined those were clouds. Weird clouds because it was a weird country up there, upside down, on her ceiling.

It occurred to Caroline that she might be going quite mad.

There was a creak in the floorboards above. A footstep. It was followed shortly by another. There was someone up there, walking slowly about. And by the sound of it, around in a circle.

Caroline sat up. She reached down beside her bed and found one of her sneakers. She threw it at the ceiling. It hit with a thud and bounced off.

The creaking stopped.

The sneaker landed on the bed, and Caroline grabbed it. She reached for the other one of the pair. She threw each shoe, one after the other, at the ceiling.

Thud.

Thud.

The sneakers landed on her bed.

After a moment, there was a thump on the floor above. And then a second. Someone had stomped his or her foot down to echo the sound of the two shoes.

Caroline's eyes widened. Whoever was there had replied.

She stood on the bed and called in a loud whisper, 'Hello?'

There was no reply from above.

'Hello?' she called out louder. 'Can you hear me? Who are you?'

143

Her bedroom door flew open, and Aunt Scarlett ran in like a runaway train. 'What do you think you're doing?'

'Who is up there?' Caroline pointed at the ceiling. 'Who is the boarder?'

'Don't stand on the bed!'

Jasper sprinted into the room. He yapped excitedly and jumped onto the bed.

Caroline bent down and affectionately rubbed the little dog's head.

Aunt Scarlett was even more furious. 'Get off the bed, the pair of you!'

Jasper bounced off the bed, and, yapping continuously, ran around the woman's feet.

'Yes, I know,' Aunt Scarlett said to him. 'You're hungry.'

Caroline stepped down off the bed.

Jasper ran from the room with his tongue hanging out.

Aunt Scarlett sighed. 'Sit down.'

Caroline noted a weird calmness had descended upon the woman.

'Sit down,' she said again.

Caroline sat on the edge of the bed.

Her aunt sat next to her.

They sat in silence.

Caroline didn't know what she was supposed to do. Her aunt appeared to be deep in thought, staring at the floor.

Jasper yapped from somewhere at the other end of the house.

Aunt Scarlett finally spoke. 'When I was a child, I wanted a doll.'

Caroline said nothing.

Her aunt spoke oddly. Disembodied. Reflective. 'I saw the doll in the window of a toy store – a little doll wearing a perfect white dress. It had a head of red hair and two large blue eyes. I asked my father if he would buy the doll for me, and he said no.'

She drew a long breath, conjuring the past in her mind.

'One week later, my father bought that doll, and he gave it to your mother.'

Another breath.

'And your mother played with it every day. Every day, until she became bored with it and threw it in the river.'

'Why are you telling me this?' Caroline asked. She wasn't oblivious to her aunt's gloom. She had always known her mother had been her grandfather's favorite, and that her mother hadn't exactly been an angel.

Her aunt wasn't listening. 'I retrieved the doll from the river and took it home. I cleaned it, dried its clothes, and even repaired its perfect white dress, where your mother had torn it. And, for four days, I played with that doll, and I was happy.

'For four days.

'And then my father saw me with it. He told me I had stolen it from your mother. He took the doll from me. And he beat me.'

More silence.

It felt endless.

'Uncle Alvin didn't go to Argentina, did he?' Caroline asked.

Her aunt stood up.

She left the room, carefully closing the door behind her.

Caroline heard a key going into the lock and the door locking.

Aunt Scarlett fell back into her armchair in the living room and pouted.

Jasper wandered into the room and went back to his rug in front of the fireplace. He flopped down and rested his head on his paws. He looked up at Aunt Scarlett and studied her face. She appeared bitter. Angry. Jasper didn't know what she was thinking about, so he closed his eyes and thought about eating a bowl of mermaid snacks.

Aunt Scarlett thought about burning.

She thought about revenge.

She thought about her list. Everyone had a list – a list of all the people who had wronged them, harmed them, or hurt them. Aunt Scarlett's list was as long as the world.

She picked up the box of matches from the table next to her, and she struck a match. She held it a few inches from her eyes and watched the flame gently dance about the match head, flickering through shades of orange and red.

Aunt Scarlett could hear the screams of billions burning.

The flame burned the match down to her fingers.

She didn't want to blow it out. She wanted everyone to burn forever.

CHAPTER THIRTY-TWO

'THERE'S A MUMMY IN THE ROOM UPSTAIRS,' THACKER WHISPERED AS Stanwick sat next to him in their first class together that day.

Thacker was studying a book from the school library.

Stanwick noted his friend wore a large Band-Aid on his cheek.

'When you say mummy,' Stanwick inquired, 'are you talking about a lady with children or a deceased person from Ancient Egypt?'

'Egypt.'

Thacker offered nothing further on the matter. The book he was flicking through the pages of was titled *The Complete Book of Four-Legged Animals*.

'What are you looking for?' Stanwick asked.

'Ears.'

'According to Thacker,' Fenella said, taking her seat next to Rosa in history class, 'there's a mummy in the room above Caroline's.'

Rosa's eyes went as wide as the moon.

The noonday glockenspiel couldn't come soon enough, and the four of them assembled in room 59.

'Why would Caroline's aunt steal the mummy from the museum?' Rosa asked.

Thacker shrugged. He leaned back against the blackboard.

Rosa noted the Band-Aid. 'And what was that noise we heard at the museum last night?'

'Yeah,' Fenella said. 'What was that all about?'

'Let's stick with the mummy,' Thacker said. 'One abnormal thing at a time.'

'Why would anyone steal a mummy?' Stanwick asked. 'What could they do with it?'

Thacker shrugged.

'And you're absolutely certain that's what you saw?' Fenella asked.

'Yup.'

'And you think it's the missing mummy from the museum?'

'How many other missing mummies do we know of?'

'And you're suggesting it's the mummy Caroline's been hearing?'

Rosa spoke with authority. 'Egyptian mummies don't walk around. They generally don't move about at all.'

'That's what I saw,' Thacker insisted. 'An Egyptian mummy. Bandages, head to toe. It sat in a chair. The chair and the mummy were the only things in the room, apart from the aunt.'

'Mummies don't generally sit in chairs, either,' Rosa added.

Thacker remembered the envelope. The letter was to go to Scotland; he had to write his address on the back for the reply. 'Where's Caroline?' he asked. 'Has anyone seen her?'

No one had.

He pouted.

'I have to go to school,' Caroline shouted through her bedroom door. 'It's after midday, and I'll get into trouble for being late.'

There was no answer.

She sat back on the edge of the bed. Her aunt's definition of 'grounded' had come straight from a federal prison instruction manual.

Squeak.

It was an odd sound, not a footstep, but something else from the room above. Caroline didn't look at the ceiling. She was fed up with it.

There was another squeak, and then a third. Something needed oiling.

There were footsteps.

And then there were footsteps and squeaking together.

And then it stopped. Half a minute later, she heard someone on the staircase.

Thud.

Squeak.

Thud.

Squeak.

A thud and a squeak, one sound slowly after the other. This went on for almost two minutes. And then it stopped, and Caroline heard nothing.

No one had seen Caroline at school. Thacker, Stanwick, Rosa, and Fenella had spread out through the building to look. They looked everywhere and asked everyone. Caroline wasn't to be found.

'Okay,' Thacker said. The four of them had regrouped on the school's front steps. 'I have a list of the things we're going to do.'

CHAPTER THIRTY-THREE

'THERE'S SOMETHING I NEED TO TELL YOU,' THACKER SAID, GAZING OUT the window at the city passing by. He and Stanwick sat on a bus. The drunk man from the night before was aboard but was now fast asleep. A face full of crumbs suggested he had eaten.

'What did you need to tell me?' Stanwick asked.

'I saw something else last night.'

'Please don't tell me you saw a daddy.'

'I think I saw a jackal.'

Stanwick glanced at Thacker. He was sober and serious. 'We don't have jackals in this city.'

'Well, I think we did last night.'

'How can you be sure it was a jackal?'

'The ears.'

Thacker offered nothing further on the matter. This, and the fact he looked troubled by the memory of it, troubled Stanwick.

The bus pulled over at a stop across the street from a post office.

'Are we getting off here?' Stanwick asked as Thacker stood up.

Thacker held up the envelope. 'The first thing on the list is to mail a letter.'

'What was that noise we heard at the museum last night?' Rosa asked again.

'Thacker thinks it was a jackal,' Fenella replied.

The two of them walked through the city, heading back to the museum. Rosa held the Christie hieroglyphics book to her chest.

'A jackal? Do we have those in this country?'

Fenella shrugged. 'He said it was big.'

'How big?'

'He didn't give me the measurements.'

They waited at a crosswalk for the light.

'He said nothing else?'

'Nothing at all.'

'That's troubling.'

Jasper was also troubled. As a dog of simple needs, he had two desires: the occasional walk and a continual supply of Captain Seadog's Salty Sea Snacks – irresistible canine treats in the shape of mermaids. Panting in expectation at the feet of Aunt Scarlett in the kitchen as she stood in front of the open cupboard, he could see that the cupboard was bare. There were no more packets of the Captain.

He wasn't impressed.

He voiced his concerns.

He also knew when to swiftly step out of the way when Aunt Scarlett's hard heel swung in his direction.

'Should we just walk up and knock?' Stanwick asked. He and Thacker stood on the sidewalk in front of the Dalrymple house.

'Yes, but I can't,' Thacker said. He tapped the Band-Aid on his cheek. 'I'm a bullseye to that woman.'

Stanwick nodded and headed to the door.

Thacker crossed the street to one of the abandoned properties and hid behind an overgrown hedge.

Stanwick had to knock five times before the door finally unlocked and opened, and an angry-looking Aunt Scarlett peered out. She wore an old smock smeared with black paint.

'That's a playful dog you have there,' Stanwick remarked. Jasper was determinedly trying to bite Aunt Scarlett's ankle. She pushed him away with her foot.

'He's hungry. What do you want?'

'I'm a school friend of Caroline's. Is she home?'

'Why?'

Stanwick shoved his hands in his trouser pockets and did his best impersonation of a 10-year-old. 'Can she come out to play?'

Aunt Scarlett's eyes narrowed with suspicion. She looked into the street and then back at Stanwick. 'Shouldn't you be in school?'

'I'm on my lunch break.'

She glanced at her wristwatch. 'Awfully long lunch break.'

'There were a lot of sandwiches. Can Caroline come out to play?'

Aunt Scarlett slammed the door.

Stanwick walked back to the street.

Thacker stepped out from behind the hedge, and they met in the middle of the road.

'Is Caroline in there?'

Stanwick shrugged. 'There's a strong smell of paint in that house.'

Thacker frowned. 'I'll be back.' He ran toward the house and around the side of the building, then along to Caroline's bedroom window.

But he couldn't look inside.

Every inch of her window had been painted black.

This troubled Thacker the most.

CHAPTER THIRTY-FOUR

PROFESSOR BACON SNEEZED. AND THEN IMMEDIATELY FELT THE PANG of another sneeze building inside his head. He hated summer. It always brought the same thing: hay fever. He took his handkerchief and wiped his nose. He glanced at his desktop calendar. Tomorrow was the summer solstice, the official beginning of summer. He would then have three months of hay fever until the relief of the fall set in.

Autumnal was a word he liked.

Winter was a word he adored with unbridled passion.

Spring was a word he found little favor with, as it always led straight back into the dread of summer.

Bacon stared again at the newspaper opened out on his desk. It was a two-day-old edition of the *City Star*. He was in the history business; he never read a newspaper on the day it was published. A curious story on the fourth page had caught his attention. There had been several reports of an enormous animal seen near the waterfront. One witness had described it as a monster. All the others described it as a large black hound.

Bacon thought again about Anput and her great beast – the beast she would beckon from the depths of the underworld and send to perform her tasks.

Kerfuffle.

His nose itched. He could feel another sneeze building.

He went to close the window to cut off the flow of that day's pollen into his room and into his head. Looking out, he saw two of the girls he had met the previous evening at the Sennefer exhibit. Four floors below, in the courtyard: the girl with blonde hair dressed in black and the girl with short dark hair dressed smartly in a pastel peach-color twinset and navy shirt.

Rosa and Fenella walked toward the museum's entrance. They were looking down the alley to the side of the building where a couple of repairmen were fixing the fire escape. It looked as though a freight train had plowed through it.

'A jackal?' Rosa asked.

'A big one,' Fenella said.

They made their way up to the third floor and the Sennefer exhibit.

When they stepped into the burial chamber, they found a gruff-looking bald man with a six o'clock shadow and a cigarette in his mouth. Detective Franks. He was studying the hieroglyphs on the chamber's walls. He turned about to survey who had joined him, and his heavily lidded eyes focused on Fenella.

'Thacker's sister,' he said. 'I forget your name.'

'It can stay forgotten,' she said. The man reminded her of a turtle.

'What brings you here?'

'We're looking for a professor.'

Franks ran his eyes down Fenella's body to her shoes and then slowly back up again until he arrived at her eyes – sapphire blue, angry.

Rosa took hold of Fenella's arm. She sensed the anger.

Franks spied the book Rosa held and the word 'Hieroglyphics' printed on the cover. He became animated. 'Is that the Christie book of hieroglyphics?'

'Yes,' Rosa answered. She held it up.

Franks confirmed the book's title. 'This is stolen property.'

'No, it isn't,' Fenella said.

'Your brother stole it from Albert Park's room at the *Blue Bear.*'

'It's a library book. We're returning it.'

'This is the museum. It's not the public library.'

'We're not taking a direct route.'

'Give me the book.' He reached out to grab it from Rosa.

'Go jump in the lake,' Fenella said.

Franks' nostrils flared in anger. 'What did you say?'

Fenella didn't repeat herself. She held out her hand and snapped her fingers in front of the detective's nose.

Franks could never understand kids and their modern lingo, but he was convinced there had been something rude about the way she had done it.

'Give me the damn book,' he blustered, getting his hands on it.

'No,' Rosa said, pulling it away from him. She and Fenella left the burial chamber and ran out of the Sennefer exhibit into the hallway.

Franks stomped out after them. 'Come back here,' he barked. 'I want that book.'

Fenella spied an open door with a sign on it: STAFF ONLY. The doorway led into a narrow corridor. She and Rosa went into it.

'Why do we always end up running?' Fenella asked.

Rosa glanced back over her shoulder. 'It's what we do.'

The narrow corridor led to a narrower staircase that only went up. They went up.

They arrived on the next floor and heard the detective's raspy breath huffing on the stairs below them.

'I have my gun out,' he yelled. 'If you don't give me that book, I will start firing.'

Rosa left the book on the floor at the top of the stairs. She and Fenella then ran along a hallway of closed doors, trying each handle to find an unlocked one. Fenella found one, and she and Rosa went in and shut the door after them. They found themselves staring at a befuddled Professor Bacon sitting at his desk.

He sneezed.

'May I lock the door?' Fenella asked.

'Why would you want to do that?' the professor asked.

'The big bad wolf is in the forest.'

He nodded his permission, no more enlightened.

She locked the door.

Rosa approached his desk. 'Why would someone want to steal a mummy?'

CHAPTER THIRTY-FIVE

'How does reincarnation work?' Thacker asked.

Stanwick bit into an apple, chewed contemplatively, then said, 'What happens when you die?'

Thacker shrugged. 'I don't know. Nothing. You take a big sleep, and you don't wake up.'

They sat on the ground behind the overgrown hedge, across the street from the Dalrymple house.

'Some people believe that's what happens,' Stanwick said. 'But the people who believe in reincarnation believe that after you die, your soul is reborn in a new body and that you get to live a new life – a brand-new life from start to finish.'

Thacker thought about that. 'From the very start?'

'Yes. As a new baby. You'd have to learn to walk and talk, and everything else, all over again because you don't get to keep any of the memories of your previous life.'

'And how often does this happen?' Thacker asked. 'How many times do you reincarnate?'

'I don't know if there is a limit.'

Thacker found the whole idea distasteful. The thought of school again, and again forever terrified him to the core of his being. 'We need to get the aunt away from the house,' he said, peering around the hedge at the building. 'We need to get inside and find out if Caroline is okay.'

'I can't honestly think of any reason someone would want to steal a mummy,' Professor Bacon said, stroking his beard. 'I assume you are referring to the Sennefer mummy?'

'Yes,' Rosa said. She and Fenella sat on chairs in front of his desk.

The professor looked out the window. After a moment's thought, he asked himself, 'Mummy brown?' then shook his head. 'Surely not.'

'What's mummy brown?' Fenella asked.

Bacon spoke quietly, with disgust. 'It's a paint color – a rich brown pigment. For a couple of hundred years, artists used it in oil paintings. It was made from a mixture of myrrh, pitch, and the ground-up remains of Egyptian mummies.'

Rosa and Fenella were equally disgusted.

'Most artists stopped using it in the late 19th century when they learned how the pigment was manufactured.'

He thought some more.

He gave a final shake of his head. 'A mummy's only real value is historic. I can't imagine too many people would want one as a decoration for their living room, and I don't think you could readily sell one. No museum worth its reputation would want to acquire one of questionable origin.'

He studied the two girls. There was something odd in their expressions. 'Do you know where my mummy went?'

The noncommittal shakes of heads didn't entirely convince him.

'I suppose,' he said, as an afterthought, 'someone might steal Sennefer's mummy if they were of a mind to use him in the Binding of the Virgins ceremony.'

'What on earth is that?' Rosa and Fenella asked simultaneously.

After confirming that Detective Franks wasn't lurking in the hallway outside the door, Professor Bacon led Rosa and Fenella back to the Sennefer exhibition. They glanced at the professor's boots. Old. Worn. They had seen a lot of miles.

Bacon led them into the burial chamber, and Rosa and Fenella took another look at Iset's image inside the coffin lid.

'It's spooky,' Fenella remarked, studying the face.

Rosa could see it, too. 'There's definitely a similarity in the eyes.'

The professor directed their attention to the hieroglyphs engraved on the chamber's walls. 'What do you think these writings say?'

Rosa knew, or thought she did. 'Is it a guide to the afterlife for the deceased? A book of the dead?'

'No,' the professor said. 'Ordinarily, that's what you would find in a burial chamber, but in this one, the writings are more a book of the undead.'

'What does that mean?' Fenella asked.

'They're a set of instructions. They detail a ceremony called the Binding of the Virgins.'

'Iset wrote these, didn't she?' Rosa asked.

'That's correct. She wrote them, and she created the set of stylized hieroglyphs they're written in.'

'And why are they written that way? Why was their meaning meant to be kept a secret?'

'Because only Iset herself was supposed to read them. Not even the scribes who engraved these hieroglyphs into the walls knew what they meant.'

'So, what's involved in the Binding of the Virgins?' Fenella asked.

The professor pointed to the ceiling.

Fenella and Rosa looked up.

A large, equilateral triangle was carved into the gray rock ceiling above Sennefer's coffin. There were hieroglyphs at each of the triangle's three corners. Rosa and Fenella recognized two of them – the hieroglyphs for 'Sennefer' and for 'bride.' They didn't know the third.

'The ceiling here, like the walls, is an exact recreation of what's inside Sennefer's tomb in Egypt,' Bacon said.

'Why a triangle?' Rosa asked.

'It's how the ceremony is performed.'

'The triangle is the strongest of all shapes,' Fenella remarked.

Bacon concurred. 'A triangle is painted on the ground. Sennefer's mummy is positioned in the first corner, the witness in the second, and the bride in the third.'

The two girls stared at the elderly man.

'What kind of ceremony is this Binding of the Virgins?' Rosa asked.

'It's a wedding ceremony.'

Fenella and Rosa followed Professor Bacon into the adjacent room where the rest of the Sennefer exhibits were displayed.

'To understand the ceremony,' he said, 'you need to know more about Iset.'

He led them to a figurine of a woman cast in terracotta and painted in pigments that had long since faded. The woman stood two feet tall and held a noble posture. She wore a white, flowing robe, with her long dark hair crowned with a string of red flowers.

'Iset of Anput,' Bacon said. 'Anput was the goddess of purification, and Iset was her follower.'

'Was Iset a high priestess?' Fenella asked, staring at the figurine's intense dark eyes.

'No. She was a chantress.'

'What's that?'

'A chantress is a singer of songs. We don't fully understand what a chantress's role was in Ancient Egypt, but we know she did more than just sing. A chantress was a type of conduit, a direct link, between this world and the realm of the gods.'

'Iset sang for Anput?' Rosa asked.

'Yes, you could describe it like that.'

He continued. 'Iset first met Sennefer at the yearly Bast Festival – a festival to celebrate Bastet.'

'The cat goddess?'

'Yes. Bastet was the goddess of the home, the protector of women and children, and cats.'

Nice kind of god, Fenella thought. 'How many gods did the ancient Egyptians have?'

'More than 2000.'

Fenella had expected 12.

'And at this festival, Sennefer performed one of his magic tricks.'

'Caroline said he was a magician,' Rosa reported.

'Yes. He was known as Sennefer the Unbelievably Magnificent

– a title given to him by the Pharaoh. His talent as a magician was said to be astounding.'

'He did more than pull rabbits out of hats?'

The professor grinned. 'Sennefer believed magic was real, and not simply just a matter of trickery and sleight-of-hand.'

'Was it love at first sight?' Fenella asked.

'Yes, and they had, what today would be called, a whirlwind romance.'

'Why did his sister kill him?' Rosa asked.

The professor gave a professorial shrug. 'His sister's name was Beketamun. Not a lot is known about her, but many historians have argued she wanted Sennefer as her own – for herself to be his bride.'

'She was jealous?'

'I suppose.'

'Could sisters marry their brothers in Ancient Egypt?'

'It was expected in royal families, but relatively rare among noble families, such as Sennefer's.'

'That's off the wall,' Fenella remarked.

'The Binding of the Virgins is a wedding,' Bacon said, 'but it's a different type of wedding to the one Sennefer and Iset would have had, had he not been murdered.'

He led Fenella and Rosa back into the tomb's antechamber and directed their attention to the four empty chests.

'This was no ordinary burial. In that era, the 19th Dynasty, you would have found canopic jars containing the deceased's internal organs here in the tomb.' He shook his head. 'Sennefer wasn't mummified in the usual way. He wasn't taken apart or disemboweled; he was left completely intact. And before being wrapped in his linen bandages, he was coated in a thick dark resin to seal him from the air.'

'He was preserved?' Rosa asked.

'Yes.'

'Why?'

'Everything about Sennefer's entombment was for the future. The preservation of his corpse, the chests with their vast treasure, and the encrypted writings in the burial chamber – it was all at Iset's command. She laid out a strict set of instructions. The Binding of the Virgins was a ceremony she planned and expected to take place in the future.'

'Why?' Fenella asked.

'Because she was dying.'

Fenella and Rosa stared at him.

Bacon led them back into the burial chamber and to the coffin lid and its image of Iset.

'Iset died thirty-six days after Sennefer. You see, Beketamun didn't just kill her brother on the morning of his wedding – she bribed a servant to poison Iset's food.' He frowned. 'Iset's death came after weeks of agony.'

'That's horrible,' Rosa said.

'So, who is the Binding of the Virgins for?' Fenella asked. 'If Iset is dead, who is supposed to be the bride?'

The professor grinned. 'Iset.'

Fenella and Rosa stared at the man.

'Reincarnation,' he said. 'At some future time, Iset planned for her reincarnated self to return to the tomb, open the burial chamber, and perform the ceremony, following the instructions she had left for herself.'

Fenella shook her head with bafflement. 'So, let's assume reincarnation is a thing, and Iset reincarnates, and she marries Sennefer's corpse. Then what? She's still married to a corpse. And don't tell me the ceremony brings him back to life.'

Bacon shook his head. 'It doesn't. The Binding of the Virgins is a ceremony of two parts. It's a marriage and a transformation. After she marries his corpse, they transcend the human plane and become gods.'

Fenella shrugged with resignation. 'I'm running out of ways of staring at you.'

The professor's grin was unflappable. 'A binding of marriage and fire.'

'I'm not detecting solid science here,' Rosa remarked with a truckload of doubt.

Bacon laughed. 'Make of it what you will. It's a fairytale inscribed on the walls of a tomb, written in an obscure form of hieroglyphic script that no two scholars can agree on as to its meaning. And the only currently accepted translation is that of Scarlett Dalrymple, who had no formal training in the language and has never set foot in Egypt.'

Rosa and Fenella shouted in unison, 'Scarlett Dalrymple?'

The rear door to the Dalrymple house opened, and Aunt Scarlett walked outside. She wore a coat and a red scarf. She had Jasper on a leash, and the little dog was a tongue-dangling, tail-wagging blur of excitement.

Aunt Scarlett locked the rear door.

She led Jasper across the yard to the yellow panel truck. It had once, long ago, been a sprightly delivery truck for small parcels and such. Now, it could charitably be described as retired. It hadn't seen a parcel, let alone a new set of tires or plugs, in more than a decade.

Aunt Scarlett opened the passenger door, lifted the little dog, and placed him comfortably on the worn leather seat. She wound down the window and shut the door.

She walked around to the driver's side, climbed in, and sat behind the wheel.

'We have some things to do,' she said to Jasper. 'And then we'll get you some more of those little mermaids.'

Jasper's smile was as brilliant as the afternoon sun.

Aunt Scarlett hit the ignition. The truck started with a backfire, and a cloud of pungent smoke spurted out of the tailpipe. She put the truck into gear and slowly followed the gravel driveway around the house to the street. Once on the road, she put her foot down and sped away with the little dog barking its head off out the window.

Aunt Scarlett didn't think to look in the rear mirror. Had she done, she would have seen Thacker and Stanwick running across the street toward the house.

CHAPTER THIRTY-SIX

PROFESSOR BACON RAN HIS EYES OVER THE BOOKS ON HIS SHELVES. THAT he had 17 bookcases in his office crammed full of 7952 books made this a lengthy procedure.

He sneezed.

He glared at the open window.

'Have you ever considered alphabetical order?' Fenella suggested. She and Rosa stood patiently by the man's desk.

'Alphabetical is inexact,' Bacon grumbled. He knew the book he was looking for was on the shelf; he had just forgotten which one. 'And order by what? Title or author? First name or last? And what if the title begins with a number?'

'How about the Dewey system?' Rosa said.

Bacon muttered something about how he needed to take a feather duster to everything. It had been one or two years since he had last done so, maybe more.

Rosa glanced at a map pinned to the wall. Little blue flags had been stuck into it, with each connected by a wobbly line of pencil. Someone had made a thorough expedition across India, Nepal, and Tibet. She glanced again at the professor's boots.

Fenella noticed that wine bottles filled one of the bookcase's cubicles. Dusty dark wine bottles. They looked vintage, like the professor.

'Scarlett Dalrymple is the principal reason there is a Sennefer exhibition,' Bacon remarked.

'Why is that?' Rosa asked.

'After the death of her father, she spent months lobbying the

Egyptian government for it to take place. The city backed the idea and offered to pay the cost.'

Bacon found the book he was after and slid it off the shelf. He presented it to Fenella and Rosa. Its worn front jacket was illustrated with an assortment of hieroglyphic writing and printed in a bold font:

The Interpretation of the Iset Writings
by Scarlett Dalrymple

'It was published five years ago,' Bacon said. 'It took her more than a decade to research and write.'

Rosa took the book. She opened it and flicked through the pages – drawings and photographs of the hieroglyphs in the burial chamber, translations, analysis, history.

'There are only two hundred copies,' the professor said. 'I believe she paid for the printing herself.'

Rosa held up the book, showing Fenella the back cover and its photograph of a much younger Aunt Scarlett.

'May we borrow this?' Fenella asked.

'Yes. It's an interesting read; however, understand that it was never peer-reviewed, and many scholars and academics have outright rubbished it. But, as it stands, it's the only complete translation of the Sennefer hieroglyphs in existence. So, make of it what you will.'

He added: 'And I want it back.'

'Of course.'

As they were leaving, Fenella asked the professor, 'The jackal was a symbol of Anput, wasn't it?'

'Yes.'

'Was it a very large jackal?'

'Well, there's the beast of Anput,' he said. 'A freak of nature used by Anput to do her work in this world. It has often been described as a large, abnormal jackal. Why do you ask?'

'My brother thinks he saw one last night.'

Bacon stared at her. He seemed a little unsettled.

'We'll make of it what we will,' said Rosa.

Stanwick glanced at his pocket watch. He stood beside Thacker, who kneeled at the Dalrymple front door. He was determinedly working the keyhole with two slender metal tools – one had a hooky end, the other blunt. Both looked like the type of tools dentists laid out on the tray next to your chair when you paid a visit.

Stanwick yawned.

'How long?' Thacker asked.

'Twenty-five minutes.'

Thacker gritted his teeth.

'Should we try the back door again?'

There was finally a satisfying clank from within the door as it unlocked. Thacker exhaled. He shoved his tools back into his trench coat pocket and opened the door.

The inside of the Dalrymple house was just as Thacker had imagined it: old, dusty, smelly, and thoroughly uninteresting. It reminded him of his grandfather's home in Dublin, which he had visited when he was five. Only his grandfather's house had been one of light and laughter; the Dalrymple house was one of gloom. Even the shadows had shadows.

Thacker stood at the foot of the staircase. He didn't see any blood, and the steps looked as though they'd been painstakingly cleaned. He noticed a black, five-gallon gasoline can standing in the hall.

Stanwick tapped his shoulder. 'We don't know how long the aunt will be away.'

Thacker nodded.

The two of them followed the hallway to the rear of the house. They found Caroline's door and Thacker knocked.

'Who is it?' Caroline called out, confused.

Thacker tried the handle. The door was locked. 'It's Thacker and Stanwick.'

He went to work on the lock with his dental equipment. It took him 20 seconds to tumble it. He opened the door, and they entered.

The room was lit by a dim bulb. Caroline stood up from the

edge of her bed. 'Are you crazy?' she whispered, her eyes looking past them into the hallway.

'Your aunt drove off in an old truck and took the dog,' Thacker said. 'Are you okay?'

She shook her head. 'I've been grounded.' She noticed the Band-Aid.

'What's with the window?'

'My aunt nailed it shut this morning and then painted it over. How did you open my door? How did you get into the house?'

Thacker held up his little metal tools. 'Want to look upstairs?'

A smile of eager expectation broke across Caroline's face.

Caroline led the way as the three of them climbed the staircase. 'Are you all right?' she asked. 'The last time I saw you, you fell off the side of the house.'

'It was nothing.'

'The boy possesses a certain amount of robustness,' Stanwick remarked.

They followed the staircase from landing to landing, and once at the top, they followed the hall down to the end. Caroline felt as though she were on another planet. She had lived in the Dalrymple house for over three weeks, and this was her first time on the second floor.

They poked their heads into the room of Egyptian hieroglyphics, gave it a quick look, and then went to the door across from it.

Thacker knocked.

There was no answer.

He tried the doorknob. Locked.

'Did you get to see inside this room last night?' Caroline asked.

'Yes.'

'Who was in there?'

Thacker didn't answer. He kneeled and went to work on the door's dentistry.

'We are about to find out if he saw what he thinks he did,' Stanwick said.

Thacker's face was concentration – teeth gritted, eyes

unblinking. He felt the tiny vibrations in his tools as they worked the inside of the keyhole.

'Where did he learn how to do that?' Caroline whispered.

Stanwick whispered back, 'First grade.'

It took Thacker a minute to work the lock and finally hear the faint clank of success. He stood up, put his tools back in his pocket, and opened the door.

The room was dark. Caroline found the light switch and flicked it on.

There was no mummy.

A chair stood in the middle of the room, and an old, ornate white gown lay slung over it. The rest of the room looked as though it had been taken to with sandpaper: bare floorboards, walls stripped of wallpaper. Even the light bulb was naked, hanging on a threadbare wire from a scratched ceiling.

Caroline scooped up the gown and examined it.

Thacker was stumped. 'That's not what I saw last night.'

Caroline admired the gown's aged elegance. 'This could be a wedding dress,' she remarked. She held it to her shoulders. 'It could fit me.'

She looked at Thacker and frowned. 'A wedding dress is not what I've been listening to walk about above me. What did you see last night?'

'A mummy.'

'An Egyptian mummy?'

He nodded. 'It sat in that chair.'

'The boarder was Sennefer's mummy?'

'Yes.'

Caroline shook her head in disbelief. 'How does an ancient Egyptian mummy walk around a room?'

Thacker shrugged. 'They don't. They generally don't move about at all.'

Caroline was bewildered.

Aunt Scarlett's black notebook lay on the floor beneath the window. Stanwick picked it up and flicked through its pages. It took only a little flicking to suggest he held something rather peculiar.

'There were odd noises this morning.' Caroline looked at Thacker. 'Squeaks and thuds on the staircase.'

It was obvious to both of them.

'She's moved it,' Thacker said. 'In a wheelchair.'

Caroline draped the dress back over the chair. 'Seriously, I heard footsteps. If it was Sennefer's mummy in this room, how did it walk around? How does a 3000-year-old mummy stand and walk around a room?'

'I always allow for the possibility of the extraordinary,' Thacker said. 'Can I see the trains?'

Caroline stared at him and then laughed. She led the way back down the stairs.

They didn't hear the panel truck's tires on the driveway's loose gravel.

Caroline opened the narrow door to the basement that stood in the hallway near the kitchen. At that same moment, the three of them heard a key go into the rear door and an unmistakable yap from Jasper outside.

'She's back,' Caroline whispered.

She knew they had seconds.

She shoved Thacker and Stanwick through the doorway and onto the basement stairs.

'Will I see you at the dance?' Thacker asked.

'I don't know.'

She closed the door.

The rear door opened, and Jasper ran into the kitchen. He ran about excitedly in circles, slipping on the linoleum, his tail a blur, his tongue flopping, his eyes crossed.

Aunt Scarlett came in after him, carrying a brown paper bag full of groceries, her attention caught by a flicker of movement at the hallway's end.

She stared.

There was no one there.

Apart from Jasper's panting and paws pounding on the kitchen floor, the house was quiet.

Aunt Scarlett frowned and closed the rear door.

She emptied the contents of the paper bag onto the kitchen

table. Of interest to Jasper were the six boxes of Captain Seadog's Salty Sea Snacks.

Aunt Scarlett ripped open a box. She poured a handful of the Captain into the dog's bowl on the floor alongside the refrigerator.

Jasper went at the little mermaid-shaped snacks with vigor and determination.

Aunt Scarlett smiled lovingly at her little dog.

She then turned her eyes back to the hallway, and the smile slowly faded. The flicker of movement she had seen bothered her.

Thacker and Stanwick stood in silence on the dimly lit concrete steps that led down into the basement. A muffled, whirring sound rose from below, and the glass panels in the door at the foot of the steps were lit up.

Thacker indicated for Stanwick to go down. Stanwick did, and he followed. Stanwick opened the door, and they entered the basement.

Thacker smiled. The whirring sound was that of trains. The aunt's room upstairs had been a room full of hieroglyphics; downstairs was a basement full of locomotives. Three tables overflowed with spare tracks, carriages, engines, repair equipment, and tools. Train memorabilia – uniforms, caps, souvenirs, books, photographs – lay everywhere, and dozens of platform signs were nailed to the walls. And central to it all was an unending miniature train track that ran around the room at waist height, set in a landscape of detailed miniature mountains, hills, valleys, and dust bowls of the American West. Three trains were in motion, moving about the scenery, pulling passenger cars, freight cars, boxcars, and Pullmans.

Thacker was in paradise. He had always wanted a train set and had asked for one every Christmas since he'd been two, but the most he'd ever gotten had been a 10-page booklet about railroad gauges.

Stanwick looked for the mummy.

Aunt Scarlett stood in the hallway outside Caroline's bedroom and stared at the door. She had a suspicion, and she tested it. The door wasn't locked. She opened it and entered.

Caroline sat on her bed, reading. She looked up.

'Did you unlock this door?'

Caroline shook her head. 'How would I do that?'

Her aunt's face soured. Evidence was mounting. She left the room and locked the door.

'There's a door,' Stanwick said for the third time. Thacker wasn't listening. He was smiling insanely, staring in awe at the trains moving along their tracks.

'There's a door. Behind it are some steps that lead to another door; it probably leads outside, but there's a padlock.'

After a moment, Thacker sighed.

He ripped himself away from his childhood. Padlocks were the most painless teeth to pull in his dentistry practice.

Aunt Scarlett made her way up to the second floor and sniffed the air. She heard Jasper clambering up the stairs behind her. She walked along the hall to the door at the end. It was closed, but she had a suspicion about that one, too. Jasper trotted after her.

She was right. The door wasn't locked.

She entered the room and turned on the light. The dress had been touched. People had been inside her house.

Aunt Scarlett's face was incandescent. She pulsed with anger.

Jasper ran into the room and excitedly ran around the chair and the wedding dress, his little paws tapping a staccato racket on the bare floorboards.

Aunt Scarlett looked for her black notebook. She had left it on the floor beneath the window. It wasn't there.

She let out a roar of anger, followed by a soaring string of obscenities.

Jasper froze and shrunk into a small ball of fluff in an attempt to vanish.

Caroline, startled, stared at her ceiling.

CHAPTER THIRTY-SEVEN

'THIS IS AN ODD NOTEBOOK,' STANWICK REMARKED.

He and Thacker rode the bus back to school.

Thacker was listening, but lost in his thoughts. He was remembering the museum and asking Caroline to the dance, and her having said 'yes.' It worried him she had now been grounded. That would be just his luck. He finally asks a girl on a date, and she gets grounded.

'Why is the notebook odd?' he asked.

'There are pages of random words,' Stanwick replied. 'None of which appears to make any sense. Some pages have only one word, but it's repeated over and over. There are pages with drawings of a little dog, drawings of the Earth, the moon, the sun, and several pages mentioning the summer solstice – at daybreak on that day, there are plans for a wedding.'

'A wedding?'

Stanwick held the notebook under Thacker's nose, open to an illustration of an inverted triangle. In one corner of the triangle was written the word GROOM. At another, BRIDE. In the lower corner, WITNESS.

'This plan is drawn on several pages.'

Thacker recognized the notebook's red spiral spine. 'That belongs to the aunt. She hit me with it last night.' He tapped the Band-Aid on his cheek.

The bus pulled over at a stop four blocks from Matheson High.

Thacker and Stanwick climbed off, and the bus pulled away. They walked along an empty sidewalk of shuttered stores and rampant graffiti – real estate near the school wasn't highly prized.

'Where could someone hide a mummy in this city?' Stanwick asked.

Thacker shrugged. 'This is a big city.'

There was a clatter and rattle behind them, and they turned to look.

They didn't like what they saw.

A block away, a trashcan rolled onto the street, leaving a trail of empty bottles and cans on the sidewalk. What had knocked it over was indifferent to order or tidiness.

Stanwick adjusted his glasses. 'Is it me, or is that dog out of proportion?'

'It's not a dog.'

Stanwick noted the pointed, elongated ears and the long, pointed snout. After a moment's consideration, he concluded, 'Yes, it's probably a jackal.'

The jackal opened its jaws. Its teeth were as red as its eyes.

Thacker and Stanwick ran.

Stanwick may have been of sizable circumference but, when he got moving, he could summon the swiftness of a gazelle, and he easily caught up with Thacker. They ran the last block to the school with timing good enough to make the state track team.

'Why do we always end up running?' Stanwick asked as they ran in through the school gates.

'It's what we do.'

They ran to the school auditorium, which stood next to the school's main building – its fire escape doors were open.

They ran inside.

The auditorium was a windowless acre of flat concrete with a proscenium-arch stage at one end. A dozen students – serious-faced due to their lofty positions as school social committee members – were installing the decorations for the dance that coming evening. They were highly offended that two non-committee members had dared to invade their private space. And that Thacker had run into the room shouting something incomprehensible.

The jackal ran in after them, and, confused by a room full of people and balloons, it came to an abrupt halt. There were balloons everywhere: dozens of balloons, each about the size of someone's head. The jackal's eyesight wasn't so good, and it found itself in a room full of heads – some with bodies, some without, some in groups, some on the floor, some high in the ceiling.

After a frozen moment and concluding that the dark creature really was there – that it really did have large red eyes, and it really was as huge as it looked – the social committee collectively screamed and ran for the doors. Any door. Any hole or crack in the building's structure that would lead them to some place where the beast was not.

Unlike its eyesight, the jackal's sense of smell was razor-sharp. It quickly sorted the students from the balloons and turned its attention to the heads of Thacker and Stanwick.

Thacker and Stanwick were clambering onto the stage.

The stage was an uneven spread of bare wooden boards with a red velvet curtain backdrop. At center stage stood an old honey-colored upright piano and a small, raised platform for a drum kit alongside it. As they ran across the stage, Stanwick hoped that Mr Grady had checked the piano's tuning.

A ladder stood against the wall at stage left, and Thacker and Stanwick ran to it and began climbing.

They could hear the jackal cantering across the auditorium floor in their direction.

The ladder led 30 feet up to a small booth where the stage's theatrical lights and sound system were operated from.

The jackal leaped onto the stage.

Once Thacker and Stanwick had both climbed into the control booth through its narrow, doorless entrance, Thacker kicked the ladder away.

The jackal was quick and strong, but it did not possess the know-how to pick up a ladder and use it. Or to fly. All it could do was jump, growl, and snap its teeth two feet below where Thacker and Stanwick gazed down at it. It then landed back on the stage with a slam that sent a tremor through the building.

'Why me?' Thacker shouted at the creature. 'Why do you keep chasing me?'

He didn't get an answer.

The jackal changed its tactic. It headed across to the other side of the stage, turned about, and then took a running charge. When it got to 10 feet from the wall, it leaped. Thacker and Stanwick jumped back as its enormous head came in through the control booth's entrance, its jaws slamming shut with enough force to snap a telegraph pole.

The jackal dropped away, then promptly trotted back across the stage for another attempt.

Stanwick glanced about. The control booth was five feet by five feet, a windowless box full of lighting controls and a reel-to-reel tape machine.

'That thing is going to kill us if it gets inside here,' he said.

A second later, the jackal's head came back in through the entrance. This time, the creature didn't drop back down to the stage. It wedged its front paws into the booth and stayed there, its torso part way in, with its hind legs scraping at the wall below.

Thacker and Stanwick kneeled, pinned to the wall, with the jackal's long, black snout barely a foot in front of them. It growled thunderously. Its breath felt like an open furnace.

Thacker thought about giving that snout a good kick. He also thought it might be hard to walk with only one leg.

The jackal made a low, guttural grunt.

It sounded to Thacker almost like a word. He realized the jackal's eyes were staring at Stanwick, and, specifically, at the aunt's notebook that he clasped to his chest.

Again, the jackal made the same grunt, with the articulation becoming clearer – beginning with a B sound and ending with a K sound.

'Did that thing just say *book*?' Thacker asked, bewildered.

The jackal grunted again. 'Book.' From the amount of strain visible on its face, it had a hard time doing what it was attempting.

'It wants the notebook,' Thacker said.

Stanwick tossed it over the jackal's head and out onto the stage. The jackal dropped away from the booth's entrance and went after it.

Thacker and Stanwick watched as, using its teeth, the jackal carefully picked up the black notebook from where it had landed by the piano. It took the book, jumped off the stage, and disappeared from their sight. They heard it run out of the auditorium.

And then silence.

Thacker and Stanwick sat patiently in the entrance; their legs dangling over the edge. The ladder lay unreachable on the stage below.

'Why balloons?' Thacker asked.

'What do you mean?' Stanwick asked, cleaning the lenses of his glasses with his handkerchief.

'Why do parties always have to have balloons?'

'People like them, I suppose.'

Thacker shook his head dismissively. 'They're just little bags of someone's bad breath. What's the point?'

There were footsteps in the auditorium. 'Thornton Thacker,' shouted an angry Undergarden.

'Up here,' Thacker shouted back.

Undergarden climbed the steps at the side of the stage and then walked out in front of them. 'What do you two think you are doing?' he asked, staring up at them. 'I have members of the social committee in tears in the administration office with some ludicrous story about you two and a dog.'

Thacker thought about trying to explain it.

He couldn't.

'Yup. There was a dog.'

CHAPTER THIRTY-EIGHT

'SO, THEY WERE BOTH VIRGINS,' FENELLA REMARKED.

Rosa nodded. 'The Binding of the Virgins.'

'Where did this ceremony come from? Did Iset just make it up?'

'I'm looking.'

Fenella and Rosa were riding a bus back across town. Rosa had *The Interpretation of the Iset Writings* open on her lap.

'Aunt Scarlett did a lot of research for this book,' Rosa said. 'It's not just a translation of the hieroglyphs in the tomb. She wrote an entire history of Iset and Sennefer.'

Fenella yawned. 'I need coffee.'

'Me, too.'

Fifteen minutes later, they walked into the *Rainy Night Café*.

Fenella noticed Sultana asleep in a chair, lit up in a shaft of afternoon sunlight. The cat liked the smell of coffee and the vibrations of music; both were always in the air at the *Rainy Night*.

Rosa took a seat at the window table and continued reading.

Fenella ordered two coffees and contemplated the slice of chocolate cake that sat on a white plate inside the cake cabinet, ready to go, ready to devour. The cabinet of cake at the *Rainy Night* was always delightful to gaze into. It stood on the counter next to the cash register. Inside lay a cornucopia of tastiness, all of it gently chilled by a thick layer of ice cubes Mimi kept replenished on a tray inside the cabinet.

Fenella glanced at the guardian of the cakes – the teddy bear that lived inside the cabinet and sat on the same shelf as the chocolate cake. He wore a winter muffler and mittens and always smiled. Fenella imagined he was drawing her attention to the chocolate cake's texture and the shininess of the chocolate icing thickly coating it.

Mimi returned with two cups of coffee.

'Thank you,' Fenella said, tearing away from the temptation. She dared not look at the caramel fudge – that would tip temptation right into the pig paddock.

She took the coffee to the table. Sultana woke and stared at the cups as they passed by.

'Iset first met Sennefer at a Bast festival at the villa of one of the city's leading politicians,' Rosa reported. 'It was the late afternoon, and there were a lot of important guests. And, on this afternoon, Sennefer the Unbelievably Magnificent performed his most famous trick of magic.'

'What was the trick?' Fenella asked, taking a seat.

'He set fire to a statue of a jackal.'

'How is that magical?'

'He stood 20 feet away from it. He set it on fire by staring at it.'

'How did he do that?'

Rosa shrugged. 'That's the point of magic, I suppose: to make you wonder. Anyway, this caught Iset's attention because the goddess she worshiped, Anput, was often depicted with the head of a jackal.'

'First impressions are important in a relationship,' Fenella said. She looked out the window and sipped her coffee. People coming and going: a man with a puppy, a woman eating an apple, an old man with a handful of books. All of them blissfully unaware a mummy was on the loose in the city.

Mimi put a new plate inside the cake cabinet. Fenella and Sultana looked. It was a slice of something green. The icing was so luminescent it probably would have glowed in the dark.

Mimi was middle-aged. She had black hair cut into a bob and was always dressed as though she was on the way to a swanky party, one that was probably taking place 30 years ago. 'Lateness is the height of fashion,' she probably would have said had you asked. After closing the cake cabinet, she went to the gramophone. It sat on the ledge behind the counter. She changed the record to another from the 1920s.

Rosa found what she had been looking for. 'The Binding of the Virgins ceremony came to Iset in a vision.'

'A vision?'

Rosa read from the book. 'On learning of Sennefer's murder, Iset gave a great cry and fell to the marble floor of Anput's temple. She twisted and turned in a turmoil of grief and fever. And, in her fever, she had a dream, and she saw wondrous things.'

'What did she see?'

'Three large burning jackals.'

'Statues of jackals?'

'No, real jackals, large ones, and, together, the three burning jackals formed a triangle.'

The two girls looked at each other.

Rosa continued. 'And Iset knew that her vision was of a ceremony, a ceremony of the gods. She knew that the goddess Anput was speaking to her directly, not in words, but in images. And, one by one, each of the burning jackals was replaced – first by the witness at the lower point of the triangle, then by Sennefer at the top-left corner, and then by Iset, herself, at the top-right corner. And Sennefer was dead, and she, herself, had been born anew.'

'She had reincarnated,' Fenella said.

'The ceremony was their marriage, where they would finally, irreversibly, become man and wife. And then Iset saw they became engulfed in flames.'

'Is that what the professor meant when he said, "a binding of marriage and fire"?' Fenella asked.

'Yes. Sennefer and Iset are set on fire.' Rosa read from the book. 'And, in their burning, they become more alive than any creature on the earth, and they transcend this world.'

'They become gods.'

Rosa nodded. 'They ascend to the realm of the omnipotent and become gods of fire and damnation. The earth becomes their kingdom, and they burn it all.'

She closed the book.

'Gods of fire and damnation that set fire to the world,' Fenella said. 'Fantastic. That's just what this city needs.'

Detective Franks sat down at Albert Park's desk and dumped the Christie book of hieroglyphics on it. He had badged his way into the newsroom of the *City Star* newspaper.

The newsroom was a humid, smoky space of crowded desks and typewriters. The windows to the street were open, and pedestal fans fluttered, with pieces of colored paper stuck to their grills to supply evidence they were switched on. Half a dozen reporters sat at their desks, typing and smoking. Park's desk was like everyone else's: a typewriter, a telephone, an ashtray, and a mess of paper.

The newspaper editor stood in the doorway to his office and stared at Franks. He was annoyed that a police officer was in the building; it distracted people from their work. What he would have liked to see sitting at Park's desk was a next of kin – someone to come and clear away his mess.

Franks went through the paperwork. Park had been a crime reporter, so his desk was a garden of criminality – stories, leads, snippets of information – all of it waiting to grow through investigation. Franks noticed a set of hieroglyphs scribbled on the blotter. Now that he had the Christie book, he would work out what all these hieroglyphic writings actually said.

Franks went through Park's desk drawers. Pencils. Typewriter ribbons. Blank paper. Empty packets of cigarettes and an empty gin bottle. And, in the bottom drawer, a fat folder with the word DUCKS written on its cover.

Franks flicked through it.

Pay dirt.

Bank records, expenditures, assets, business records, offices, factories, audits, and tax returns. Park clearly had contacts at the tax office and a bank or two. Franks lit a cigarette and read through some of it. There were annotations in red, in the same sloppy handwriting as in Park's notebook, and in the other bank records Franks had found in his room.

Franks spent an hour at Park's desk smoking and studying the bookkeeping.

He had found the end of the rainbow.

CHAPTER THIRTY-NINE

'IT WASN'T MY DOG,' THACKER SAID, LOOKING ABOUT AT THE PADDED walls of Principal Puddle's office. He had never noticed before how dirty they were. Row upon row of dirty beige felt panels; the dirt went all the way to the ceiling.

'It accompanied you onto the school grounds,' The Puddle said, staring across his desk at Thacker with regret. Being a respectable member of the education profession, he had to let his pleasant thoughts of torture and dismemberment remain locked in the dank vault of his imagination.

'It followed me.'

'From all accounts, the dog was a wild and unkempt beast, as are you. It's often been said that dog owners take on the characteristics of their pet.'

Thacker thought about Philip and Dash. The man had a point.

'It wasn't my dog,' Thacker said. 'I don't have a dog. My sister has a cat, but that was not the dog that followed me.'

'Following you would suggest it knew you.'

'Well, I didn't know it.'

'Then where did it come from?'

'I have no idea.'

'This is all rather vague, Thacker.'

'Don't I know it.'

P.P. Puddle sighed. A great intake of breath followed it, one that Thacker feared would inhale the room's supply of oxygen.

There was an exhale, and the big man's face became somber. Thacker knew what was coming. A migraine, to start with.

'Do you know what those are?' Puddle pointed to a stack of letters piled on his desk.

Thacker could see handwritten letters and a handful of typewritten ones on letterheads. 'They're letters.'

'They're letters from parents. I have been reported to the Department of Education, the American Medical Association, and the FBI – because of my decision last week to delay summer break.'

Thacker relaxed. Relief gushed through his soul.

'I wouldn't smile just yet, boy.'

'No?'

Puddle shoved a wad of loose blank paper and a pencil across the desk in front of Thacker. 'There are alternative punishments.'

Thacker felt the migraine punch the clock inside his head.

'I want you to write this down.'

Lines.

The Puddle dictated: 'I must amend my ways unless I should descend into the pits of hell.'

Thacker wrote that down.

'Hold it up.'

Thacker held up the sheet of paper.

'Correct.'

'How many times do you want me to write this out?'

'Four hundred thousand times.'

Thacker threw the pencil and paper onto the desk. 'What about a suspension? Could we do a deal on that?'

Puddle shook his head. 'All this is by the by. Writing lines is merely a matter of procedure. A policeman is waiting for you at the administration office.'

'Because of the dog?'

'No, because he wants to arrest you, and, frankly, that is the best thing that could happen to you and this school.'

He fluttered his hand, dismissing Thacker.

As Thacker left the office, Puddle added a footnote. 'After you are released from jail, the lines will be waiting for you.'

CHAPTER FORTY

IT WASN'T DETECTIVE FRANKS WAITING OUTSIDE THE SCHOOL administration office for Thacker. Sitting on a bench in the corridor was the man Thacker had seen at the library and the museum: the dark jacket, the polka-dot tie, the worn-out face, and the broken nose. The man now wore a trilby on his head. He saw Thacker and stood up.

'You're a cop, aren't you?' Thacker said, walking toward him.

'Lieutenant Bendix.' He held out his badge. 'And you're Thornton Thacker.'

Bendix spoke as he looked: sharp, choppy, punchy sentences. There was a sparkle in his eyes – like he knew he'd win if you picked a fight with him.

'What am I under arrest for?' Thacker asked.

'I'm not arresting you. Who told you that?'

'A man I went to see about a dog.'

'I want you to take a drive downtown with me.'

Thacker noticed Miss Xavier in her lair behind the counter, peering contentedly at him. She all but wagged her finger.

Downtown meant one thing: the city police department. Lieutenant Bendix drove with one hand on the wheel and an elbow out the open window. He drove slowly, like someone's grandmother.

'You're new here, aren't you?' Thacker asked.

'I transferred in a month ago from San Francisco. You have a reputation in this town, Thornton.'

'Nobody calls me Thornton.'

183

'Okay.'

Bendix stopped for a light.

'What kind of reputation?' Thacker asked. 'What have you heard?'

'Stuff.'

'What kind of stuff?'

The lieutenant's face said: where do I begin? He cut to the chase. 'The stuff I'm interested in is the stuff about the Dalrymple house. I know you're a friend of Caroline Greer.'

'How do you know that?'

'I know things. You've seen a dead body before, haven't you, Thacker?'

'One or two.'

'I have a new one to show you.'

Thacker frowned.

The stoplight changed to green.

The police department stood on the corner of Brett and Hardwicke in the heart of the city's downtown. It was a drab building of four floors that occupied a city block. The structure was the definition of uninspiring. A bored three-year-old had probably drafted the thing with a crayon on a wet afternoon.

Lieutenant Bendix parked in front.

They climbed the steps to the entrance. There was a sign above the door:

City Police Department

Crime & Punishment, since 1888

The morgue was in the basement. It was brightly lit, clean, white tiled, windowless, and frigid. It was like walking into a refrigerator where everything was past its use-by date.

Bendix took off his hat. He led Thacker to a trolley. There was a plump body laid on it under a white sheet – a plump man's hand with fat fingers hung out the side.

'Who is this?' Thacker asked, although he had a hunch.

'We think it's Alvin Dalrymple.'

'I expected something like this. Why isn't the aunt making the identification?'

'I want to keep everyone at Walnut Street out of this for the moment.'

'Why?'

'This is an investigation within an investigation. Think of this as an onion.'

Thacker didn't like onions.

'I'm being careful about who gets to see the layers as I peel them back.'

Thacker knew peeling onions made you cry. 'Pull back the sheet. Let's see him.'

'The body has no head.'

The words felt like a punch. 'Where did you find him?'

'He was in the Cinnamon River. Do you know if the uncle had any distinguishing features? Tattoos, birthmarks?'

'I never met him.'

Bendix's jaw slackened. 'You never met him?'

'Nope.'

The lieutenant's face was: I have just wasted the last 45 minutes of my life.

'I've seen a magazine photograph of him,' Thacker offered.

'The body has no head,' Bendix repeated.

'Pull back the sheet. Let me see what he's wearing.'

'There was an autopsy. He's naked. Why do you want to see his clothes?'

'Was he wearing a locomotive engineer's uniform?'

Bendix's eyes snapped to Thacker like he was a magnet. He retrieved a cardboard box from a table at the other end of the room. He placed the box at the end of the trolley next to the dead man's feet. He rummaged inside and pulled out a pair of wet blue-and-white-striped overalls. 'He was wearing this.'

'It's the uncle.'

Bendix dumped the overalls back in the box.

'About that onion,' Thacker said. 'The other layers include Albert Park, Caroline's mother, and a hieroglyphic message written on a wall in blood, don't they?'

Bendix didn't answer the question. 'You're not to tell anyone about what you've seen here. Not Caroline Greer, your sister, or any of your other friends who get mixed up in things none of you should get messed up with.'

Thacker nodded.

The lieutenant put his hat back on.

'Can I give you some advice?' Thacker said.

'Like what?'

'The aunt is the key to all of this.'

'Is that a fact?'

'It's a hunch.'

'Based on what?'

'Blood on a staircase.'

'At the Dalrymple house?'

'Yes.'

'You've seen this?'

'No. I heard about it. And don't trust Franks.'

Bendix smiled. 'Detective Franks doesn't like you, does he?'

'It's mutual.'

For a moment, Bendix forgot he was a professional law enforcement official. He went off the record. 'Let me tell you about Detective Franks. He has to be the stupidest OBSCENE OBSCENE OBSCENE I've ever met. He seriously needs to be kicked in his OBSCENE OBSCENE. And kicked OBSCENE hard.'

Thacker smiled radiantly. He could do business with the man with the polka-dot tie.

CHAPTER FORTY-ONE

ROSA TURNED HER DRUM KEY AND TIGHTENED ONE OF THE TENSION rods on her snare drum. She knew exactly how tight to wind each rod to get that crisp snap out of the skin when she hit it. She wore a sleeveless blouse with a tropical print, jeans, and blue sneakers. She had dressed to perform.

It was 10 minutes after eight in the evening, and the school auditorium was a blur of activity. The social committee members hurried to have everything prepared for the evening's dance. Every balloon had to be in its place, every streamer hung correctly, every colored light bulb screwed in, and the refreshments table had to be suitably laid out with a giddy assortment of beverages and snacks. Such was the busy life of the school social committee members. And every one of them had one eye on the door, just in case any other large dog, beast, bird, or brontosaurus should decide to wander into the room.

'Did you know tonight's dance had an Ancient Egyptian theme?' Fenella asked, staring across at the three-foot-high golden pyramid on the food table. It was presumably a cake.

'I didn't,' Rosa replied, glancing at the row of life-size papier-mâché mummies that three social committee members were attempting to stand uniformly upright.

Fenella wore her black sweater, black cropped pants, and black flats. She helped Rosa finish assembling her set of red-shelled drums on the stage's drum riser – a raised platform wide enough to accommodate drums, cymbals, and stool. Some musicians had it easy. They could stroll into a venue with a guitar slung over their back or carry a small case housing a flute or violin.

Rosa's drum kit had more than a dozen pieces; each one had to be carried individually into a venue and arranged in combination with the others. She was grateful her uncle drove a taxi.

Thacker walked into the auditorium. He wore a clean shirt under his trench coat. His beloved Epiphone B4 upright bass came in a case, but it had the weight of a dead cow. He didn't so much carry it as drag it. He also dragged a heavy fear that Caroline might not show up. He dragged his instrument case up the stairs at the stage's side and across to Fenella and Rosa.

'Did you find Caroline?' Fenella asked him. He didn't look happy.

Thacker laid his instrument case on the floor behind the drum riser. 'She's at the Dalrymple house. She's been grounded.'

He paused. 'Her uncle was murdered. His body is downtown in the morgue.'

Fenella and Rosa were shocked.

'Oh, no.'

'Esto es terrible y triste.'

'Do the police know who killed him?'

'No. We need to get Caroline out of that house.'

Fenella and Rosa nodded in complete agreement.

'When?' Rosa asked.

'Tonight. After the dance. We go there, we kick in the window, we get her out.'

'She can come and stay at our place,' Fenella said.

Thacker agreed.

Audrey Beech-Whale passed by the front of the stage, holding several sheets of paper and quietly rehearsing a speech. Audrey was the head of the school social committee. There was always a speech.

'Audrey,' Fenella called out. 'Why the Egyptian theme?'

Audrey smiled. 'Yes, we don't usually have a theme for end-of-year, but the committee decided to celebrate L.L. Carnaby and his Egyptian expedition. He's one of the city's heroes. Did you know there's currently an exhibition at the museum about the tomb he discovered?'

'We know,' Rosa said.

Audrey returned to her passing by and rehearsing.

'We went to the museum,' Fenella said to Thacker. 'The hieroglyphs inside Sennefer's tomb are instructions for a wedding ceremony.'

That caught Thacker's attention. 'We found a wedding dress in the room above Caroline's.'

'Did you find the mummy?' Rosa asked.

'No. The aunt has moved it.'

'Where to?'

He shrugged. 'Whose wedding is it?'

'Iset and Sennefer. The ceremony is the Binding of the Virgins.'

'Sennefer and Iset were virgins?'

'Yes. And that's why someone might steal Sennefer's mummy – to use it in the ceremony.'

'How does that work?'

'Iset marries the mummy.'

'Wouldn't Iset be dead by now?'

'Sennefer's mummy is wed to the reincarnation of Iset.'

'Huh?'

'And after they're married,' Fenella said, 'they're set on fire, and they become gods of fire and damnation.'

Thacker stared skeptically at them both.

'This is according to Aunt Scarlett's translation of Iset's hieroglyphic writing,' Rosa said.

'The aunt's translation?'

Rosa plucked the aunt's book from her bag. She held it up for Thacker to see its title and author's name.

Thacker was stunned. He screwed up his face. He felt like he had physically become a row of exclamation and question marks.

Stanwick wandered in. He wore his pork pie hat and a neon-blue shirt under his jacket. Some musicians had the most effortless lives of all. Thacker, Rosa, and Fenella watched him as he strolled across the room with his hands in his pockets. He ambled over to the honey-colored Ellington upright that stood waiting for him to the right of Rosa's drum set.

'Hello, my old friend,' Stanwick whispered to the piano, taking a seat on the stool.

'The mummy is used in a wedding ceremony,' Thacker said to him.

'Oh, really?'

'And the wedding is performed in a triangle,' Rosa added.

Stanwick recalled the pages of the notebook. 'I think we've seen the floor plan.'

'And then they're set on fire,' Thacker said.

'How odd.'

'Can I borrow some chalk?' Fenella asked Rosa.

Rosa kept a supply of leftover chalk teachers had discarded. She would grind the pieces into powder and apply it to her hands for a better grip on her drumsticks.

She handed Fenella a piece.

Fenella drew a triangle on the stage's wooden floor. The others gathered around.

At one corner of the triangle, Fenella wrote: WITNESS.

'The person who will witness the wedding,' Rosa said.

At another corner, Fenella wrote: SENNEFER.

'The mummy. The groom.'

At the last corner, Fenella wrote: BRIDE.

'Iset.'

'Wouldn't she be dead?' Stanwick asked.

'Not Iset from 3000 years ago – her reincarnation.'

Stanwick nodded. 'Okay, and who is Iset's reincarnation?'

Everyone looked at Thacker.

He shook his head. 'Caroline doesn't believe in reincarnation.'

Fenella thought of something. 'Wait a minute. Maybe the aunt does.'

'She has the mummy,' Rosa said, nodding. 'And she truly wrote the book.'

'And she's probably insane enough.'

Thacker shrugged. It was giving him a headache. 'When is this wedding supposed to take place?'

'At daybreak on the summer solstice,' Stanwick said.

Everyone stared at him.

Stanwick wiped his glasses with his handkerchief. 'It was in the aunt's notebook we found.'

'You have a notebook written by the aunt?' Fenella asked.

'We did, but a large jackal came and asked for it back.'

'When is the summer solstice?' Thacker asked.

'Tomorrow.'

CHAPTER FORTY-TWO

SOMETHING SHINY CAUGHT CAROLINE'S EYE. SOMETHING SMALL WAS wedged between two floorboards and had been caught in the room's light. She climbed off her bed, kneeled, and used a fingernail to pry the object loose.

It was a silver paper clip.

Caroline sat back on the bed and straightened the little piece of metal as best she could until its length was about three inches.

She stared across at the keyhole.

How hard could it be?

She put on her cream sweater and her tightly tapered, tartan-patterned pants. She slipped on her red sneakers. It was after nine, but if she could get out of the house, she was going to the dance.

And then she couldn't find the paper clip. She had left it on the bed, but it wasn't there anymore. She looked about on the floor and under the bed, but she couldn't find it.

There were footsteps in the hall.

Caroline sat back on the bed.

The door unlocked, and Aunt Scarlett entered, carrying a tray of food. 'Here's your dinner.' She presented Caroline with a small mountain range of mashed potatoes and several lumps of congealed green – possibly boiled cabbage, but who could tell.

Caroline took the tray, rested it on her lap, and waited for her aunt to leave.

Her aunt didn't leave. She sat on the edge of the bed next to Caroline and stared at the wall.

Caroline took her fork and used it to move the dirty white

hills of mashed potatoes about. It was an excuse to be doing something, anything, other than having to talk to the woman.

'Destiny,' Aunt Scarlett grunted loudly after a minute's silence.

The fork flipped out of Caroline's hand and plopped on the floor.

'Leave it,' Aunt Scarlett snapped. She stared at her niece. 'Do you believe in fate?'

Caroline was cautious. 'Sometimes.'

'We have to accept our role in this world; the part we are born to play. Do you understand this?'

Caroline didn't know what the woman was talking about. 'Sure.'

'And you accept this?'

'Sure.'

Her aunt noticed Caroline's tartan pants. 'Why are you dressed like that?'

'I felt like wearing something different,' Caroline said. She changed the subject. 'I need to use the bathroom.'

'Again?'

'What am I supposed to do, pee in the corner?'

Her aunt was mortified. She sprung to her feet and grabbed Caroline by her throat. 'When I was a child,' she yelled, 'I would have had the skin thrashed off of me for talking like that.'

The two women stared at each other. Caroline with knives.

Aunt Scarlett let go.

Caroline rubbed her neck.

Aunt Scarlett begrudgingly nodded. 'Go to the damn bathroom, if you must.'

Caroline walked down the hall to the bathroom, with her aunt following her.

'I may be some time,' Caroline announced with a shovelful of sarcasm. 'I'll try to get it all done for the day.' She went in, shut the door, and slid the bolt to lock it.

She really did need to go. And after she had gone, she quietly washed her hands.

She then took the plug out of the bathtub and slowly turned on the faucet. She let a gentle stream of water tinkle into the tub.

She doubted that she could have opened a locked door with a paper clip, but climb through a window – that she could do. She quietly opened the bathroom window.

And then she was gone.

CHAPTER FORTY-THREE

MUSIC FILLED THE AIR.

Thacker watched Fenella. She stood by the refreshments table, lit by the auditorium's soft, multi-colored party lights. She wore a face of expectation. She was waiting for her boyfriend.

Thacker tried to remember the guy's name.

Bob.

Bruno.

Douglas.

Uriah.

Ebenezer.

Filet Mignon.

Kevin! That was the name.

Students filled the auditorium – dressed up, made-up, animated, and eager. Some students danced, some did not, some were too shy to ask. The end-of-year dance was the only time anyone in school looked like they were alive rather than perfecting the recently risen-from-the-grave look, while meandering to and from class with the eyes of the dead. This was the last day of school before summer break. Freedom began at this dance.

Thacker looked for Caroline.

He didn't see her. There was little expectation on his face.

Stanwick played an odd note. It was neither out of key nor wrong in any sense; it just wasn't a note needed in the tune they played at that moment.

Thacker studied the faces in the crowd. The great unwashed of Matheson High – his fellow students, the teachers, the odd parent.

Stanwick played the odd note again.

It got Thacker's attention. It seems he had slowly been losing the tempo. He had his trench coat off. He stood on the stage alongside Stanwick at the piano and Rosa, who sat at her drum set and lightly kept the rhythm with her snare drum and hi-hat. Thacker slid his bass playing back in time with the beat. It was a slow dance number, an old standard that was in every musician's repertoire.

Thacker spied a guy walking toward Fenella. The Kevin-guy. The poet. Bored look on his face, hands in his pockets. Slouch.

He arrived.

They talked. Fenella, mostly.

The Kevin-guy barely looked at her.

Thacker couldn't hear the words, but he could read his sister like a newspaper.

And then the Kevin-guy walked away.

Thacker could tell by Fenella's face he wasn't coming back. Expectation had been canceled.

Thacker glanced at Stanwick and Rosa. There was a nod from both; they had read the same newspaper. Thacker laid his bass on the floor behind Rosa's drum riser. Stanwick added more bottom end to his piano playing, and Rosa added deeper stabs of her bass drum and adjusted her rhythm.

Thacker left the stage and walked to the refreshment table.

'Want to dance?'

'You can't dance with your sister,' Fenella said.

'Yes. I can.' Thacker took her by the hand and led her into the crowd of students on the dance floor. They danced under the light of a slowly rotating mirror ball.

Fenella had a brave face.

'Dancing is a metaphor for the whole of life,' Thacker said.

Fenella was impressed. 'That sounds like something the Man Upstairs would say.'

'Thanks.'

'What does it mean?'

Thacker shrugged. 'I have no idea. It's something I heard the Man Upstairs say.'

Fenella laughed.

Her attention was caught by something behind her brother, on the other side of the room. She whispered in Thacker's ear, 'Caroline is here.'

Thacker turned around and spied Caroline standing near the door. She was looking about – looking for him. The first thought that entered Thacker's head was that Caroline was the prettiest girl in the room. He hadn't had thoughts like that before.

He whispered to Fenella, 'I've never asked a girl to dance.'

'You asked me.'

'You're my sister.'

Fenella shoved the boy in the girl's direction.

Thacker walked over to Caroline. He was going to tell her how stunning she looked, but all that came from his mouth was: 'Your aunt let you out of the house?'

'I let myself out. Let's dance.'

Thacker smiled. He noted the tartan pants.

Caroline took his hand and led him onto the dance floor.

Stanwick traded a nod with Rosa. They changed gears down to a slower tune – the slower the tune, the closer the dancers. Stanwick played a leisurely melody, and Rosa accompanied him with the slow brush of her snare drum and the light taps of her hi-hat.

Thacker held Caroline close. Close enough to look right in her eyes.

Neither of them knew what to say. They let the dancing do the talking.

She had the prettiest eyes.

The prettiest smile.

She was the prettiest girl in the room, and Thacker wanted to tell her that. He guessed from her smile she knew what he was thinking.

A trumpet joined in with the piano and drums. Stanwick switched to playing chords, and the trumpet played a soulful melody above it.

Caroline looked up at the stage.

Fenella stood next to Rosa and Stanwick. A spotlight from

197

above lit the three of them, with Fenella's golden trumpet glowing in the downlight. She had pulled off her sweater to reveal her latest T-shirt. Across the front in bold letters: DEAD WORDS.

'Does all your family play an instrument?' Caroline asked.

'No. My father only plays gramophone records.'

That smile again.

'What's the song they're playing?'

'Gershwin's *Summertime*.'

And it was summertime, and Thacker had never thought about it before, but maybe summer was the most perfect season. But then, it could have been the dead of winter at the North Pole. It was the dancing with Caroline that made it right. It was the holding her in his arms, feeling her arms embracing him. It was the looking in her eyes.

And then her smile faded, and she frowned. 'I'm worried about that wedding dress.'

'So am I,' Thacker said. 'I don't think you should go back to that house.'

'Where can I go?'

'My house.'

There was no hesitation. She nodded.

The trumpet stopped, its mellow tones replaced with words. Fenella stood at a microphone. She held her trumpet loosely at her side. She sang from her soul.

There were no more words between Thacker and Caroline.

If Thacker had been thinking straight, he'd have thought the whole thing was as silly as ballet shoes on a bison. But he wasn't thinking straight, and he hadn't been since that day he had slammed into Caroline in the corridor. Weirdness and mystery. He moved his face toward hers. She moved toward him. They kissed.

An angry scream.

Caroline knew that anger off by heart. It was Aunt Scarlett.

All sound and movement in the auditorium ceased.

'Take your dirty hands off her,' Aunt Scarlett shrieked as she stormed across the room with bloody murder in her eyes, her heels hammering the floor.

Everyone jumped clear of her path.

The woman came up on Caroline and Thacker like a bulldozer. She punched Thacker in the face and sent him flat to the ground. She stood over him and thundered, 'I will not have her among boys. I will not have her made unpure!'

'We were only dancing,' Caroline yelled at her. 'He's my boyfriend.'

Aunt Scarlett slapped Caroline across the face. She grabbed her wrist and dragged her to the door.

And then they were gone.

Teachers and parents stood motionless with mouths agape and, frankly, no idea what to do. Students crowded around Thacker where he lay. Rosa pushed through and kneeled at his side, gripping his arm. 'Are you okay?'

Fenella arrived a moment later, and the two of them helped Thacker sit up.

Thacker had a punch-drunk smile on his face and Caroline's words echoing in his head: *He's my boyfriend.*

'Unpure?' Stanwick questioned, stepping up alongside them.

Fenella looked up at him. 'I have a bad feeling about that.'

'The Binding of the Virgins,' Rosa said.

'Yeah, with the aunt as the witness. And the one holding the matches.'

CHAPTER FORTY-FOUR

THE YELLOW PANEL TRUCK SPED ACROSS TOWN WITH ONE OF ITS headlamps out.

'How long did you think I was going to stand waiting in the hallway?' Aunt Scarlett growled. She had a cigarette, a sour face, and her foot hard down.

Caroline sat in the passenger seat, gripping the dashboard. 'How did you know about the dance?'

'Do you think I'm stupid? Your friends mentioned rehearsing music for a dance, and I telephoned the school.'

'And what did you mean by saying, "I will not have her made unpure"?'

Aunt Scarlett wasn't listening.

They ran a stoplight and sped through the busy cross traffic. There was a chorus of brakes screeching and car horns.

'You're crazy,' Caroline yelled above the engine's whine.

Aunt Scarlett wasn't talking.

Two minutes later, they drove onto Walnut Street.

The truck's single headlamp lit up the loose gravel of the driveway, and they drove around to the rear of the house.

Caroline was insistent. 'What did you mean by unpure?'

Aunt Scarlett parked the truck, killed the light, and turned off the ignition. She climbed out, walked around, and opened the passenger door. She reached in, grabbed her niece's arm, and yanked her from the seat.

'I've had enough,' Caroline yelled as her aunt shunted her across the yard to the house. 'You can't treat me like this.'

The lights were still on. Aunt Scarlett opened the kitchen door and dragged Caroline inside.

Caroline struggled to get free from her aunt's vise-like grip.

Aunt Scarlett wasn't letting go.

'You're a bitch,' Caroline yelled at her.

Aunt Scarlett slapped her.

Caroline glared and said it coldly: 'A nasty, foul, cruel bitch.'

Aunt Scarlett surged with anger. Her eyes widened. Veins stood out. Teeth protruded. She was beyond words. She made a gargling noise and punched Caroline in the face.

And then punched her again.

She dragged her to the kitchen sink and kicked open the cupboard under it. With her free hand, she pulled out an old metal bucket.

She dragged Caroline through the house to her room.

She dragged her in and threw her onto the bed.

'The next time you need to use the bathroom,' she howled, 'you can use this.' She threw the bucket into the corner.

There was a knock at the front door.

Aunt Scarlett's head snapped to one side, cocked toward the door at the other end of the hall. She was like a wolf that had heard a sound in the forest.

There was a second knock.

She left Caroline's room and locked the door.

Caroline felt her face. She was amazed she didn't have a bloody nose. She climbed off the bed and went to the door and put her ear hard against it.

She heard the front door open.

She heard muffled talk.

She could make out a man's voice, but she didn't recognize it.

Detective Franks stood on the doorstep. He put his police badge back in his pocket. 'I don't think we should have this conversation outside.' He flicked his cigarette into the front yard.

Aunt Scarlett was milk white.

She let Detective Franks inside.

He followed her down the hall and into the living room.

She went to the fireplace and grabbed her cigarettes from the mantel. She lit one. Her hands were shaking.

Jasper looked up from his rug. He sensed her distress.

Franks smiled at him. 'Cute dog.'

Jasper gave the detective a dismissive look.

'Let's get this straight,' Franks said, pulling out his gun from under his raincoat. 'I'm not here in any official police capacity.'

'I guessed that,' said Aunt Scarlett.

Franks smiled smugly. He had the look of a man who had bet the farm on a horse, and that horse was about to gallop home into first place. 'I've been putting the jigsaw together.'

'What jigsaw?'

'Albert Park had many of the pieces, and that's why you had him killed. He'd put them in the right order, hadn't he?'

Aunt Scarlett didn't answer. She stared at the gun.

'What did you do?' Franks asked. 'Hire someone to set a pack of Rottweilers loose on him?'

She didn't answer.

'We'll ignore that for the moment,' Franks said, returning his gun to its holster. 'That puzzle piece isn't important.'

He moved closer. 'What is important is Egypt. This is all about Egypt, lady, and what your family found there.'

Aunt Scarlett smoked. She stared at him.

'I know your family found more than a mummy inside that tomb.'

Her breathing increased. Her pulse accelerated.

Franks grinned. He moved closer, close enough to be related. 'And that's the most important piece of this jigsaw puzzle.'

Aunt Scarlett had nowhere to go. She stood caught between the detective and the fireplace.

Jasper barked. The little dog was furious at the man browbeating the woman who fed him. He got up, trotted behind, and stood staring up at the back of the man's head.

Franks ignored the yapping.

'What do you want?' Aunt Scarlett asked.

'Your father set up a manufacturing plant in Egypt to make plastic ducks for export back to this country.' Franks shook his head. 'There was no manufacturing plant. I had the police in Cairo check the address. It's a vacant lot. And why would he want to make ducks in Egypt when he already made the things here?'

Franks' grin became majestic. 'But there were two dozen shipments of ducks from Egypt to this country, to this city, and I'll guarantee the contents of those wooden crates weren't made of plastic.'

Jasper barked loudly. Raw anger rippled through his muscles.

Aunt Scarlett took a drag on her cigarette. She no longer looked scared. 'You shouldn't play with jigsaw puzzles unless you have all the pieces.'

Franks shoved her against the mantel.

She dropped her cigarette and swung at his face.

He grabbed her wrist mid-flight and pushed her back harder.

'I want some of the loot,' Franks snarled.

She tried to hit him with her other hand. He grabbed that, too.

'I want some of the gold and silver.'

Jasper gave a deep growl that rattled and shook everything in the room. Franks finally looked behind him, and he didn't like what he saw.

The fluffy little dog was now as big as a mastiff and completely black. Ripples surged through Jasper's body like sped-up waves along a shoreline, and with each wave, he grew larger.

Aunt Scarlett got her hands free.

Jasper's black marble-sized eyes grew into two large ovals of deep, fiery red. His head grew larger, with his ears elongating and his snout growing longer and pointed. He opened his jaws. His teeth were fiery red.

He was now taller than Franks and roared thunderously.

'No,' Aunt Scarlett shouted. 'Stop!'

Franks stared into the face of the enormous black jackal growing larger in front of him.

He instinctively reached inside his raincoat and pulled out his gun. He aimed at the jackal's head.

The jackal lunged and bit Franks' hand clean off at the wrist.

Blood sprayed.

'Not in my living room, Jasper!' Aunt Scarlett screamed.

CHAPTER FORTY-FIVE

MOUTH GAGGED. HANDS TIED BEHIND HER BACK. CAROLINE SAT IN the rear of the panel truck with a potato sack over her head. She couldn't see anything. The old truck took a sharp corner, and she toppled onto her side.

'Ouch,' she grunted through the gag tied tightly around her head. She already had a sore face from where her aunt had punched her. Now she had a sore shoulder.

Jasper barked. The little dog was somewhere in the truck, probably seated in the front next to Aunt Scarlett. Caroline couldn't see – she hadn't seen anything since her aunt had burst into her room, tied her up, gagged her, and pulled a sack over her head.

She had fought, but her aunt had been stronger.

The panel truck took another corner.

Caroline didn't know where they were going or why. She guessed they had been on the road for 10 minutes.

Everything was guesses.

The truck slowed, and Jasper barked again.

Caroline tried to free her hands – her wrists were bound with a thin rope. There was a tiny bit of slack, and she worked it, moving her hands behind her back, trying to make the small amount of slack bigger.

The truck slowed to a crawl, took another corner, drove maybe 50 feet, and came to a stop.

The engine turned off.

A door opened.

After a moment, the truck's rear door opened.

Caroline felt her aunt grip her ankles. The woman dragged her across the floor to the opening.

'Where's your other sneaker?' Aunt Scarlett grunted.

'It fell off when you hauled me out of the house,' Caroline snarled, but her words were muffled behind the sack and the gag in her mouth.

'What?'

Caroline didn't repeat herself.

Aunt Scarlett dragged Caroline out of the truck and stood her upright. Caroline's left socked foot came down in a puddle of water.

Jasper barked.

Aunt Scarlett took Caroline's arm and led her across a rough surface – a roadway.

They walked 20 feet and stopped.

Caroline heard a car horn in the distance.

Aunt Scarlett unlocked a door, which squeaked as she opened it.

Caroline was led inside a room. The ground under her socked foot changed to cold, flat concrete, and tiny pinpricks of light through the sack speckled her face.

The squeaky door closed.

Aunt Scarlett led Caroline a couple of dozen steps across the concrete floor, then stopped and let go.

Caroline turned about on the spot and tried to get her bearings, but it was impossible. She couldn't see anything and couldn't tell how big the room was. She heard something being dragged across the floor, and sensed from the echo that the room was bigger than her bedroom.

The noise stopped, and Aunt Scarlett shoved Caroline backward. She came down hard on a wooden chair.

Caroline felt her aunt grab her ankle. She felt a rope slipping around it and her aunt tying her ankle tightly to the chair leg.

Her aunt did the same to her other ankle.

Jasper barked. The sound echoed. The room was big.

Aunt Scarlett ripped the sack off, instantly exposing Caroline to a harsh bright light.

Caroline blinked rapidly.

As her eyesight came into focus, she discovered she sat in the middle of an empty warehouse. A bank of floodlights mounted high above lit up a room big enough to park a fleet of buses. Scraps of paper and packing materials littered the floor. Thirty feet to her left stood a wooden pallet laden with a dozen cardboard boxes. Jasper sat perched on top of them. Directly in front of her hung a tall metal roller door, and next to it stood a door with red peeling paint – the squeaky door.

Aunt Scarlett walked in front of Caroline and bent over, her head only a foot away. She untied Caroline's gag and pulled it free from her mouth.

'Where am I?' Caroline asked.

Her aunt studied her – eyes hung low, unblinking, corners of her mouth rising slightly.

Caroline knew the smile.

'You can scream if you want to,' Aunt Scarlett said. 'No one will hear. No one will come.' She glanced at her wristwatch.

'Did you kill Uncle Alvin?' Caroline asked.

Her aunt didn't answer.

'Are you going to kill me?'

Her aunt walked over to her dog and whispered something. She then went out the red door and closed it behind her.

The key clicked in the lock.

A moment later, Caroline heard the panel truck start up and drive away.

Silence.

'Hello?' Caroline called, her voice echoing.

No one answered.

'Hello,' Caroline shouted.

No one heard. No one came.

Jasper made himself comfortable on top of the boxes and rested his head on his paws.

'Where am I, my little friend?' Caroline asked him.

If the little dog could have, it would have shrugged.

Caroline considered standing, but with her hands tied behind her back and her legs tied to the chair, she'd probably have fallen over, and she had enough bruises already. She leaned forward and continued wriggling her hands to open up the slack in the rope.

She heard something behind her – the sound of someone adjusting themselves in a chair.

'Who's there?' she called out.

Silence.

Caroline strained her neck to see who was behind.

'Truthfully, who's there?'

She shuffled her chair, inching it, and then her eyes widened.

Twenty feet behind her sat an Egyptian mummy in a wheelchair, its bandaged hands resting in its lap, its head slightly tilted to one side.

Sennefer.

CHAPTER FORTY-SIX

THACKER, FENELLA, ROSA, AND STANWICK WALKED BRISKLY. IT WAS well after midnight, and there was no plan, only a goal: to get Caroline out of that house and away from her aunt. They entered Walnut Street, and the first thing they saw was a police squad car parked at the curb by the Dalrymple mailbox.

'That could be a good thing,' Rosa said.

'It looks like Detective Franks' car,' said Thacker, breaking into a run.

The four of them sprinted to the Dalrymple's front door, where Thacker knocked by punching it.

No one came and opened it.

Thacker tried the handle. Locked.

He kneeled in front of the keyhole and went to work with his dental equipment.

'I'll check the back door,' Fenella said, running off along the front of the building. Rosa ran with her.

A black car pulled up behind the squad car.

Stanwick watched as a thickset man climbed out and put on a hat. He headed up the footpath in their direction.

Thacker glanced.

It was Lieutenant Bendix. He looked annoyed. 'What are you doing here, Thacker?'

'Looking for Caroline. Why are you here?'

Bendix poked his thumb over his shoulder. 'I have a man in the house across the street on stakeout. Detective Franks went into this house, and he didn't come out again. Are you illegally trying to unlock that door?'

'I knocked, but the aunt didn't come and open it.'

'The aunt's not here. She drove away in an old yellow panel truck.'

Rosa and Fenella returned. 'The kitchen door is wide open,' Rosa reported. She and Fenella stared suspiciously at Bendix.

'I'm a policeman,' he grunted.

Thacker ran off along the front of the house.

'Why are you trying to get inside?' Bendix called out, running after him.

'My girlfriend is in danger.'

Everyone followed Thacker around to the rear and in through the kitchen door.

'Caroline?' Thacker shouted, running down the hallway to Caroline's bedroom.

Her bedroom door was open.

She wasn't there.

Thacker heard the others calling for Caroline in other parts of the house. He spotted one of Caroline's red sneakers lying discarded in the hallway. He picked it up.

'Franks?' Bendix called out at the foot of the staircase.

Thacker walked to him and held up the sneaker. 'This is Caroline's.'

Bendix shrugged. 'It's a shoe. People wear them.'

Rosa and Fenella came down the stairs.

'There's no one upstairs,' Fenella said.

'There's nothing in the room above Caroline's,' Rosa added.

Stanwick headed toward them from the direction of the living room. 'You had better come with me,' he said urgently to Bendix.

Everyone followed Stanwick into the living room.

A wide splattering of blood had been added to the room's sparse decor.

Detective Franks lay on his back on the floor. He was barely conscious, his left hand gripping the end of his arm where his right hand once had been.

Fenella kneeled alongside him. 'I need a knife.'

Thacker gave her his pocketknife.

'We have to stop the bleeding. Take off your tie,' she said to Bendix. She cut away the sleeve of Franks' raincoat and the shirt beneath it at the shoulder.

Bendix kneeled alongside and took off his polka-dot tie. He passed it to Fenella, and she tied it around Franks' arm above the elbow.

'It's a tourniquet,' she said, tying the tie as tightly as she could manage.

'Who did this to you?' Bendix asked.

Franks' eyes were unfocused and distant. He whispered, 'A jackal.'

'The beast of Anput,' Fenella said.

'Beasts? Jackals?' Bendix shook his head in confusion.

Rosa came back into the room. 'I've telephoned for an ambulance.'

'Where is Caroline?' Thacker asked Franks, kneeling at his head. 'Do you know where Caroline is?'

Franks didn't answer. He'd passed out.

'Where's the phone?' Bendix asked, getting to his feet.

'It's in the hallway on the wall.'

'You kids need to go home.'

Thacker looked up at Rosa. 'Telephone Uncle Diego.'

'I already have.'

'This is a big city,' Stanwick said.

Thacker didn't need reminding.

'Caroline could be anywhere.'

CHAPTER FORTY-SEVEN

'HELLO,' CAROLINE SHOUTED AGAIN.

Again, there was no reply, just the echo of her voice fading into the warehouse walls. Caroline didn't know where the building was located, but she figured it wasn't in the heart of downtown.

She looked back again at the mummy and its hands.

Were the fingers moving?

She kept working her own hands, trying to slacken the rope binding them.

She had seen countless photographs of Sennefer's mummy and had heard her father describe every inch of the linen bandages binding him, but he didn't seem as big as she had expected. He had a slight build and was probably well short of six feet when standing.

The thought of Sennefer standing did not amuse Caroline.

She took another look.

His head was wrapped in bandages, but she felt like he was staring at her with those vivid, intense eyes pictured on his coffin lid.

The rope binding Caroline's wrists slackened, and her hands sprang free.

She examined the dark red rings the rope had burned around her wrists. They would sting for days. She untied the ropes binding her legs, stood up, and headed to the red door.

It was solid metal and locked.

She went to the tall roller door next to it. She grabbed the chain that hung from the roller and pulled it. The door rose two inches, and the chain went taut. There was a padlock.

Caroline looked about.

There were no windows. There was a smaller roller door on another wall, but she could see another padlock. A wooden staircase behind Sennefer's mummy led up to a door on a second floor and a row of windows that looked out into the warehouse.

There was one other door – a blue one on the far side of the room. Caroline ran to it.

Solid metal.

Locked.

Caroline walked across the warehouse looking for a tool or a lever – something she could use to break the roller door padlock. She found nothing.

She went to the pallet laden with cardboard boxes and a sleeping Jasper. She pulled one of the dusty boxes from the pile. It was sealed. She pried her fingernails under the sealing tape, loosened it, and ripped open the box. Out spilled 20 yellow rubber ducks, scattering across the warehouse floor.

Jasper woke and raised his head.

Caroline stared at the ducks and their familiar off-yellow color, and she knew at once where she was. She was back in her childhood. She was in her grandfather's abandoned factory. The processing plant where the rubber ducks had been made lay behind the smaller roller door.

Jasper went back to sleep.

Caroline stepped around Sennefer's mummy and climbed the wooden stairs. The door at the top wasn't locked, and it led into a dark corridor of brown wooden doors. Caroline opened the first and went in.

It was an office. Six desks stood in a row – typewriters, notepads, telephones, and layers of dust. Caroline picked up a telephone. The line was dead. She tried another. Dead. Someone was still paying the power bill, but not for the telephone. She went across to the row of cobwebbed windows and looked down into the warehouse. Sennefer's mummy still sat in his wheelchair. Jasper still slept on top of the boxes.

Caroline went back into the corridor. A fire exit stood at the end. She went to it. Locked. She tried another of the brown doors. It opened into another office and more desks. She entered and crossed to a row of broken windows that looked out to the street below. It was a deserted neighborhood of factories and workhouses lit by flickering streetlamps. It was too high to jump from the window. She heard a train rumble on its tracks and remembered that the factory stood near the railroad yards.

A headlamp lit up the street, and the panel truck came into view. Aunt Scarlett had returned.

Caroline ran back down the corridor to the first office she had entered. She went across to the windows and looked down into the warehouse.

After a moment, the red door opened with a squeak. Aunt Scarlett entered. Following her in was an old man dressed in a black blazer – tall, thin, with a cigarette in his mouth and a clump of white hair on his head. It was the old man she and Thacker had seen leaving the Dalrymple house the previous night.

Jasper barked. He stood on the top of the boxes with his tail wagging.

Aunt Scarlett saw the empty chair and the rope lying on the ground.

Caroline stepped back from the window. She needed somewhere to hide, and quick, and the only thing she could think of was the crooked cat.

She tried the other doors in the corridor until she found it – her grandfather's office. She darted in and shut the door.

Her grandfather's office faced the street and was lit by moonlight. The nameplate, L.L. Carnaby, still sat on his large antique desk; his pungent pipe smoke still hung in the air. The room wasn't as big as Caroline remembered, but the black cat sconce still hung on the wall, and it was still crooked.

Caroline didn't need a chair this time. She straightened the cat. The bookcase quietly slid to one side, and the darkened room Caroline had peered into briefly in her childhood reappeared.

She went inside and looked for a switch. 'If I can open it,' she whispered, 'I can shut it.'

She heard the door at the top of the stairs open.

'Where are you?' she heard Aunt Scarlett yell angrily.

Caroline found a small panel on the wall. There were two buttons. She pushed both. A dull light came on inside the room, and the bookcase quietly slid back into place along its track.

Caroline turned about.

The room hidden behind the bookcase was no bigger than a bathroom. There were no doors or windows, and the air was stale. There was a table, and spread across it lay a handful of golden, glowing objects – Egyptian jewelry, ornaments, and trinkets.

Caroline knew what they were. Treasures from antiquity.

'Wonderful things, indeed,' she whispered.

CHAPTER FORTY-EIGHT

UNCLE DIEGO LOOKED LIKE A MOVIE STAR – 36, A HEAD OF PERFECT dark hair, a pencil mustache, and a scar on his cheekbone where a bullet had gotten a little too close on a beach in Normandy in '44. His taxi was a shiny forest green, with a cream roof and checkered stripe.

'What's going on?' he asked after he had parked outside the Dalrymple house.

'Trouble,' Rosa said, climbing into the front.

'My girlfriend is getting married to a mummy,' Thacker said, taking the window seat behind him.

'Is that legal?'

'No,' Fenella said, closing her door. She sat behind Rosa, with Stanwick sitting between her and her brother. Stanwick placed his pork pie hat on the rear dash behind him.

Uncle Diego didn't understand, but that was a typical day for his niece and her friends. 'So, where do you want to go?'

'Two-twenty-one Parker Street,' Thacker said.

Fenella looked across at him. 'Who lives there?'

Thacker didn't answer. 'Drive,' he said. His face was solemn.

Uncle Diego put the sedan into gear. They headed across town. It was the middle of the night, the streets were empty, and the moon hung in a cloudless sky.

'Let's start with what we know,' Rosa said, pulling Aunt Scarlett's book and a flashlight from her bag. She started flicking pages.

'We know that the wedding takes place tomorrow morning,' Stanwick said.

'Triangle, mummy, bride, witness,' Fenella said.

'And matches,' Thacker added. 'They're married at daybreak, and then set on fire.'

He stared out the window at an empty city sidewalk slipping by, desperate for any glimpse of Caroline.

'The garden at the back of the aunt's house is a triangle,' Fenella said. 'But the house is now a crime scene, so it's unlikely to take place there.'

'She moved the mummy,' Thacker said. 'She had a place planned. Somewhere else.'

'It needs to be outside,' Rosa reported, reading the details in the book. 'The Binding of the Virgins ceremony needs to be performed somewhere that has a clear view of the horizon, to see the first glimmer of the morning sun.'

'In a park, maybe?' Stanwick said. 'Or on top of a hill?'

'Armstrong Hill,' Uncle Diego suggested. 'It's the highest hill in the city.'

'Baker Hill is only five feet shorter,' Stanwick pointed out.

'This is ridiculous,' Fenella said. 'You only have to drive out to the city limits or into the Silverdales, and you'll find taller hills than any of those in the city. And anyway, you can see the sunrise from the top of almost any building, even ours.'

They drove in silence, everyone thinking of high places.

'Who lives at 221 Parker Street?' Rosa asked Thacker.

'A boy and his dog. How long until daybreak?'

Uncle Diego knew. 'About three and a half hours.'

CHAPTER FORTY-NINE

JASPER SNIFFED THE BOOKCASE. HE KNEW SOMEONE WAS BEHIND IT. THE only way he could communicate this information was by wagging his tail, sniffing, and scratching at the foot of the bookcase. Aunt Scarlett wasn't conversant in dog, but she had her suspicions, and she knew about the cat on the wall.

Mr Strudel entered the office. 'There's no one in any of the other rooms.' He took a silver hip flask from his pocket, unscrewed the lid and took a swig.

'Don't you get drunk,' Aunt Scarlett snapped.

Strudel put the cigarette back in his mouth and smiled at her. The smile was borderline gleeful, borderline crazy, and clear across the border into *I don't care*. He inhaled his cigarette and his face lit up.

Aunt Scarlett had never noticed before how bloodshot the man's eyes were. They reminded her of illustrations she had once seen of the planet Mars.

She picked up Jasper. 'We'll look downstairs,' she said in a loud voice to the bookcase.

She left the room, and Strudel followed her.

CHAPTER FIFTY

PARKER STREET LAY IN ONE OF THE CITY'S NEWER PRECINCTS. IT WAS a long street of identical brick apartment buildings: five floors and row upon row of identical windows. At this time of night, only a handful were lit up. The small hours before dawn were the domain of insomniacs, lunatics, and book readers.

Uncle Diego parked the taxi in front of building 221. Concrete steps led up to a large glass door and a brightly illuminated lobby.

'Does Philip live here?' Fenella asked her brother.

'Yes.'

Thacker climbed out of the taxi and shut the door. He leaned back in through the open window. 'Why would Aunt Scarlett want to turn her niece into a god? What's in it for her?'

'That's a good question,' Stanwick remarked.

Thacker walked along the sidewalk, counting the windows. He stopped when he came to eight. A third-floor light was on. He reached into his pocket and found a quarter. He took aim at the window and threw the coin.

The coin hit the window frame and fell to the ground.

The window opened, and Philip's round face appeared. He wore pajamas and held a book about knights. He had been far away in a distant land dealing with a dragon.

'Thacker?'

'Is Dashiell home?'

'Dashiell? Why?'

'Is he at home?'

'Yes, he's here.'

'We need him.'

Philip glanced at his wristwatch. 'It's the middle of the night.'

Thacker held up Caroline's red sneaker. 'The game is afoot.'

Philip grinned enthusiastically, then disappeared from the window.

Thacker retrieved his quarter.

CHAPTER FIFTY-ONE

CAROLINE PRESSED HER EAR TO THE BACK OF THE BOOKCASE. SHE HAD heard nothing for several minutes. Not a sound.

She was certain there was no one in her grandfather's office. And she was feeling nauseated – the hidden room had no windows or doors or any ventilation. It was a sealed room, a tomb, and the air had been sour when she had first walked in. She had to get out of there, and then out of the building.

Caroline looked again at the table and the handful of Egyptian artifacts that lay on it – a scattering of leftovers, a sale table in a department store long after the rush. She didn't want to think too hard about it; the story had always been that tomb robbers had raided Sennefer's tomb. Right at that moment, she was more concerned about breathing.

She pressed the two buttons on the control panel. The light went out, and the bookcase slid to one side.

The office was empty.

Caroline stepped out of the small space and breathed. She listened, but heard nothing.

She crept into the corridor and made her way along to the office by the staircase. She went in and stepped up to the window. Looking down into the warehouse, she couldn't see her aunt or the old man in black, or even Jasper. Even Sennefer's mummy and his wheelchair had gone.

The red door on the other side of the warehouse was wide open, and, through it, Caroline could see the wet street outside flickering in the streetlamps. The open doorway was more tempting than all the chocolate in the world.

Caroline quietly opened the door and carefully made her way down the wooden stairs. The fifth step from the top creaked loudly. Caroline gritted her teeth and stood rigid.

There was no hue and cry. No one came running.

She breathed again.

There was a possibility she was going to get out of this place.

CHAPTER FIFTY-TWO

UNCLE DIEGO DROVE THE TAXI BACK ACROSS TOWN AND ONTO WALNUT Street. Thacker now sat in front next to Rosa, who had moved into the middle, and Philip had taken Thacker's place behind Uncle Diego. He sat unseen behind Dashiell's wall of mustard-colored fur – the dog sat in his lap.

Uncle Diego parked in front of the Dalrymple house, and Thacker, Dashiell, and Philip climbed out.

'Where do we start?' Philip asked. He still wore his pajamas under a dressing gown, with sneakers on his feet. He had Dashiell on a leash.

Thacker walked over to the Dalrymple driveway. He imagined the panel truck pulling out and speeding away. But then, which way did it turn when it arrived at the end of the street? Left or right?

'Here,' Thacker said.

Philip led Dashiell to the driveway.

Thacker kneeled and presented the red sneaker to Dashiell.

The old dog looked at the shoe and didn't seem interested in it.

'He's tired,' Philip said. 'He had a busy day.'

'Doing what?'

'Sleeping.'

'How old is that dog?' Uncle Diego asked. He stood leaning against his taxi, hands in pockets. Stanwick leaned with him.

'Dog years or human years?' Philip asked.

'Dog years.'

Philip did a quick mental calculation. And guessed. 'About 100.'

Thacker put his hand on the back of Dashiell's neck. He held the red sneaker under the dog's nose. 'This shoe belongs to a friend of mine, and I really need you to find her.'

Dashiell begrudgingly took a sniff of the sneaker, but remained uninterested. He yawned and thought about his comfortable pale-blue pillow with a bone motif.

Stanwick poked his head in through the passenger window. 'What do we know about the witness?' he asked Rosa.

Rosa held up the book. 'I'm looking for that.'

'Please,' Thacker pleaded with the dog. 'Please find her. Her life is in danger.'

Dashiell yawned.

Philip had never seen Thacker so distressed. He kneeled alongside Dashiell. He lifted one of his dog's floppy ears and whispered in it. The pooch paid attention.

Fenella's eyebrow raised. 'Please tell me he can't actually talk to that thing.'

Thacker had no idea what Philip had said, but Dashiell's eyes widened and focused. He took another sniff of the shoe and then raised his head and took in a deep snort of the night air.

He stood motionless, with his nose raised.

'What's he doing?' Thacker whispered to Philip.

'Calibrating.'

Suddenly, with a burst of energy that startled everyone, Dashiell took off. In a heartbeat, Philip went from kneeling to running.

'He's found the scent,' Philip shouted as he ran, gripping the leash with Dashiell straining it tight at the other end.

Thacker ran to the taxi. 'Follow that dog!'

CHAPTER FIFTY-THREE

CAROLINE STOOD AT THE BOTTOM OF THE STAIRCASE AND LOOKED ACROSS at the open red door. She took a deep breath. She didn't know where her aunt and the man in black had gone. It was now or never.

She ran.

She made it halfway across the warehouse floor when Aunt Scarlett stepped in through the doorway, holding Jasper.

Caroline came to an abrupt halt.

Aunt Scarlett closed the door and locked it.

'You knew where I was hiding.'

Her aunt nodded. She put Jasper on the ground, and he ran to his stack of boxes.

'So, you know what's in that room.'

Caroline found herself caught in a cloud of cigarette smoke. Strudel grabbed her from behind. He pulled her hands behind her back and held her firm. Caroline didn't know where the old man had been hiding, but she didn't take her eyes off her aunt. 'Sennefer's tomb wasn't empty, was it?'

Aunt Scarlett walked over, smiling at Caroline. 'No, it wasn't. How do you think your mother and father could afford to live their lives of spoiled leisure? Or for your grandfather to own three Bentleys and a beach house in Hawaii?'

'What are you two talking about?' Strudel asked.

Caroline turned her head to look at the man standing behind her. 'Who are you, anyway?'

'Never mind him,' Aunt Scarlett rasped. She placed her hand

around Caroline's throat. 'No, Sennefer's tomb hadn't been raided; that was just a story your grandfather made up. He and your parents were the tomb robbers.' She laughed. 'You surely didn't think this family made its fortune from rubber ducks?'

She took her hand away. 'You can let go of her,' she instructed Strudel. 'There's nowhere she can go.'

Strudel released Caroline.

Aunt Scarlett walked across the warehouse toward the blue metal door.

Strudel took a white clerical collar from his blazer pocket and fixed it into place around his neck.

Caroline was incredulous. 'You're a priest?'

'Father Strudel. And despite what people have claimed, I have never been defrocked.'

Aunt Scarlett unlocked the blue door and opened it. 'Take her up.'

Strudel clamped his cigarette between his lips and grabbed Caroline's arm.

'Let go of me!'

He dragged her across to the doorway.

They passed a smiling Aunt Scarlett and went through into a shadowy, windowless stairwell.

'We go up,' Strudel said, pushing Caroline toward the concrete steps.

She had no choice but to climb them, with Father Strudel behind her, gripping one of her hands behind her back.

'Where are we going?' Caroline asked.

'Up to the roof.'

'Why are we going to the roof?'

'It's where it's going to happen.'

It was like pulling teeth out of the man's head.

'What's going to happen on the roof?'

'A wedding.'

'Whose wedding?'

'Sennefer and Iset.'

Caroline felt ill. 'I'm not Iset.'

'I don't care.'

At the top of the stairs, Father Strudel shoved Caroline through a doorway and onto the factory roof – a flat expanse dotted with skylights and ducts.

In the cold, gray moonlight, Caroline saw Sennefer's mummy waiting in his wheelchair.

She screamed: 'I don't believe in reincarnation!'

CHAPTER FIFTY-FOUR

DASHIELL LED PHILIP AND THE TAXI HALFWAY ACROSS TOWN AND INTO the city's industrial district – the city's backside. A labyrinth of dark streets and dirty factories, warehouses, and offices coated in a layer of grime and shrouded in a cloud of industrial-strength smoke.

And then he led them into the railroad yards, where old freight cars went to die, surplus tracks were left to rust, and everything was the color of soot.

'I've found it!' Rosa exclaimed. She looked up from the book. 'The witness is Sennefer's sister, Beketamun.'

'How does that work?' Fenella asked.

'Not his actual sister – a substitute. The witness represents Beketamun. And what she is witnessing is the wedding that she stopped.'

'Got it.'

'The witness needs to be two things. She needs to be a similar age to Beketamun–'

'How old was Beketamun?' Stanwick asked.

'She was Sennefer's youngest sister,' Fenella said. 'And Sennefer was 20.'

'And she needs to be a virgin,' Rosa said.

Thacker remembered the aunt's words at the dance: *I will not have her made unpure.*

'The Binding of the Virgins is the binding of Sennefer, Iset, and the witness. All three of them are virgins.'

The taxi slowed. Its headlamps lit up Philip, who had come to a stop. He stood next to Dashiell, who stood rigid, staring into the darkness underneath an old Pullman car.

'He's found something,' Philip shouted, pulling out a flashlight from his dressing gown pocket. 'There's something under this railway carriage.'

The taxi stopped, and Thacker climbed out. He came over. 'What's under there?'

Philip shrugged.

And then they both saw it. Philip's flashlight beam caught a pair of eyes in the darkness staring at them.

'Caroline?' Thacker called out.

The eyes blinked.

Thacker ventured toward them and climbed under the carriage.

A moment later, there was an angry shriek.

Thacker sprinted back out into the moonlight with an angry ginger-colored cat running behind him.

Dashiell barked.

The cat overtook Thacker and raced past Philip, who just managed to keep a grip on Dashiell's leash and stop the old dog from tearing off after it.

'It's a cat,' Thacker barked. 'He found a cat! We're running out of nighttime!'

They bundled themselves back into the taxi and sped back across the city to Walnut Street. They had to try again. Dashiell had to be reset at the beginning.

'Is the witness burned as well?' Thacker asked, studying the sky through the window, fearing daybreak.

'No,' Rosa said, studying the book. 'Only Sennefer and the bride are set on fire.'

Thacker suddenly felt an enormous wave of relief, as though it was Christmas and he had just walked into a room full of presents.

'Tell me I'm wrong,' he said, 'but Caroline is the witness. She must be. It's the aunt who thinks she's going to become a god – become a god and burn the world. This is all about her. It must be. Surely?'

229

'It sort of makes sense,' Stanwick said.

Rosa held up the book with its photograph of a much younger Aunt Scarlett on its back cover. She pointed her flashlight at it, with her fingers covering the woman's face so that only the eyes could be seen.

Aunt Scarlett had the same eyes as Caroline – the same eyes as Iset.

'The aunt is the bride,' Thacker said. 'It's the aunt who must be stopped.'

CHAPTER FIFTY-FIVE

AUNT SCARLETT STEPPED ONTO THE FACTORY ROOF. SHE APPEARED ethereal in the moonlight, with her hair dyed black, her lips red, and her dark eyes exaggerated by thick black makeup. She held three long-stemmed poppies.

The moonlight also lit Caroline's face, and she wasn't happy. Strudel had tied her standing, hands behind her, to an air-conditioning duct that rose out of the roof and, for some reason, did a parabolic arc straight back into it.

Caroline couldn't mistake the way her aunt was now dressed – like an Egyptian high priestess, and exactly like the woman painted inside Sennefer's coffin lid. She wore the ornate, flowing white gown Caroline had seen back at the house, sandals, a gold sash about her waist, and a thin band of gold cloth embroidered with stripes of blue about her head. Holstered behind the gold sash was a long kitchen carving knife – a fat blade with a pointed end.

Aunt Scarlett looked east, out across the jagged, crenelated silhouette of the city. A slender, bare hint of daylight lit the horizon. She closed her eyes and inhaled.

She whispered, 'Soon.'

She went to Sennefer, where he sat in the wheelchair, and kneeled in front of him. 'This poppy is for you.' She placed a poppy at his feet. 'This poppy is for me.' She placed a second. She kissed the third poppy and placed it with the others. 'This poppy is for our binding and our destiny. I pledge my eternal soul to you.'

The woman was quite mad, Caroline thought. Romantic, but nuts.

Slowly, the mummy's right hand rose and reached out to Aunt Scarlett.

Caroline froze with astonishment. She wasn't imagining it.

Aunt Scarlett took Sennefer's bandaged hand and kissed it. 'Soon we will be together. Together for eternity, and the world will be ours.'

The woman *was* quite mad, but also a 3,000-year-old mummy had just held out its hand to her.

Aunt Scarlett placed Sennefer's hand back on his thigh. She walked over to Caroline. With one hand, she grabbed her by the throat. With the other, she pulled out the kitchen knife and pressed its tip under Caroline's chin.

Aunt Scarlett leaned close and whispered: 'The beast of Anput was unleashed into this world, and it sought Beketamun. But it could not find the little sister; she had vanished into eternity, and the glimmer of her soul was never to be found.

'You, Caroline, will stand in Beketamun's place. And, in her place, you will play your part in the Binding of the Virgins.'

'The binding of the what?' Caroline asked.

'You will witness this marriage and this revelation of my destiny.'

'Wait? What? *You're* going to marry the mummy?'

Aunt Scarlett stabbed the pipe two inches from Caroline's head. The knife's blade was so sharp, it slid into the metal as though it was made of watermelon.

She left the knife sticking there and went back to Sennefer.

A sickening wave of realization swept over Caroline.

Behind Sennefer's wheelchair stood a cardboard box – the rope Strudel had used to tie Caroline to the duct had come from it. Her aunt reached in and took out a can of paint and a paintbrush. She came back and popped the can's lid. Starting at Caroline's feet, she began painting a white line.

'You are the bride of Sennefer,' Caroline said.

Her aunt said nothing.

'You killed my mother.'

Her aunt said nothing. She painted a white line 20 feet across the roof until she came to the poppies at Sennefer's feet.

Caroline wanted to vomit.

Father Strudel appeared in the doorway, out of breath, with a cigarette butt clenched between his lips. He had hauled a black gasoline can up the stairs – the same can Caroline had seen at the house. Strudel stood it on the ground and exhaled a gust of air.

'I'm getting too old for kinky horseplay.' He walked away to look at the view and to start a new cigarette.

Aunt Scarlett came back to Caroline, and, starting again at her feet, she painted another white line, this one at a 60-degree angle from the first. And like the first, she painted this line out to a length of 20 feet.

She then painted a white line across the roof that connected the two ends.

Caroline realized she stood tied at the sharp end of an inverted equilateral triangle.

Aunt Scarlett threw the paint can and brush away. She stormed back across the roof to Caroline.

'I killed your uncle, too.' There was glee in the woman's eyes. She went to the gasoline can and took off the cap. She poured gasoline into the triangle. She walked about, splashing the fuel everywhere. The air reeked of its sickly odor.

Caroline struggled to get her hands free. They were tightly bound behind her, and her wrists already throbbed from the previous binding.

Aunt Scarlett emptied the can, then threw it away. She walked to the edge of the roof, held out her arms, palms open, and looked to the eastern horizon.

'What is she doing?' Caroline called out to Father Strudel.

He looked bored but he glanced at Aunt Scarlett. 'I imagine she's waiting for the sun to come up.'

'She's insane. Don't you understand that?'

'Her money's good.' He unscrewed his hip flask and took a drink.

'Why the gasoline?'

He shrugged.

Aunt Scarlett strode across the roof to Caroline. Her eyes were wide and unblinking. She screamed spittle and anger in Caroline's face, 'Witness this, little sister!' She then marched back to the edge of the roof to wait for sunrise.

CHAPTER FIFTY-SIX

UNCLE DIEGO DROVE HIS TAXI OF DOG AND HUNTERS BACK TO THE Dalrymple house. And, once again, Thacker presented the old canine with the red sneaker. And, once again, Dashiell dashed off after the scent of Caroline's foot, with Philip jogging behind, clutching his leash.

'That fellow can run,' Fenella remarked, staring ahead at Philip as they trailed behind in the taxi.

'We've been doing this all night,' Thacker growled. 'How long until daybreak?'

'Soon,' Uncle Diego said.

'Is Aunt Scarlett a virgin?' Stanwick asked.

'They had no children,' Thacker said.

'And the uncle slept in his own room,' Rosa said. She looked at Thacker, sitting next to her on the front seat.

He caught her look.

'There's something you need to know.' There was something serious in her eyes.

'What?'

'I've just read what happens to the witness at the end of the ceremony.'

Thacker felt that room full of Christmas presents circling and draining away down the plughole. 'What happens to her?'

'Before Iset and Sennefer are set on fire, the witness has her throat slashed. It's revenge for what Beketamun did to Sennefer.'

Thacker's body and soul sank into the seat. His life was heading down the plughole, too.

CHAPTER FIFTY-SEVEN

DAYLIGHT CAME. THE FIRST SLIVER OF THE MORNING SUN SLID OVER the distant horizon and cast a golden ray across the tops of the city's buildings...

And Aunt Scarlett's face.

She closed her eyes and smiled with a sense of profound achievement. She had been waiting for this moment for many years. In her soul, she had been waiting all her life. All her lives.

She savored the excitement.

'How many other people have you murdered?' Caroline shouted at her.

The old priest was so startled by Caroline's outburst, he almost dropped his hip flask.

Aunt Scarlett walked calmly over to Caroline.

'I kicked away your grandfather's walking stick; he was never good with staircases. And killing him answered the question: How do I get Sennefer to come to me, rather than me going to Egypt?'

Aunt Scarlett grinned as if it were an obvious thing.

'A Sennefer exhibition to commemorate my late father!'

'You're insane.'

'The Egyptians consented, the city paid, and the mummy was shipped. They put him right where I could get my hands on him.'

'You're completely insane.'

'And killing your mother meant you would also be brought to me.'

She put a gentle hand on Caroline's cheek. 'I first saw you on the day you were born, and right from that day, I had a feeling

236

you were special. When I translated the tomb's hieroglyphs and recognized my true path in this life, it became obvious. You were to be my witness.'

Caroline spat in the woman's face.

Her aunt slapped her, and her grumpy face returned. She spun around and barked at Father Strudel. 'Let's get on with this.'

Strudel concealed his flask in his blazer pocket.

Aunt Scarlett walked across the triangle, through the puddles of gasoline, and took her place in the triangle's empty corner.

'Where am I supposed to stand?' Strudel asked.

'In the middle. And you're drunk. You're swaying like a daffodil.'

'I'm medicated, madam.' He stepped inside the triangle and took a position at the center, facing Aunt Scarlett and the mummy, with his back to Caroline.

Caroline felt a little slack in the rope. She kept working her hands to free them.

'Shouldn't you and the groom be standing side-by-side?' Strudel asked.

Aunt Scarlett shook her head. 'The triangle is the way this will be performed.'

Strudel shrugged. He didn't care. He reached into his pocket, pulled out a Bible and opened it to a bookmark.

He cleared his throat. 'Dearly beloved, we are gathered here in the sight of God.'

He looked at the mummy and then at Aunt Scarlett. He closed the Bible.

'In the sight of the gods. Come one, come ye all.'

He took a puff on his cigarette.

'To join this woman and this ancient, dusty man. To enter them both into the sacred covenant of matrimony.'

Caroline's hands strained against the rope. She was desperate.

'To live happily ever after, forever and ever.'

CHAPTER FIFTY-EIGHT

'WHY HAS HE STOPPED?' FENELLA ASKED.

They were back in the middle of the industrial district, and Dashiell had come to an abrupt halt. He sat in the middle of the road, head resting on paws, yawning. Uncle Diego parked at the curb in front of Philip, who was bent over, clutching his knees and inhaling great gasps of oxygen. He was so red-faced from all his running, he looked like a beetroot.

Everyone climbed out of the taxi.

'Daybreak,' Thacker growled at the dawn sky.

The street was empty, lined with bland buildings. The streetlamps went out, their work done for another night.

'It's just factories,' Fenella said, looking around. 'We drove through here the first time.'

Stanwick tapped Thacker's shoulder. He directed his attention to the entrance of the beige building they stood in front of.

Thacker looked.

Realization grew in his eyes.

He smiled.

Suspended above the entrance hung a large, badly weathered rubber duck.

'Ducks!' Fenella said.

'It's a duck,' said Uncle Diego. 'So what?'

'Rubber ducks,' Rosa said. 'The Carnaby family financed the Egyptian expedition from money made from selling rubber ducks. This must be their factory.'

Fenella ran to the entrance – a tall double door with large, rusted handles.

Thacker couldn't see anything at the top of the building, just the edge of the roof.

'Caroline?' he shouted.

A heartbeat later came Caroline's distant reply. 'Thacker!'

'They're on the roof,' Thacker said.

'The door is locked,' Fenella reported, coming back from the entrance.

'I'll look for another way in,' Stanwick said, heading to the alley that led behind the building and to the warehouse entrance.

Uncle Diego ran to his taxi. 'I'll radio for the police.'

Thacker ran his eyes up a drainpipe – it went up the wall to the roof.

'No.' Rosa grabbed his arm. 'That's at least 80 feet.'

'Don't even think about it,' Fenella said sternly.

'We don't have time,' Thacker said. He took off his trench coat and gave it to Rosa.

He went to Uncle Diego, who stood by his driver's window with his radio microphone in his hand. 'I need your tire iron.'

CHAPTER FIFTY-NINE

FATHER STRUDEL TOOK A PUFF ON HIS CIGARETTE. 'DO YOU TAKE THIS man to be your husband, in the best of times and the worst, in sickness and health, to love, honor, and obey him all your days?'

'I will be his bride,' said Aunt Scarlett. 'I will be his consort, and together we will take our place in the pantheon.'

'Thacker!' Caroline shouted.

'Shut up,' her aunt barked at her.

Strudel looked at the mummy. 'Do you take Scarlett to be your wife? Good times, bad times. Sickness, health. Love and obey?'

Strudel took another puff. He glanced at Aunt Scarlett. 'He's supposed to say something.'

The mummy moved. It leaned forward in the wheelchair, and then slowly rose to its feet.

Caroline's eyes couldn't get any wider.

Strudel felt the hip flask in his pocket and decided to stop drinking that specific brand of whiskey.

Now standing, Sennefer raised his bandaged arm. He extended his hand to Aunt Scarlett in the other corner of the triangle. She extended hers.

'With this ring,' Strudel said.

'There is no ring,' Aunt Scarlett snapped.

Strudel swayed on his feet. 'With this triangle, receive this as a sign of both your love and fidelity.'

'*Thacker!*'

'I pronounce you man and wife.'

Aunt Scarlett's smile was as bright as the sun.

'You may now kiss.'

Aunt Scarlett went to Sennefer. He took her in his bandaged arms, and they hugged. He leaned her back, and they kissed. It would have been wonderfully romantic had it not been that he was a 3000-year-old corpse wrapped from head to foot in bandages, and she was bananas.

And then Caroline saw Thacker's unmistakable blond head, and his hands too, as he hauled himself up over the two-foot-high safety guard that ran around the roof's perimeter.

Aunt Scarlett stomped across to Caroline and yanked the knife out of the duct. 'Your mother was the one who broke the tomb's seal. Yes, I killed her. But I didn't kill your father.'

Strudel noticed Thacker, too.

'Your father drank too much. And did you ever wonder why?'

Caroline was watching the knife. It was inches from her throat.

'He drank because of what happened to Harwood.'

Thacker rolled onto the roof. The tire iron was tucked under his belt. He heard hammering below in the street. Stanwick was breaking his way into the building.

'Harwood didn't die of blood poisoning a week after they unsealed the tomb; that was a story your father and grandfather made up.'

Caroline knew of Harwood – the expedition photographer on the Sennefer dig. 'What happened to him?'

'They killed him. Your grandfather, your father, and your mother.'

Caroline felt numb.

'Harwood wanted to report what they had found inside the tomb. They killed him and destroyed his photographs.'

'They found the treasure.'

'Yes, *my* treasure. They broke the tomb's seal, my seal, and now all four of them are dead.'

'You really think you are the reincarnation of Iset?'

Aunt Scarlett reeled back. She bellowed thunderously in her magnificence, 'I am Iset! I am the bride of Sennefer!'

'And the bride must be stopped,' Thacker shouted.

He swung the tire iron and struck the aunt's arm. The knife flew from her hand.

The woman lunged and snatched it back up. She turned about and stood in front of Caroline, slicing the air in front of Thacker.

A loud growl came from deep within the building.

'How dare you,' Aunt Scarlett screamed. 'No one interrupts the Binding of the Virgins!'

'Who are these virgins you keep talking about?' Caroline demanded.

'The three of you are virgins,' Thacker shouted. 'You, her, and the mummy.'

Aunt Scarlett turned to Caroline. 'And now, little sister, you are going to die.'

'Who said I was a virgin?'

Her aunt stared at her.

Caroline stated the fact plainly: 'I am not a virgin.'

Aunt Scarlett was shocked.

Bewildered.

Bulldozed.

Thacker came up behind her and slammed the tire iron down on the woman's outstretched arm. The knife hit the ground and slid away across the roof.

A second loud growl erupted. This time from the stairwell leading to the roof.

Aunt Scarlett turned about and screamed unintelligibly at Thacker.

The jackal smashed its way through the doorway at the top of the staircase and let rip a deafening roar that echoed throughout the city.

'Kill him,' Aunt Scarlett shouted at it, pointing at Thacker. She ran to get the knife.

Thacker went to Caroline and frantically unraveled the rope binding her wrists.

Police sirens sounded in the distance.

The jackal stepped into the triangle. Its enormous eyes glanced at Strudel, then trained on Thacker. It growled again.

Strudel decided everything he had seen on the roof was on account of the whiskey. He reached into his pocket and found another cigarette.

'Kill him,' Aunt Scarlett commanded the jackal. She couldn't find the knife.

Strudel put the new cigarette to his lips. He lit it with the butt of the previous one.

Thacker pulled Caroline's hands free.

Strudel tossed the butt over his shoulder, and it landed in the gasoline.

Whomp.

A wave of flames spread out.

In a flash, Strudel, Aunt Scarlett, Sennefer, and the jackal's backside were ablaze.

Rosa, Fenella, and Stanwick arrived at the top of the stairs and ran through the smashed doorway.

Thacker dragged Caroline away from the burning triangle.

The jackal, yelping, galloped across the roof and disappeared over the side.

Strudel hopped across the roof, ripping off his burning clothes.

Aunt Scarlett and Sennefer were engulfed in flames. She appeared calm as her gown and his bandages burned. She had found her place. She was truly happy. She went to him, and they embraced.

'The earth becomes their kingdom, and they burn it all,' Rosa whispered.

The binding was incomplete. Burning was the final thing Aunt Scarlett and Sennefer the Unbelievably Magnificent would ever do. By the time anyone from the city's fire, police, and sanitation departments could get near them, they had become a blackened clump of ashes and smoke.

And, as the poets say, nevermore.

CHAPTER SIXTY

TWO WEEKS LATER A REPLY FROM SCOTLAND ARRIVED AT THE THACKER house. It unfolded that Aunt Lillian had received the first two letters Caroline had sent and had replied, but her letters had never made it into Caroline's hands. After which Aunt Lillian had received no other letters from Caroline until the one with Thacker's return address. Clearly, Aunt Scarlett had not been a good postmaster.

The police undertook a thorough investigation of the events that had taken place. Fingerprints were collected, crime scene photographs were taken, and everyone was questioned.

The aunt had been fixated on Ancient Egypt and a fantasy that she was the reincarnation of Sennefer's bride. She had stolen his mummy from the museum, murdered her sister, her father, and her husband, and had attempted to murder her niece.

No one could explain the jackal.

Sennefer's and Scarlett's ashes were swept up, poured into a glass jar, and quietly shipped back to Egypt along with the rest of the pieces from the exhibition.

There was an international diplomatic kerfuffle. The Egyptian government was furious.

Father Strudel's last known whereabouts was aboard a cargo ship bound for Antarctica, where he planned to swear off alcohol and teach penguins how to yodel.

Detective Franks spent a week and a half in hospital and blamed Thornton Thacker for every wrong thing that had ever happened to him in his entire life.

The *Christie Big Book of Egyptian Hieroglyphics* was returned to the library.

Professor Bacon at last had an explanation for the three poppies.

And Caroline inherited everything. She instructed a lawyer to remit the remaining – stolen – Sennefer treasures to Egypt. And to sell everything else. She bequeathed most of Uncle Alvin's train set and collection of locomotive memorabilia to the city's transportation museum.

She gave a box to Thacker.

This tale of weirdness and mystery began when Thornton Thacker walked into Caroline Greer – Matheson High, between classes, busy corridor, boy slams into girl. And it ended with the pair of them standing together on a busy platform at the city train station at sunset. A locomotive throbbed and gushed great spurts of steam. People were climbing aboard the carriages, finding seats, stowing luggage in the overheads, waving from windows. An agitated stationmaster on the platform stared at his wristwatch.

'I'll write,' Caroline said.

Thacker nodded.

Caroline held Jasper. The little dog tried affectionately to lick her face. 'Don't look so glum, Thacker. I'm only going to Scotland. It's not like I'm going to Jupiter.'

Thacker couldn't help it.

The stationmaster blew his whistle.

Caroline waved to Rosa, Fenella, and Stanwick – they stood on the platform outside the train station's restaurant. The five of them had had a long goodbye lunch.

'Will I see you again?' Thacker asked.

'Of course.' She kissed him. A long, lingering kiss. Jasper squirmed between them.

'Move it,' barked the stationmaster.

Caroline smiled at Thacker. She and Jasper climbed aboard. After a moment, she appeared at the window and waved.

Thacker put his hand to the glass. She to his.

The stationmaster blew his whistle again, and the engine driver unleashed the locomotive's might. With deep belches of energy, the heavy machine began to move.

Caroline waved again. She looked sad.

The train rolled out of the station. And she was gone.

'She'll be back,' Stanwick said, putting his hand on Thacker's shoulder.

'No. She won't,' Thacker said, staring at the empty track. 'That's what love is all about. Wanting what you don't get.'

He turned about to see Fenella and Rosa walking to him across the deserted platform.

Fenella hugged her brother.

'*Rainy Night Café*,' Rosa said with authority.

Everyone was happy with that.

Fenella put on her sunglasses. 'Cool. Let's roll!'

They walked to the exit, Thacker sluggish at the rear. He thought about buying a hat.

The others left.

There was a cough.

Thacker recognized the tie. Lieutenant Bendix stepped out from beside a newsstand, where he'd been standing unobserved.

'This is a mean city,' Bendix said to Thacker. 'It's full of mean people doing mean things. You have to walk these streets and not let the mean attach itself to you.'

Thacker nodded.

'And try to stay out of trouble.'

Thacker smiled. 'Yup.'

ABOUT THE AUTHOR

Stephen Ross had a misspent childhood. He played a lot of electric guitar and piano in bands no one's ever heard of and, using his dad's movie camera, shot a bunch of crime movies with his high school friends. One day, he wrote a short mystery story and sent it to a magazine. They bought it and published it.

Since then, Stephen has written over three dozen short stories and novelettes, which have appeared in *Alfred Hitchcock's Mystery Magazine, Ellery Queen's Mystery Magazine*, several Mystery Writers of America anthologies, and many other publications, including *Dark Deeds Down Under*, the first ever anthology of New Zealand and Australian mystery fiction.

Stephen has been nominated for an Edgar Award, a Derringer Award, a Thriller Award, and has been an Ellery Queen Readers' Award finalist.

A member of the Mystery Writers of America and the New Zealand Society of Authors, Stephen was recently a contributor to Lee Child's multi award-winning handbook: *How to Write a Mystery*.

Stephen is currently having a misspent adulthood. He lives in Auckland, Aotearoa, and believes it is entirely appropriate to eat chocolate while reading.

www.StephenRoss.net

ACKNOWLEDGEMENTS

I warmly thank the following people who made this book possible.

You, dear reader. A book is just a bunch of words until it's picked up and read.

Vicki Marsden, my fantastic literary agent at High Spot Literary.

Lindy Cameron, my fantastic publisher at Clan Destine Press.

Jason Nahrung for his guru-level editing and wisdom that raised the book's game.

Andrea 'altocello' Farley for her wonderful cover design.

My mother and father (Bev and Eric).

And Mina, my first reader, for her encouragement, inspiration, proofreading, and perceptions.

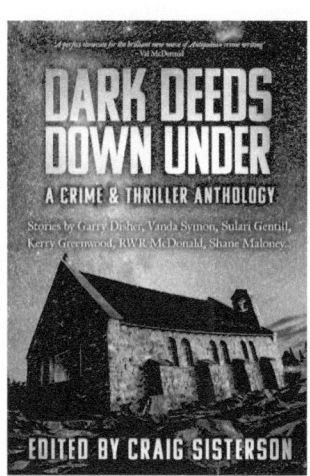

Stephen's story 'Mr Pig' features in *Dark Deeds Down Under,* Clan Destine's first anthology of Aussie & Kiwi crime fiction.